UNCIVILIZED

SUPER SOLDIERS

REBECCA ROYCE

Uncivilized

Ebook 978-1-960447-03-6

Print 978-1-960447-14-2

Copyright @ 2023 by Rebecca Royce

Cover art by Original Syn

Print Cover Art by Original Syn

Content Editing: Virginia Nelson

Copy Editing: Jennifer Jones at Bookends Editing

Final Proof Editing: Viv Jackson

Formatting: Ripley Proserpina

Published by Rebecca Royce

www.rebeccaroyce.com

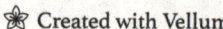 Created with Vellum

1

A GIRL NAMED RAVEN

The rain pounded on my head, making it harder than I would like to check my surroundings. Still, I made the effort. I'd come too far to be waylaid by a would-be assailant or some pickpocket with a hard-on for my coat. I was almost there—the weeks of travel to get to the small town on the edge of the galaxy couldn't be for naught. I'd lived through broken- down vessels threatening to fall from space and sketchy cargo ship captains who spent too much time noticing my legs *and* somehow had managed to survive on the meager rations I brought with me when I escaped in the middle of the night to make the journey.

All because I promised Amias I would deliver his message. I intended to keep my word—I would find The Five and give them the note in my pocket. It was the last thing he ever asked of me, so I wouldn't let him down. He'd saved me a million times, and that wasn't an exaggeration. The least I could do was find my way to the bar in the small town where I would hand over the note he'd been so desperate to have delivered in the end.

So far, the coast was clear. No one tried to assault or stop me. Actually, out of the few people I passed on the street, none seemed to even care that I was there. Theirs was an enhanced planet, for the most part. That meant one of the places without authorities trying to catalog and watch their every move, lest they destroy the universe.

Of course, monitoring by the authorities wasn't a terrible idea. I saw firsthand what happened when we let the former Super Soldiers take over planets.

The mark on my forehead was a forever reminder of just how badly things could go, but I couldn't control any of that. I was one woman alone and likely to be that way forever. All I could do was put one wet foot in front of the other and deliver the note in my pocket.

Afterward, I would have to go back to do what I could for the others for as long as I could.

I stopped short, staring at the building in front of me. It was just as Amias had said it would be. *The Frog and The Bull*. Not that I could read the sign, but the picture of the frog seemed a good indicator, and it eerily resembled the picture he'd sketched for me. I'd spent hours memorizing it until I could see it in my dreams.

From where I stood, I could hear music playing inside the building—it was the pub where The Five hung out, their home base, so to speak. Amias had explained all of it to me over the years. He, Stone, and I had talked late into every evening, even when Stone and I should have been sleeping to prepare for the next day's heavy burden. Amias never needed to sleep very much, because the enhanced people needed so much less rest than the rest of us. Despite my being the third wheel, they never made me feel that way, not even once.

And now they were both gone.

Tears threatened again, and I managed to shove them

down. I wouldn't successfully manage to hold them back forever, but for the moment, I would keep holding on. Everything I knew about the small town was because Amias had told me about it. I'd never been in a bar or anyplace like one before. The Five did business there, though, and it was the only place Amias could guarantee they would return. I hoped they'd be in residence, as I didn't have the time or resources to stay and wait for them to arrive.

Not that hope ever really amassed much of a result for me in the past.

It seemed likely everyone in that bar knew I was outside already. They could hear, see, smell, taste, and react better than I ever could.

They'd been made to be that way. In labs. When those labs threw them all away, the rest of us had to learn to contend with the Super Humans who lived among us. Ruling us, hurting us, except in those few places that controlled them.

And I had no idea how they managed it in those places.

It didn't matter. *I'm one woman with no power.*

But I would deliver the letter. I flung open the door and walked in with more confidence than I actually felt. *There is no point in showing these men weakness.*

I'd never experienced walking into a room and having everyone turn to look at me—realistically, I usually wasn't even noticed. But a room full of what looked like enhanced people all turned to stare at me at the same time, practically in unison, and my heartbeat kicked in response to the weight of their combined stares. The music inside the dark pub blared louder in here than it did outside, jangling my already jagged nerves. *How do these people, with their extra-sensitive hearing, stand this noise?*

Or maybe that was the point? Maybe they chose to blast

the music so they didn't have to hear the other parts of the universe they'd really rather just tune out. Either way, it bugged me.

With my ears ringing from the noise, I stepped further into the room. I was wet, dripping, and on display, but not in the way that I usually was at home. Being dressed and stared at was somehow worse than what I was usually forced to do.

I swallowed and walked toward the bar. The interior wasn't a surprise, as it also matched my best friend's description—dark, rundown, yet clean. Someone had made the floors shine, and the bar was immaculate. What they didn't care about was keeping up the burgundy walls, which were peeling, and the barstools were taped together. I would have to be careful where I sat.

A tall man worked behind the bar, and so far, all I'd seen were men. The planets that catered to enhanced men sometimes had women on them, like ours did, but no women had been invited to this particular meeting.

Then again, there hadn't been any female Super Soldiers. The three that had been made had all been killed shortly after birth.

Or so the stories said.

The bartender's chestnut brown hair and neatly trimmed beard caught my attention, but it was his ocean blue eyes that held my gaze the longest. The only positive of living where I did was seeing that color every day out my window. I hadn't been in the ocean since I was a small girl, but I could smell the salt and see the views in my mind. They saved me, daily.

At least my sanity.

Water dripped off my clothes, hitting their neatly kept floor in a puddle under my feet. I abruptly became acutely aware of just how wet I was. I swallowed, not that I could do anything about the dripping. If I'd had the means to stay dry, I would have done so.

"Hi," I said. The bartender ignored me. There was no way he couldn't hear me. Hell, every man in the room probably could hear my heartbeat. Many found their senses intrusive, but I'd gotten used to it over time and it usually didn't bug me anymore. Between Amias and the other enhanced that I dealt with daily, those sorts of things were commonplace for me.

However, that usually meant I had their full attention rather than them completely ignoring me. *First they all stared, and now no one will look at me at all.*

It was almost coordinated. *They must have done this before.*

I tried again. "Hello. I...I need to find The Five. Can you please point me in their direction?"

No one was looking, but boy did I have their attention again. The hairs on my arms bristled and stood at attention. They were listening to me. *They don't have to be looking at me to hear.* Despite knowing they could hear me, their silence amplified my tension, making me utterly aware that I stood in a room surrounded by predators. If even one of them so chose, I would become their prey, so I needed to get out of there before that happened.

The bartender sauntered over to me. "Sorry, I can't help you with that. The Five? Never heard of them." He pointed toward the door. "Out."

This is bad. He was either lying—my preference—or things had changed so much in the past years that they were all gone. Surely, someone would remember them?

That meant that this man was lying.

I tried again. "Listen, if you are...declining to tell me the truth for whatever reason...and I'm sure it's a good reason...I need to, please, ask again. I'm here on a task that I have to complete. I just have to." *With every fiber of my being.* "I can go. I know I don't belong here. I get it. And I don't want any trouble. If you could just tell me who any one of them are, or where I can find them, I will go and never come back."

Chairs screeched and wobbled as several people—seven of them to my count—quickly left the bar. Were The Five among them? The joke of the whole situation was that there were now only four of The Five left. They just didn't know it yet. I knew their names, nothing else.

The bartender narrowed his eyes in what best could be called a threatening expression. "Let me give you a piece of advice, girlie. When someone like me tells someone like you to get out, you get out." He pointed at the door. "Or there are consequences."

Tears threatened again. I tended to cry when I got really angry, like my signals got crossed in my brain, and I couldn't tell the difference between anger and sadness. With the burden I carried, it was even harder for me to decipher the two feelings. I couldn't start the tears. Wouldn't. *Not here.* Not with these people throwing me out in the rain without even letting me do the last thing my best friend ever asked of me.

I nodded, my lips wobbling despite my determination. "Okay. I'll go."

"Ransom," a man who sat in the corner said as he rose. He knocked twice on the table and even more of the bar exited, fast. I lost count of how many, but they left in a hurry, like a drove of fleeing enhanced men. *That can't be good.*

In the end, that left four men in the bar with me. Ransom was certainly one of The Five—I recognized the name. He was the youngest of them, and Amias had said he was like his little brother.

Of course, the big, strong, intimidating man who told me to go didn't look like anyone's little brother. Not to me, at least.

That meant the other three were Crew—and he was in charge. Gunnar. And Mace. I didn't know who was who, but I'd guess the one who made everyone leave was Crew. I tried not to look at them. Now that I knew that Ransom was Ransom, I would simply hand him the letter and get on with it.

Everyone would be glad to see me leave.

I pulled the letter out of my pocket. It was dry, at least—the only thing I'd managed to keep that way. In what was absolutely not a swift move, I extended my hand to pass the letter to Ransom.

He stared at me and didn't move.

The man who had spoken walked toward me. Like Ransom, he didn't seem to be in the least bit of a hurry. My hand shook, and I dropped it, still holding the letter to my side. My stomach growled; I was hungry. It had been hours and hours since I'd eaten anything.

"Who told you to bring that to The Five? That's not a name we've used in a long time. Where did you hear it, and who gave you that note to give to us?"

I turned to the man. He was as tall as Ransom, with longish black hair and green eyes. They were striking, but I couldn't read anything from him. Barely there interest at best? He crossed his arms over his chest, like he was bored.

My tears fled easily in that second. This was just...awful. I wanted to curse at him for being so cold and disinterested when I had come so far to do this job. I'd learned over the years to hide what I thought, and I schooled my features into careful neutrality, but I should really thank him. Just his one look saved me from the humiliation of sobbing in front of him.

"Amias. He sent me here to give you this." I held out the letter to him this time.

They all shifted slightly at the sound of Amias' name. I let myself look at the other two men in the room. One of them was blond, and the other more of a light-haired redhead, like a strawberry blond. They were as tall as I expected them to be—Super Soldier sized.

"It has been a long time since any of us have heard that name. Where is he? Why did he send you instead of coming himself?" Their leader wasn't bored anymore. No, he pulsated fury, his jaw hard, his gaze threatening to tear me apart.

It is my job to deliver this news. I'm not sure how I made it that far without it ever occurring to me that I'd be the one responsible for telling them. I'd thought of the note...not about having to tell them why I brought it. Grief clouded my brain—I'd been just trying to put one foot in front of the other up until that point, rather than processing any of it.

I let out a breath I'd been holding. "I'm afraid I have to tell you he is dead." It was hard to speak the words, and my voice cracked on the word *dead*. "He died a little over a week ago, and his last request was that I give this to you."

The man I thought was likely Crew grabbed the note out of my hand. My fist clenched, but far too late to be of any good. His movement had been so fast, I barely tracked it, but the note was in his hand, and he read it quickly.

I almost cried out as a sob caught in my throat. That piece of paper...small and delicate as it had been...represented my last link to Amias.

With it out of my possession, the wave that I held off for so long struck me so hard, it might have knocked me over if

I hadn't been leaning against the bar. I blinked. How did I not begin to process what losing Amias and Stone actually *meant*?

I had to get out of there. Turning on my heel, which squeaked because I was such a soaked mess, I ran for the door.

"Wait."

I stopped. The power of his order rendered me practically unable to disobey him. He wasn't a man that people didn't listen to. I turned to stare at him.

He held up the paper for a second before he passed it to the strawberry-blond who took it, read it, and then passed it to the one with white, blonde hair. He finally passed it to Ransom.

"Did you read that note?"

I shook my head. "No. I can't read."

Why teach women to read when we were only around for one reason? Men weren't paying Clarke for me to read to them.

White-blond man blinked rapidly. "Then how did you get here?"

I pulled out another note. "Amias wrote down things, and I just matched his words with the ones I needed as I went. He anticipated what I would have to see. When it varied, and it didn't much, I asked for help."

"You're smart." Strawberry blond smiled at me. It was a sad smile, like Amias' death rode on the edges of it.

"She's a sex worker, " Ransom supplied. "In case you missed the brand."

I touched my forehead, an instinctive move I made whenever someone brought it up. "I'm not a sex worker. I don't go out on the street and sell myself. Yes, Clarke owns my body and gives it out as he sees fit. He owns all of us on our planet. None of us are free." That thought spurred me forward. "I have to go."

I didn't know why I even wasted the time to justify myself to them. What difference did it make what they thought about me? If a woman had to sell herself to survive, then that was her fate. I wasn't better or worse than they were. It just was what it was.

The leader spoke again. "I said wait." He took a step toward me. "We haven't heard from Amias in years. He vanished, leaving just a note to tell us he was never coming back. Then you arrive, and you've delivered this blow. It's going to take a moment. What is your name?"

I sighed. "I have to get back. There is no time to lose. I've been gone for a week. They can only cover for so long before it will be noted, and then everyone who helped me will be punished."

Ransom held up the note. "Do you want to know what it says?"

"He didn't tell me. It was for all of you." And I'd learned long ago to mind my business. Why would I want to step in other people's trouble when I had plenty all on my own?

Ransom crumpled up the note, and my heart split in two. "No." I rushed forward and then skidded to a stop. What was I doing? Still, I spoke before I could stop myself. "That is the last thing he did. Please don't throw it away. Please keep it. Forever."

He slammed it down on the table. "It says, *I'm sorry*. Nothing for years and years. I'm sorry. And he's dead. Fuck. This. Shit." Ransom stormed out of the room, slamming a door in his wake.

I forced myself to swallow. *Okay. Time to leave.*

I ran from the bar, and no one tried to stop me. The rain pounded down on me with even more force than before, or maybe I'd started to dry off, making it feel even worse. It didn't matter. I had to make it back to the shuttle before it left. My feet burned since the heels on my borrowed shoes were worn thin. I couldn't think. I just had to get there.

The streets were once again empty, and the face the shuttle pilot made when he dropped me off made sense. Why had I wanted to be here? I didn't.

But I'd done what my friend asked of me. *I did it.* I wiped at my eyes. The last and really only thing he'd ever requested, and I hadn't failed him. It felt important, somehow.

I skidded to a stop. There was a sign where the shuttle sat parked, but I couldn't read it. Why was it dark? Why wasn't there anyone waiting for the shuttle? I made it back on time—he'd said it would take off again in two hours.

It had not been two hours.

I looked around. There was no one to ask about the sign. What was happening? Thunder blasted its loud trumpet in the night sky.

What was I to do? Amias had left no instructions on how to find my way back home.

"They don't fly in weather like this."

It was the redhead from the bar. I turned to look at him through the downpour. He didn't seem to be bothered by the onslaught. In fact, as the water hit his chest, practically gluing his shirt to his body, it somehow became an even better look for him. My hair wasn't as blond as his when I wasn't wet. It was a darker shade of red.

"He said they'd take off in two hours."

He shrugged. "Bill Dryer is a con artist and a liar. He's also a shuttle pilot, but right now those first two things matter more. You wouldn't have come if he'd told you that he wouldn't take you back tonight." He pointed at the sky.

"It's not the rain. Who cares about that? It's the layer of electricity. See it?"

I followed where he pointed. Sure enough, a whole layer of the sky lit up again and again in strobing electrical pulses. "Will that stop when the storm clears?"

"No." He shook his head. "We're lit up like that for the next six weeks. We call this the quiet time here. If you're here, you're here until *that* goes away."

I covered my mouth to stop my scream, but I was unsuccessful. Panic and dread braided themselves through my chest, restricting my ability to breathe, to think. "No. I can't be here for six weeks. Why did he let me come? Why?"

"Bill? He needed what you paid him to get drunk, most likely. He's not one of us. He's like you, so he can actually get drunk. Anyway, he got you down here just in time, and now you're stuck."

I sunk to the ground, my legs finally giving up. I had enough money to eat maybe one more meal. I had nowhere to stay, and even if I didn't eat with what little money I had, I wouldn't have enough for even a night's stay anywhere.

Not getting home meant others would die. What was I supposed to do?

Redhead walked toward me. "What's your name?"

He knelt so we were eye-to-eye. I swallowed. "What would you like my name to be?"

That was what I always said to the men who came and were granted time with me. Most of the men liked it. It flew from my lips with practice, like a muscle memory.

"No. Try again. Real name. What is it?" He held my gaze.

I sighed as another burst of thunder hit. "My name is Raven. I don't have a last name that I remember, just Raven."

"Okay, Raven. My name is Gunnar."

I blinked. "Weapons and tech."

He smirked. "So Amias had things to say, did he? Yes, that was and is my specialty. Who were you to him, that you made a trek like this with no one to help you at the worst possible time? Were you his lover? His wife?"

"Not me." I laughed. I kept having to deliver them news. "He was my best friend. My person. He was married to my brother, Stone. They're both dead now, and without them, there is no one to help me in the world anymore. They're gone. They were it. I am Clarke's property, and right now, I'm lost. Look for me in a week, since I'll still be sitting here."

He put out his hand. "No, you won't. Come on. We have a lot to talk about. You're coming back with me. If he was married to your brother, that would make him your family. For most of my life, Amias was my brother. Clearly, there were years that I didn't know him. You can tell me about those years, and I'll tell you about mine with him. He saved my life many a time. The least I can do is watch out for his family for six weeks. It's the least any of us can do."

The last part seemed like it wasn't directed toward me. It might not be. The enhanced could hear lots of things I couldn't. Sometimes they had conversations we couldn't even hear.

Almost as soon as he spoke, the blond man arrived. He carried a sweatshirt with a hood in his hand. Gunnar tugged me to my feet, and the blond man put the shirt over my head, placing the hood over my hair.

"I'm Mace," he said in a low voice. "I'm really good at killing people. Sounds like you already know that."

With no choices—not that I ever had any—I followed them back to their bar. I'd delivered Amias' note and doomed myself in the process.

2

MY NEW HOME...FOR NOW

Their leader opened the door when we arrived, nodding at me as I came close to the door to the bar.

"I'm Crew," he said, and although I already suspected his name, it was nice to have the official introduction. "Let's put her in the guestroom, the one next to Amias' old room. It's clean."

Mace nodded. "That's what I was thinking."

They led me through the bar to a door that opened to a set of stairs. I hadn't known they lived above the bar, but it was a huge space. I counted six bedrooms as we walked down the hall. From the outside, their bar seemed deceptively small.

I rubbed my face as the first shiver hit me. The cooler air sliced through my wet clothes, clacking my teeth together before I clamped my jaw.

"It'll be okay." Mace touched my back. "The hot water will help."

I blinked, surprised. "You have hot water?"

"You don't?" Gunnar opened a door for me then ushered

me inside. A big bed with brown sheets and pillows covered in matching pillowcases stood in the center of the room. Other than the table next to the bed, no other furniture adorned the space. He passed by me to enter another room, then looked over his shoulder to speak to me. "Bathroom is here." I followed him and watched as he put on the water. "Like I said, plenty of hot water." Then he stared at the water and stepped back. He stuck his hand in it again. "What the fuck?"

"What's the matter?" Mace called from the doorway to another bedroom. "Not working?"

"No, it fucking isn't." He turned off the water and stormed out the door. "Of all the fucking times for the hot water to go out."

Gunnar rushed past me and back down the stairs. I could hear him banging on them as he sped from the room.

Crew shook his head and crossed to the window. "Well, there went that idea. Okay, we need to get you warm. Off with the wet clothing. Give them to me and get under the covers. That's a start."

My teeth chattered, and it was like my whole body vibrated, my hands shaking. I should have some modesty, but that fled years ago. In my position, nudity didn't matter anymore. Even if, in the back of my mind, a little voice suggested I should protect myself from being seen by everyone. It didn't matter, though, since these guys could pay Clarke, if they were so inclined, to see me naked any time they wanted. Any man could.

But when I tried to pull my shirt over my head, the shaking proved more of a problem than I expected, as though my muscles didn't want to comply with what I needed them to do.

"Let me help." Mace approached with his hands spread

in a calming way. "You're safe with us, naked or otherwise. You would have been anyway, I believe, but we actually use a machine to keep our sexual urges at bay. You could walk around this city all day long completely nude, and no Super Soldier would want to do anything with you. I can't speak for the regular humans, but the rest of us are fine."

Some time, when I wasn't about to die, I should ask questions about that whole explanation. *Oh, forget it.* I needed to know right then, despite the shakes. My curiosity wouldn't allow for anything else. "What?"

"We'll get into it later," Crew said as he walked over and helped Mace. Between the two of them, they very systematically undressed me until I stood in front of them shaking and freezing. Mace grabbed a towel from the bathroom and ran back out, wrapping me in it.

Crew nodded toward the bed. "Come on. Under the covers will be warmer."

I tried to walk to the bed, but my legs, like my arms, didn't want to cooperate. In the end, Crew picked me up and carried me to the bed, although it wasn't far away. It was like my body was just shutting down from the cold. Truthfully, I'd never felt so cold before. My planet was much warmer than theirs. It almost never rained, and when it did, it wasn't heavy or cold, because of the drought.

I wrapped the blanket around me, appreciating its softness, but my skin didn't warm. I tugged it tighter against me, pulled it over my head like a hood, and I still didn't begin to warm. I felt slow, sluggish with the chill, but I continued to quake with violent shivers.

"She's really frozen." Mace strode to the bed, taking off his shirt and pants with each step. I gaped at him. Only seconds ago, they assured me they didn't think about sex. *Now he's stripping?* What fresh hell was this? I was grateful for their help, but I'd be damned if I was having sex with them right then. No one was there to order me to do so, and besides, I was freezing.

But, as he crawled under the covers with me and tugged me against him, he didn't hold me in a sexual way.

"Skin to skin warms the fastest. We used to do this when we were on missions, if one of us was accidently frozen."

I found my voice, and although it shook, I used it. "Accidently fr-r-rozen?"

"Sure," Crew answered, stripping down to his underwear. Just like Mace before he crawled into bed next to me, so that I was officially sandwiched between their bodies. Their deliciously warm bodies, which felt like actual heaven against my chilled skin. "Amias once spent two days locked in a freezer. All sorts of strange shit used to happen to us. Super Soldiers have notoriously bad luck in some ways. Anyway, this will warm you."

We lay there in silence for a few seconds. The three of us. Under the covers of their bed, waiting for my shivers to stop. "Th-thank you for this."

Mace shook his head. "Make that the last time you thank us. Gunnar told you outside, you're Amias' family. We'll see to your health until you leave. And you can tell us things about him, if you want. Things we would never have known otherwise."

I could do that, if only I could think past my shivers. They pressed closer to me. Their bodies were hard, but I was used to that from the enhanced. They were all built like gods, but it didn't mean they weren't actually demons on the inside.

"What would you like to know?" If my shaking bothered them, they weren't indicating it.

Mace spoke first. "He married your brother..." He

paused. "What was his name, your brother? You said it earlier, but my head was buzzing from the news of Amias' death, and I don't remember it."

My breath caught in my throat as grief came in on a wave. Their deaths were a wound that was never going to close. It was new pain, yet already I knew it was permanent. The grief dug a hole inside of me that I would just have to live with because there was no way it was going away, ever.

Still, despite my shakes and pain, I answered. "His name was Stone."

"Was he your older or younger brother?"

This time it was Crew who asked, so I glanced at him as I answered. "Older. By three years. We were always together when we were young, and since Clarke takes women into service three years before he does men, we entered his service at the same time."

Crew shifted slightly on the bed, his foot finding mine under the covers. "Can we put a pin in what you just said? I'd like Ransom to be here when we discuss how Clarke is running his empire, and right now he's off in the mountains handling himself."

"Sure." Presumably, we'd have lots of time to talk. Weeks and weeks while I would remain stuck here at their mercy. They could ask me anything, though. I didn't have any secrets, since my life had been laid out for me from the day the enhanced lost their place in the world and took ours. Well, not these guys, although I really didn't know who lived in their town before them. Had they all been ousted, so that these four and those like them could live here? It didn't matter. This was the world. The strong took; the weak tried to survive the taking.

Mace placed a gentle hand on my arm. "How old are you, Raven?"

That was a good question. I needed to think for a second. "I'm either nineteen or twenty. We don't keep track of time. Wait...I know the fall passed into winter. So, I'm twenty. That's right. Twenty."

"Twenty," he whispered after I said it. "What was I doing at twenty?"

"Nothing good," Crew answered him. "You were probably battling on the other side of the galaxy. That timing is probably about right. How did Amias die? Let's just get to that. How did he die?"

I closed my eyes for a second. Too cold still to sleep, the jitters hadn't left my body, and I wasn't a fainter. That meant I would actually have to answer them, which meant talking about the terrible time that would live with me forever.

"Stone got the flu. It swept through the housing units, and it seemed like everyone got sick. I don't know why I didn't catch it. I just didn't. I took care of everyone with it, so presumably I was really exposed. But Stone got it. Clarke made sure that the higher ups didn't get sick, or if they did, he put them in the med machine. The real money makers are too important to lose." I was on my way to becoming a money maker, but I wasn't one yet. He wouldn't have spared the power for me. If I got sick, I would've been on my own. "I tried to take care of him. I did. Amias did, too. You guys obviously don't get sick, so he wasn't at risk. We stayed up for days, trying to get that fever down. It just wouldn't budge. He got so weak. Then he was gone. They took him right away. They didn't even let us say goodbye, his body just disappeared." I swallowed. They were not moments I cared to remember.

"Take a second if you need one," Mace whispered.

"I'd rather rush through it, if it were me." Crew's hand was on my hip, as if he intended to anchor me to the present

—to where we were and not where my head wanted to go. That was, however, impossible, if I was going to tell the rest of it.

I caught my breath, and then I spoke quickly, shoving the words out past my heartache and shivers. "I should have realized what was going to happen, but I was lost to my grief. I couldn't think, could hardly put sentences together. There were still so many people to take care of, but Amias was so quiet. He sat down and started writing things. I already told you I can't read. None of us who were under five when Clarke came can at all. It didn't occur to me to ask what he was doing, but he was..."

"Making plans," Mace supplied. "That's what he did when he made plans. When there was strategy to create, he'd sit down and start writing."

"Yes. He was doing that. He was furious. You have to understand, when Amias showed up on our planet, it wasn't to fall in love. He was there to work for Clarke, like all of the other enhanced that live there. It takes a lot of enhanced to make Clarke's empire work."

Mace sat up on his elbow. "Why would he do that? Why would he have gone and done that?"

"I don't know. It's not something we ever discussed. I just knew he left his team—you guys—because he sometimes spoke of you. Regardless of all of that, he went to Clarke. Those of us who aren't like you? We tended to avoid the enhanced. Don't be offended. It's just a lot, and they can really hurt us, if they so choose. I guess, the same way you could hurt me if you wanted."

Crew shook his head. "No one will hurt you."

"Amias was assigned to us, to watch our grouping and make sure we behaved. His job was to see to it we followed orders without complaint. That our clients were satisfied when they left. But he and Stone made eye contact, and that was that. They both fell off the cliff into loving each other. I couldn't believe it. That kind of love, marriage? That's not part of our life, but that was it for them. *Boom.* Clarke's people knew about it. Amias worked harder than anyone, so that they could stay as they were, with him living with us. For the most part, the whole housing area made sure to behave, because everyone loved Stone, and no one wanted to hurt him by having Amias taken away."

The room was so silent, I could practically hear my still thudding pulse in my ears. Crew spoke quietly. "It's totally foreign to me to imagine such a thing. Love, what did your brother do for Clarke?"

"The same as me. All women and men are given out sexually on request to Clarke's business associates, although some also perform other functions. I did my best to be a healer, although clearly, I'm not a very good one." *A better one would have saved Stone.* That was on me, something I would have to live with, despite my constant guilt. Somehow. I didn't know how, but maybe I'd figure it out in time. Tears threatened again, so I blinked them away fast. *No crying. Not here. Not yet.* "Amias came to me on day three. He had made his plans, so he handed me the note to give to you. He took the time to detail everything, including instructions on how to get here. Everything was drawn out, so I just needed to match what he'd drawn with what I'd see. He asked me to do this for him." My voice shook, but it had nothing to do with my chill. "I begged him not to, got down on my knees, but he was set on his course. If they just opened the med machines up, Stone wouldn't have died. They let a hundred people die, and they didn't blink, but he didn't want to live without Stone. So, he decided to make them pay for taking him."

I let out a breath. "I didn't get to see it. He set up people to sneak me off planet—all of those plans, while I had no idea." One tear slipped past my guard, and I brushed it away roughly with a shaking hand. "My best friend, but he didn't let us grieve together. He took himself from me, too. Sorry, that's selfish of me to say. That's not my best."

"Don't apologize." Mace put a hand in my tangled hair. "He went after Clarke."

I nodded. "Took out three of the other enhanced, damaged Clarke, but in the end, they sliced him in two. That's what I've been told, anyway. I wasn't there, but he's gone. They're both gone." I rubbed another tear away in irritation before I blew out a breath. "And now you're stuck with me. I can't get off the planet, and the people who helped me will be hurt when whoever replaced Amias reports my absence. The only thing I can hope for is they might assume I'm dead, too. Best case scenario, I could get really, really lucky and hope they don't have a good count of all the bodies."

Mace pushed my head against his chest. "We've got to get you warmer." His arms wrapped around me like a hug. Crew scooted closer, hugging me against him from behind me.

They didn't ask me any more questions, and if I was honest, I was grateful for the quiet. Eventually, I became warmer. That thought crossed my mind about two seconds before my eyes closed. Not that I intended to go to sleep or anything, but because my eyelids felt so very heavy...

My brief respite from consciousness didn't last long. The door swung open to bang against the wall, awakening me just in time to see Gunnar run into the room. "Fixed! The water is fixed," he crowed in pride.

I jolted awake when he entered, if my brief rest could be

called sleep. "Sorry. Sorry," I sputtered, shoving myself up onto my elbows.

Mace pulled me back down, snuggling me into the curve of his body with an easy familiarity that soothed my jangled nerves from the abrupt awakening. "Why are you sorry? You've been through an ordeal. You're cold. Your body likely needed the rest, which you were getting before someone ran in like a freight train and woke you up."

Gunnar held up his hands. "Sorry, Raven. Sorry. I listened to your story. I'm sorry about your brother. What Amias did? That's just what he *would* do. He went out as he would have wished to go, though I'm sorry you had to lose both of them. Thank you for bringing us his note, and the news. We never would've known, not ever, if you hadn't taken the time to come to us."

Crew got out of the bed. Immediately, the cold air hit my back, and I shivered. "Trade with me, Gunnar. I need to go find Ransom. We've all lost him, everyone in this room has. He needs to be here. I'm going to bring him home. Come on, lie down."

Gunnar kicked off his shoes before he took off his shirt and pants. He slipped easily into the position Crew abandoned, but his energy felt strangely different than Crew. We sort of fell into a cozy easiness as we lay there, despite the topic of conversation.

But Gunnar was wide awake.

My lethargy vanished, too, surprising me, but I've always been good at going without sleep. Sometimes men wanted to stay days with me, yet I never dared sleep in the same room with one of Clarke's associates. They might wake up themselves, see me asleep, and get angry about the lack of attention.

"The water is warm now. I bet that would help you feel warmer."

It would certainly make a huge difference in how bad I likely smelled. Was it...days ago that I last managed to get a bath? "I don't get hot water at home unless we warm it over the stove, so I'll take advantage of the offer, if that's okay."

"It's okay." Gunnar nodded as Crew left the room, redressing himself as he went.

"Yes," Mace let me go so I could get out of the bed as well. "Take all the time you want. Despite the fact that it wasn't working, we don't usually suffer from lack of hot water here. You'll have the basics to meet your needs, nothing fancy, even though we're cut off from other planets. We can offer hot water, a bed, food, and safety."

I climbed around him and slipped my feet to the floor, chuckling. "I don't have a bed at home, just a pad on the floor, a blanket, and a pillow. What you've just described is my definition of luxury, not basics. Thank you. I realize you don't have to do anything for me."

Gunnar widened his eyes, his expression a mixture of stunned confusion. I didn't imagine he often found himself befuddled, which made the expression bizarrely adorable. The enhanced rarely felt any confusion whatsoever, so far as I could tell.

"Amias lived these last years without a bed and hot water...?" He made the words a statement, but I could pick up on his unspoken question.

"He could have had one. I think most of the enhanced do, but he preferred to share his pad with Stone."

Mace cleared his throat. "Raven, if Stone also was used by Clarke's associates sexually, how did Amias react? Your description makes it sound like he was very attached; yet he just let that happen?"

I nodded, not surprised it didn't make sense to someone who never lived our life. "The men that Stone serviced for Clarke—well, anyone we touch because of our orders? They're meaningless to us. We do what we must to survive, because he owns us, and he owns the whole planet. I'm sure that Amias didn't like the situation, but Stone loved only him. Whatever went on between the two of them, it was different than what Stone had to do for Clarke."

"Why didn't he just take you two and leave?" Gunnar crossed his arms over his chest. "That's what I would have done. Grab the husband. Grab the sister. Come home. You could have been learning to read and bathing in hot water for the last five years. Whatever went down that last day that Amias was here when he announced he just had to leave, he knew he could come home. That he could *always* come home."

Mace nodded. "He had to know."

"It wasn't just us, though," I tried to explain. "A whole housing area counted on him. Stone loved all of them, all of us. They...tolerated me as Stone's sister. He never would've left them. He really believed that we were all better together, and that we could survive better as a unit. If Amias even suggested leaving the planet, Stone would have refused him. Amias loved him, so he would've understood that to take Stone away from the people who relied on him would be to destroy him. Stone would never choose to leave us behind."

They didn't understand, and I could tell. Honestly, I didn't really understand it, either. I never loved anyone the way Stone and Amias loved each other. Despite knowing their choices, I had to admit I would've chosen differently if I was in their position. If I had been Amias, I would've picked up Stone and left the second I spotted him.

I would have asked forgiveness later.

If I'd been Amias, I would've left me behind the first week we met, but he was a better person than me. *They both were.*

I stopped short about a second after I stepped into the bathroom. In theory, I knew how the shower worked. The older people talked about them all the time, reminiscing about how it had been *before*. I guess technically it was only fifteen years since everything changed on my planet, but before seemed like a different world to me.

Twisting the faucet as Gunnar had done earlier, I let the water pour out of the gilded device. It occurred to me that I didn't have a change of clean clothes, and despite my lack of concern over nudity, I didn't want to spend weeks naked.

I poked my head out of the bathroom, spotting Mace quickly. "I have two changes of clothes on the shuttle. I didn't bring them because I didn't want them to get wet, and I intended to come right back to leave the planet."

Mace nodded. "I can get those back for you by tomorrow. You'll have your clothes."

"Thank you." Then I remembered, *no more thank yous.* "Never mind. I didn't say that."

He smirked at me. "Good."

The hot water proved to be glorious. I closed my eyes and let it roll down my back. I cried out from the joy of it, probably the closest I'd ever been to an orgasm. I smiled at the thought. The cold fled my body. Yes, this was exactly what I'd needed.

My weariness from traveling swirled down the drain with soap and filth. Although I'd need to board another shuttle to get home, I had to admit I didn't look forward to the experience, and I silently vowed to myself that I'd never be on one again, if I could help it. The noise. The constant feeling of knowing I wasn't on the ground...all of it unsettled me in a way I didn't like. I liked real, planetary gravity.

That was a word that I learned only recently. *Gravity.*

I turned off the water and wrapped myself back up in the towel before I exited the bathroom, expecting the guys to be gone from the room they'd loaned me. But they hadn't moved, still lying right where I left them. Gunnar patted the bed where I sat previously, inviting me to join him.

With no reason to fear them, I obeyed. I dropped the towel and climbed back into the bed, where they wrapped me under the blanket, before they both enveloped me in a hug, sandwiching me in their embrace. I wasn't cold anymore, but I didn't mind the feeling of their bodies against my own. Stone had been a hugger, a big one, and I missed him. My breath caught, and I realized I didn't know how I'd live the rest of my life without a hug from my big brother.

"Do you guys give hugs out regularly?" I joked, trying to lighten the moment.

Gunnar laughed. "I don't think I've ever given one before, to be honest, so the answer would be no. Not me. And not Mace, either."

"You're so much warmer. Your skin feels better." Mace spoke quietly. "Now you need to sleep, because your body is telling me you haven't in a very long time. I can hear the strain in your breath, in the swoosh of your blood, in your heartbeat. You are aching to sleep, and I know, because I have lost more people than I can count, that you don't want to be alone right now. I don't want to, either. Neither does Gunnar, so lie here with us and fall asleep. Maybe we will, too, but no matter what, you won't be alone with the grief tonight. We can share it, like Amias never let you do."

3

MAYBE I CAN BE HELPFUL

I wish I could say I instantly fell asleep after Mace advised I should rest, but sleeping with two strangers in my bed wasn't normal for me. In fact, I'd been all but trained not to sleep if it meant my partner's needs might not be met, which meant I continued to be wide awake.

And so did they.

Minutes passed before I spoke again. "Can you just fall asleep anytime you want to? Like, if you had to go to sleep, could you force yourself to do it?"

"We need very little sleep," Gunnar supplied. "Much less than you, but we tend to try to quiet down into acting like we're going to bed around two in the morning every day to keep a similar sleep-wake schedule as the regular humans. Years ago, if we were ordered to bed, I could sleep instantly because of an order."

Mace snorted. "Or else we did a really great job of faking it."

"Did you?" Gunnar shifted to stare at Mace. "Did you really manage to fake it?"

With a shrug, Mace answered him. "I did. I was never

the type to just knock out when my head hit a pillow. Unless they put me in cryo, because then, obviously, yes, out cold till they thaw us."

I tried to make sense of his words, but he lost me with about half of them. "Cryo?"

"Back before the company went under, we used to be put in extended sleeps. They basically halted our aging until they woke us, pretty much a cold freeze. It sucked, but those days are long over."

The idea seemed unfathomable to me. Our home was very low tech, sometimes no tech. It was there, if Clarke and his people wanted to use it, but it wasn't for us. Freezing people technology? How did that even work? There were med machines, but other than for my sterilization, I never got in one. Apparently, they also got into some sort of machine to keep themselves from wanting sex, a mind-boggling idea for technology. Then again, since we had so little, it didn't take much to impress me. If I were being honest, they amazed me with their constant electricity and hot water.

It was like time stopped and started moving backward when the enhanced became part of general society, or at least that was how it felt on my world. Or maybe I was over-thinking things? Maybe they just were what they were.

"I have a question. When you talk about us, you call us the enhanced." Mace leaned on his elbow, his head tilted in careful consideration of my face. "Why that? I've never heard the term before. We're just Super Soldiers. It's what we were always called, and you guys are normal humans."

At least one of their questions was easy to answer. "Clarke doesn't like the term *Super Soldiers*. He finds it offensive, so we call you *enhanced*. He prefers that. Every once in a while, I think or use *Super Soldiers*, because my mother always said it, but I'd say ninety percent of the time, I don't even think it."

I hadn't heard that term spoken since my mother died when I was ten—a decade without her. I knew grief cooled. Even if the pain never really left, we got used to carrying it. *Will that happen now? Can anything ease the ache that was in the place in my heart Stone and Amias used to fill?*

Gunnar rubbed his eyes. "Do I want to know why he finds it offensive?"

I shrugged. "You're not soldiers anymore. Now you're out in the world and you're just better. More gifted. Stronger. Better able to exist."

Mace scrunched down in the bed. "Our so-called *better* comes at a huge price, and the price seems more offensive than using the name we were gifted when we were made. I don't know. Clarke was always such a douchebag."

I laughed and then covered my mouth. "Sorry."

"Why? I'm the one who said it." Mace shook his head. "You woke up apologizing. What do you think is going to happen to you if you do something wrong?"

My head swam. Maybe I really was tired? "Anything could happen. You have to be careful to never offend your betters."

"We're not your betters." When Gunnar spoke, he actually sounded sad, even though his face remained passive. "Did Amias make you feel as if he was better than you in some way? Like he expected you to treat him as a superior?"

I shook my head, almost laughing at the idea of it. "No, he was my best friend. Taught me to play games. I helped him clean up when it was called for, made him laugh. We talked all the time. He made sure I was okay after jobs. He loved my brother but didn't leave me out of their life together."

Mace nudged me. "I hear a *but* in there."

Did he? Is there one? Yes, there was. "It feels disloyal to say it."

"He's dead. The only person you have left to be loyal to is yourself." Gunnar sighed. "The dead don't care if we tell the truth or if we lie for them. They aren't here anymore to deal with any kind of consequences. They've left it all for us."

I knew that was true. First my father had been taken down by Clarke's men in the initial surge. Then my mother and then my brother, both gone from illness. Now, Amias from his attack on Clarke. The dead never came to tell me what to say or not say, and perhaps all I owed them was the truth. It was so much easier, anyway.

"I've always wondered why he was there in the first place. You had that question, too. Why would he come work for Clarke? If he didn't fall in love with Stone, would he have hurt us like all of the rest? None of them ever cared what happened to me at one of my appointments. What would he have been like?"

I spoke the words aloud for the first time, and then I burst into tears. I hadn't felt them coming, hadn't known it was going to happen, but there it was. Tears flooded out of my eyes, streaming down my face as sobs wracked my body. My grief swallowed me whole, and I didn't have it in me to fight it.

Wasn't I the most selfish person ever? What did it matter that he came under different circumstances? What mattered was he'd stayed and been my friend. I cried harder.

"What are we supposed to do when someone cries?" Gunnar asked Mace.

"I don't have any idea."

I shook my head trying, and failing, to stop myself from crying. "Nothing. You don't have to do anything."

Pressing my head against my knees, I gave in to the need and just cried because I had to—because the shut-off valve for my tears was broken, and I'd never be able to stop them until they stopped themselves. A strong hand touched my back, rubbing gently in circles. A few seconds later, Gunnar tugged me into his arms.

I shook my head to tell him he didn't have to hold me, but it was pointless. I couldn't get the words out, and with my head pressed against his chest, I stopped trying. Mace scooted close, and like earlier, they pressed me between them.

After that, I wasn't really sure what happened. The pressure felt good, stabilizing somehow. Maybe I slept or just left mentally for a while, but it was Crew's return that brought me back to myself.

"She okay?" His voice was low.

"You woke her." Mace answered in an equally soft voice. He rubbed my back. "Go back to sleep, Raven. It's just Crew and Ransom coming home. You're fine. Go back to sleep."

The bed dipped, once, then twice. I would have lifted my head, but Gunnar kept his hand to the back of it, holding it against him. I closed my eyes again. His heart beat slowly, steadily in my ear, like it could be trusted to never stop beating.

But I knew that wasn't true. Sometimes the enhanced lost their heartbeats. Sometimes they died.

A sob reared up again. How did I even have anything left to cry?

"Sshh," Gunnar whispered.

I needed some air, and I needed it right then or I was going to throw up. I managed to somehow pull away, or perhaps Gunnar let me go because he could tell I needed to move. I jumped off the bed, once again naked without caring, and rushed toward the door.

Making it downstairs, I almost got outside before Ransom grabbed my arm.

"Here." He shoved his shirt over my head. "Can't go out there like that. We're safe, and I'm ninety percent sure all the other Super Soldiers who live nearby won't bother you. We don't actually make sure that they all take their treatments, though, as that is their own choice. Everyone makes the same choice, because I don't know how you live otherwise, but they might not be able to look at you without wanting you like this. I'd like to think they'd still behave, that they would control themselves, but people are monsters when it comes down to it. I think you probably know that better than most." He visibly swallowed. "Plus, there are non–Super Soldier males living here, too. Who knows with them? Monsters come in all shapes and sizes, and not all of them were made in a lab."

"Thank you." Some of my nausea fled with his words, not that I could explain why.

He pointed with his chin. "If you go out the side door, there's an awning to keep you dry."

"Side door?" I glanced around, not sure which way was the side.

"I'll show you."

I followed Ransom across squeaky floors to the kitchen, a clean, dark, and currently empty room. Did they serve food there or just booze? Wasn't it next to impossible for an enhanced to get drunk? Didn't Amias tell me that at one point?

Not that it mattered. I followed him out the door he advised at the bar, and then stood under an awning listening to the patter of rain. I closed my eyes. The air outside was warmer than earlier, or maybe it was more tolerably dry. In any case, I closed my eyes and just breathed the scent of wet and earth.

Ransom didn't leave my side, remaining there with me. The breeze lifted tendrils of my hair in a damp kiss, and I exhaled slowly, reveling in the sensations. With my lids closed, I couldn't see him or what he was doing, but his presence was a comfort, and for that I was glad. Sometimes, I just needed to breathe.

Finally, I opened my eyes to look around. Darkness surrounded me on all sides, and I couldn't see anything around us. Everything, erased by inky blackness, and I realized someone had turned off the streetlights.

"Why turn off the outside lights?" My voice sounded hoarse from all the crying. My head ached between my eyes, and all in all, I felt struck down by heavy machinery. I wouldn't recover from the emotional outburst with just a few breaths, apparently.

Maybe it was better to not feel things. Maybe there was a treatment, like sterilization of your emotions, I could buy. It would be worth it, if just to ease the pain.

"Look up." He nodded toward the sky. I obeyed, and sure enough, I could see the electrical storm they pointed out earlier. The same storm which kept the ships grounded until it was finished, apparently. "We turn off the lights down here so we can watch the show. If we happen to be awake, anyway. For the next six weeks."

I never would have guessed they'd do something just for the pleasure of it, but as I watched the lightning—yellows, purples, reds all bleeding together as they danced across the sky—I could see why they would want to look at it.

It was beautiful. Deathly beautiful. *Why are so many of the most lethal things the most appealing to watch?*

"Amias never told me how you guys came to be here, just that I should look for you here. That this was your spot, the place where you did business and lived." Although I'd never grasped it at the time, I now understood they lived at their business. I wondered why Amias didn't make it clearer to me. I rubbed at my face. "Did you come here right away, after things changed?"

The light from inside the house illuminated him a little, enough that I could see him raise one eyebrow as he regarded me. "When the corporation went under, we were slated to be executed. Hundreds of us were, but Crew led us away. In the dead of night, we escaped together. We made the journey in a barely space-worthy, dingy old ship, and then yes, we made our way here. It was an all but deserted planet, with a few families here and there who didn't bother us, so we didn't bother them. Eventually, we came to know them, and they got to know us. Others joined us over time, and we rebuilt this town, all of us together. Everyone who came here shared our purpose, which was just being away from everyone else. If someone wants to hire us for a job only we could do, they seek us out here. Otherwise, we keep to ourselves, live our lives, sell what we make here to others, and don't get involved in things that aren't any of our business."

"I see." I sort of understood. I didn't know what it all meant, or how the corporations made people in labs. What did that even mean when it came down to it? But I didn't have to understand every intricate detail to know they had to run. They'd built a life on a planet so private, it entirely shut out the rest of the universe for six weeks out of the year. Amias had left them behind for some reason, and then I came uninvited to bring them pain.

I touched the door behind me. "Did you build this or was it already built, just needing repair?"

"The latter. Some of the houses in town were built by us, but this one lasted through neglect. We made it sound again. It needs a new paint job none of us feel like doing, but it's sound and steady." He touched the wall, not looking at me . "I was rude to you when you arrived, but that's because we don't answer to the name The Five anymore. Mostly, we dropped it because Amias is gone, which leaves only four of us." He shook his head. "So you knowing that name...it made me wary. I apologize. For that, and for all my actions afterward. I'm not usually so rude. At least, I think I was rude. It isn't always clear to us how our words and actions are interpreted. When we arrived, the humans here helped us understand some things, but we're still men bred and born to kill. Battling to have any sense of other is a constant issue for us."

I nodded, since I understood. Being trapped by circumstances of birth or creation seemed pretty similar, in my opinion. "It's hard to escape a purpose, or to run away from what you're supposed to be."

"Do you think you're supposed to be a whore? Is it what you were born to do? Do you think you were created with no greater purpose than to open your legs because Clarke or others tell you to?"

I stiffened my spine. I hated the word, even though it only had what power I gave it. "I suppose I'm supposed to be one, like you were supposed to be a mindless killer. What does it say about either of us, if our very existence was dictated by people and powers we didn't choose, yet we have to follow their directions? I'm glad life took you in a different direction, but I also wonder which is worse—being ordered to sleep with people and obeying or killing people for the same reason? I don't have blood on my hands...do you?"

I bit off the words, a hard answer to his mean question, before I second guessed myself. Once I thought it through, my eyes widened, and I clamped my hand over my mouth. Why did I say that to him, one of the few people standing between me and literal death on my own?

I dropped my hand, panicked about making it right. "I'm sorry. So sorry."

He smirked at me, actual amusement glinting in his hard eyes. "Don't ever apologize when you're telling it like it is. Also, quit cowering. I'm not going to hurt you, not ever. No matter what you say to me, okay? I guess I owe *you* another apology."

I shrugged. I'd heard far worse, honestly. "I do seem to trigger you. I don't mean to, for what it's worth. Is there something about me that you just didn't like right off the bat?"

He sighed, loudly. "Before was different than now. I think I'm jealous of you. There, I said it. And I'm not overly familiar with the emotion, so I don't like how it feels but there it is."

My mouth fell open, my eyes wide, while my brain tried to digest the information. I sputtered for a second before I finally managed, "What?"

"You spent the last five years with him. I'm jealous of that." He spoke through gritted teeth, tension tautening his already hard jaw. "Not proud of it, but there it is. His last five were with you, not me."

He spoke in a low, rough voice, one laced with pain, and I could feel the grief coming off him as though it were my own. I thought of Amias and Stone, and a realization hit me.

"Were you in love with him?" I knew they couldn't be

sexual because of their machine here, but love was so much
more than just sex. I continued quickly, hoping I didn't
offend him, but very curious. "Did he leave you for my
brother?"

Ransom blinked rapidly, then seemed to understand.
"Not in the way that you mean. I didn't know that Amias
loved men. That's how little we discussed such things. It just
wasn't part of our lives, so not even the option of that kind of
thing crossed our minds. No, he was my brother, like they're
all my brothers. We made promises to each other on the day
we got away. We all agreed we would do this thing...this life
that we weren't designed for, one where we weren't even
sure how to exist...together. Then he took off, saying he
needed some space to consider things. He said he was never
coming back, but I always thought— But he didn't. Because
he fell in love, which is hard to even consider as a possibility.
Then you got all that time with him, the time he'd promised
to share with us."

I hugged him, because he looked like he needed one.
Ransom caught his breath and didn't move for a good three
seconds—which felt really long in the moment—before his
arms wrapped around me.

But then his body sighed against mine, so I snuggled
into his neck.

"I'm sorry that he hurt you," I whispered to him. It
wasn't a lie; I was sorry for it. "I'm sorry the way you heard
about his death was by me showing up like that."

We stayed quiet for a little longer before his grip on me
eased, and we stepped away from each other. His voice
sounded a little gruff when he spoke. "Let's get you inside.
It's been a long time since you slept. I can hear your exhaus-
tion. The little bit that you fell asleep earlier wasn't
enough."

Mace had said he could hear it earlier, too. I tried not to resent the fact they knew more about my physical state than I sometimes did.

He continued. "I get needing air, but now you need to sleep."

It seemed likely he was right, especially since my mouth opened just then in a jaw-popping yawn. We walked back upstairs in silence. Although I sort of expected to find the bedroom empty, I instead found them all on the bed, none of them moving. Ransom's words from earlier resonated with me. They didn't always know how to do human-y things, even though they were technically human.

Taking a hard look at them, I noticed the same wounded look in their eyes as I saw in Ransom. They were hiding it because they didn't know how to otherwise, but Amias' death had hit them all.

"Do you ever share a bed? All of you, together?" It was certainly big enough to fit everyone.

Crew ran a hand through his hair. "Lie next to each other? On missions, sometimes, we might sleep together. Been a long time, but yes."

"Do you want to now? With me?" I asked because, worst-case scenario, they would say no. I liked the idea of spending the night with four people who loved Amias, who didn't seem to mind that I'd criticized their friend, and because my brother wasn't there to hold me. There was strength in sharing pain.

Mace patted the bed next to him. When I began to climb in, I remembered I wore Ransom's shirt. I tugged at it to take it off, but he grabbed my arm. "Keep it. For tonight, I'm good."

He kicked off his shoes and Crew followed suit. They were all shirtless, big, broad, muscular men made for battle.

And as lost in this room as me.

I climbed into their bed. It jostled several times as they all got comfortable around me. I ended up back in between Mace and Gunnar. Crew took the spot next to Gunnar, and Ransom snuggled next to Mace. We were sharing a bed because we all missed Amias. I had five years they missed with him, and they had most of his lifetime.

The six weeks I stayed here could be a time we used to share stories, I hoped.

Maybe I could help them out in some way, even make things work out so they became glad I visited them. I yawned, and Gunnar pressed my head back against his chest. I closed my eyes, and I didn't try to fight the need to sleep. They were all there, so maybe five of us together could keep the bad thoughts away for a night.

When I awoke sometime later, light streamed through the window. It wasn't bright, but it was morning, none-theless. Thunder boomed in the distance, and I remembered the rain. *Will it storm for the entire six weeks?* That was my first thought upon waking. My next was that I was still pressed against Gunnar's chest, and Mace was tight against my back, his arm around my waist. Someone—it took me a second to realize it was Ransom—had his hand in my hair. His arm was above Mace's head on the pillow.

Crew was asleep, his face turned away from us, his arm flung over his eyes like he was keeping out the light.

My muscles were tight. I hadn't moved in a long time, and I didn't normally sleep for very long. I wasn't used to being able to lie still for so long. Men usually woke up very erect, in my experience, always hard in the morning.

But not this group. Whatever they did to control their sexual urges, it meant they weren't hard even as they lay against me in the dawn.

It was an interesting experience, a novel one for me. When they woke up, they wouldn't want to fuck me once or twice more before they left. I could just *be there* with them.

I stretched luxuriously, reveling in the freedom of the idea of having company in my bed without pretending I felt like having sex with them.

Gunnar sighed and his arms on my back tightened around me. His heartbeat was slow and steady. His eyes opened slowly, and as I leaned back just a little bit to look at him, he smiled at me, so I smiled back.

"Hey," he whispered. "Morning."

"Morning, " I whispered back. "Did I keep you up?" It couldn't have been easy to sleep with me pushed up against his chest.

He scrunched up his face. "No. Slept great. You are very...comfortable to rest alongside. I actually fell asleep. I even dreamed, and I haven't in a long time."

We whispered, but the other three woke up almost simultaneously in that moment. Mace squeezed my stomach and dug his head into my back. Ransom gripped my hair tighter and Crew flipped over to stare at us.

"Hi," Mace said. "Good morning. Can't believe how long I slept."

Ransom groaned. "Could still be sleeping, if you guys weren't so loud."

"Not being loud," I giggled. "Whispering actually."

He groaned again, a longer sound this time. "Same difference."

Crew sat up and grinned at me, but then his face became serious. "Last night was intense. It needed to be. Today we get back to it. There are so many things to do."

Mace squeezed me tighter. "When are there not a million things to do? Let's just lie here and be lazy. No one liked a good lie around day better than Amias. We can make it his memorial."

Then they all sat up all at once. It startled me, so I did the same. What was going on?

"Something wrong?"

Crew jumped out of the bed. "Someone is very sick. Did you tell me you could heal?"

My drowsy brain struggled to keep up, but I got there. "Yes. But I've never had to help an enhanced person."

He shook his head. "Regular human, a young child, aged five." He pulled me from the bed. "They need help."

4

FAIRYTALES ARE WARNING STORIES

One of them had washed and dried my clothes the night before, not that I knew which one or when. Maybe when I'd gone outside with Ransom—but they were dry enough for me to pull on my pants. My shoes, however, were still damp, so they squeaked as I struggled to keep up with the guys. I tried ignoring my discomfort, striding as quickly as possible.

Crew stopped running and turned to me. "Don't be insulted."

What did he mean? Then he hauled me into his arms, and I yelped. What was he doing? I understood in seconds —he needed me to move quicker than I physically could. I clung to his neck as he ran. Whatever was happening, it must be very, very bad.

The scene when we arrived was bustling. The enhanced surrounded the house, talking in low voices. As Crew pushed through the crowd to get me to the patient, I immediately saw the problem. A little girl on the ground struggled to breathe. She lay flat on her back and a blue, foaming liquid pooled out of her mouth.

I pushed out of Crew's arms and landed on the floor next to the little girl. She was five and small for her age. Her parents—neither enhanced, I noticed—cried and screamed. I caught my breath. So much power pulsed around me, yet no one there knew the first thing about helping a child? No matter, I could handle it...I hoped.

"Get her on her side." I began to roll her over and her father, seemingly coming out of his stupor, took over and helped me get her to her side. I quickly inspected the child, trying to figure out what caused her distress.

"Who are you?" the dad asked, but I didn't have time to introduce myself. I needed to focus on his kid.

"This is Raven. She can help, maybe. She's staying with us." Mace spoke succinctly, but his words flowed over me as I continued to examine the child. I needed information.

Crew knelt, and I grabbed his arm. "Med machine?" Surely if they had one, she'd already be in it, but it was worth asking just in case.

He shook his head. "None on the planet. We've tried to procure some several times, but they're the rarest of the rare finds. I can't get one anywhere."

He should come visit my planet. Clarke had twenty or more lined up in a back room. I never used one when I was sick, only to make it so I never had kids, but they were there and in perfect working order. It didn't matter in the moment, though, as I would have to improvise.

"What's her name?" I asked her dad directly.

He blinked rapidly, emotion clogging his voice when he said, "This is JoHanna."

"Okay, JoHanna. You're going to be okay. The adults are going to make this better." Maybe me saying it aloud would make it true, would make the universe stand up and listen for once. "This is poison. She has ingested something that is making her sick." I'd seen it, unfortunately, many times before. "It would help to know what she ingested. Is there any chance she got into cleaning products or found a plant that she might have eaten?"

Her mother finally spoke. "N-no. Nothing. We were all here. We ate breakfast. She went outside to play, but she never eats plants. She knows better."

All kids knew better until they didn't, but I didn't say it aloud. With our death rate so high, it became a communal effort to raise the young.

I whirled around. With no obvious answer, we'd have to treat for general toxic substances and work out the specific poison later. Too many people crowded around, their voices and anxiety making it even harder for me to concentrate. I reached out a hand and placed it on Gunnar's arm. "Gunnar, could you organize the bystanders to look to try to find the substance? Where I'm from, most of the time, poisonous plants have similar qualities. We can hope that's true on your planet, too, since they were formed by the original settlers, who supposedly modeled the planets after Earth." Or so I'd heard. Earth might as well have been a legend for as much as it mattered in my life. Of course, every planet was different, and their location in relation to their sun and more could change things like weather patterns—as seen with their six-week yearly electrical storm. "Let's see if that holds true here. Try to figure out how far she strayed this morning. Could she have made it into a nearby wooded area? Use your judgment. She's not enhanced; she's normal, like me. Small legs and big hearts, these kids can go further than we think." I took a breath. "Milky sap. Shiny leaves. Yellow or white berries. Umbrella shaped. Anything like that, or anything brightly colored. Okay? It could be anything, but make sure you're looking for things a kid would find interesting enough to stuff in their mouth. Get everyone looking. It would help to know what is causing this."

I jumped to my feet, since I knew what I'd do at home. We had very little, but what we accumulated was purposeful, and I'd been trained in using it. Behind me, I heard thundering footsteps of Super Soldiers and humans all searching for the cause of the child's distress as I'd asked.

Without knowing about the specific toxin, I had to hope I would find what I needed and not something that might make the situation worse. I missed the old women who trained me in medicine. They always seemed to know the right thing to do, but maybe they were still directing my hands in a way. Their teachings followed me wherever I went, after all.

First things first, we need water. "Get her some water. Not too hot, not too cold, about two ounces. Start with that, and we're going to try to flush this out. Once we get some fluids into her, I'm sorry to say, we're going to make her puke. This could be the worst thing to do, and I need you to understand that. I could be absolutely wrong, or it could save her."

The dad nodded, gripping my hand with desperation. "We have no idea what to do. At least you have an idea of something to try."

I did, and I had to hope it wasn't going to kill her. Grabbing a toothbrush—some things looked pretty similar everywhere, apparently—I pushed it toward the back of her tongue. Once. Twice. Three times. Finally, four times.

She puked. And puked. I grabbed the water from her dad. We were going to have to repeat the process, and the child wasn't going to like it.

Crew, who remained inside, met my gaze over her heaving body. I knew it likely looked pretty awful, and I didn't have any idea if it would even work, but at least I wasn't alone. We were in this together.

JoHanna sat on the couch sipping water. After a very long few hours, I would guess the last of the poison should be out of her system. Her mother held her, and her father sat next to them, his head in his hands. "I just don't know how this could have happened."

I shook my head. She was alive, and that was key, but we didn't know what poisoned her. How could her parents prevent it from happening again, if they didn't know what caused it the first time? She remained quiet, and so far, she wasn't sharing any information.

Ransom burst through the door. "Nothing. I'm sorry. We haven't found any poisonous plants within a ten-mile radius. I can't believe she'd be able to have gone further than that." He stared at JoHanna for a moment. "So glad she's doing okay."

"Thank you so much for helping her." Her mother's voice shook. "I don't know how I'll ever be able to thank you. Do you live here now?"

I blinked. Almost no one ever thanked me, so I had no idea what to do with her gratitude. "Um, for the next six weeks? Because of the storm."

Her father's eyebrows shot up. "Oh, that's right. I never think about it, because we would never want to leave. But, yes, I guess you're stuck, aren't you?"

Crew shook his head. "We're all clearly lucky she arrived when she did. In the meantime, she's staying with us. Speaking of which, it's time to get her back. I'm glad the child is improved."

I was, too, but it still ate at me that we didn't know what she'd ingested. We got lucky this time, but that didn't mean we would be if another child sickened. We had one real healer back home, a woman about ten years older than me. She was amazing at what she did, and Clarke almost never let her out of his palace, keeping her just about locked inside. We could beg, and sometimes he'd let her come help people, but the times he agreed were few and far between. The rest of us made do with what little knowledge we could pass between us, since the old women who knew the most about healing were gone as well.

"A man gave it to me," JoHanna said in a soft voice, almost a whisper. Though her words were quiet, the child managed to silence the entire room. The enhanced all likely heard her, since there were no secrets with them around.

I thought about how Clarke's men had known Amias would come for Clarke, but then again, he hadn't bothered to hide it.

He walked into his execution with his weapons drawn knowing what would happen to him. I shook my head. I couldn't afford to go there in my head when the child needed me in the present.

Crew knelt, taking her small hand in his own. "Which man?"

"A man like you. A man with special powers. One of the tall men."

I cleared my throat. "An enhanced?"

"What's that?"

Right. The vocabulary is different here. "A Super Soldier?"

She nodded. "He held out a flower and said it was beautiful. It was. Then he said it also tasted good. He told me I should try it. We're supposed to listen to all of you, because you take care of us, and you keep us safe. I ate it, but it didn't taste good. He told me to go home and not to tell anyone or he'd hurt my parents." She lifted her gaze to meet mine. "Is he going to hurt my parents because I told you?"

Crew shook his head, his lips thin in irritation. "No. He's not. Who was it? You know everyone who lives around here, JoHanna, so which man did this to you?" A muscle ticked in his jaw. I wouldn't want to be on the other end of Crew's temper, that much was clear, even as he restrained himself and stayed gentle.

"I don't know him, but he was like you, and you're to be trusted."

I winced internally. Few could be trusted. No way should an entire small-town's worth of people be treated as safe. Why were they raising the child to be so vulnerable?

It wasn't my business. I wouldn't be there very long. I wouldn't be there for the ramifications of what they did and didn't do, obviously.

Crew rose. "So he was a stranger? Someone who doesn't live here. What color was his hair, JoHanna?"

She pointed at Crew. "Brown, like yours."

"Brown. Okay. Thank you." He turned to her father. "I'll take care of it."

Her father nodded. "Thank you."

Crew stormed toward the door and then stopped, turning around to regard me. He held out his hand, offering it to me. "Time to go."

I nodded. If he hadn't suddenly remembered me, would I have been able to find my way back to their bar on my own? I wasn't sure, but it seemed doubtful, especially since we'd rushed and he'd carried me part of the way.

Lacing our fingers together, I let him lead me outside, where more enhanced than I'd ever seen surrounded the house.

"We obviously have a problem. A stranger. Someone who didn't announce themselves in the proper way went after one of our kids. It can't be allowed." He nodded toward Mace. "I'll trust you to handle finding him. Twenty-four-hour security here until he is found. He doesn't get near this family or that little girl again. Assign people."

Mace nodded once. "On it."

Crew stared at the group in front of us. "We made something here, all those years ago. Some of you followed me here, others of you stumbled upon us or brought others in. We were all clear on how we meant to live, and no one has ever been forced to stay. This place and how we live isn't for everyone, and I get that. We maintain our equilibrium. We take jobs that use our skills, when asked, we maintain this place, and keep the non– Super Soldiers safe. In turn, they teach us things that we don't know how to do, and they take care of us, too. It's a circle, and we maintain it. This is the first time I've ever seen the way things work get challenged. The first time in *fifteen years*. I'll defend our way of life. Now is your only chance, did any of you bring someone here and not report it? Or do you know someone was here and didn't tell? This is the amnesty moment, and it will be the only one I offer."

Everyone was quiet. I couldn't hear a thing, but they probably could. Any changes in heartbeat or catching of breath—everyone would know. After a moment, Crew nodded. "That is fantastic. I want to keep trusting all of you. I plan on doing so, but if you've betrayed us, then you're due for a reminder of who we used to be before we settled down."

What was that exactly?

"And this is Raven. I know you've all heard that by now,

but she's staying with us. Anyone bothers her and you'll answer to me."

I raised my free hand. "Hi."

Mace stayed behind with Gunnar and Ransom, but Crew left with me, walking slowly this time. I made some mental notes about my surroundings even as the rain drizzled down on our heads. It wasn't like the night before. This was more like a misting. Glancing up, I could see the electricity sparking in the atmosphere, the sky just dark enough for the tracery of vein-like light to be visible.

Off in the distance, I could see a town. Nearby, mostly forested lands spread out, but other houses sat back from the road.

"You saved her. I couldn't have done that."

Crew's voice filled the quiet around us, and I jerked in surprise before considering him. I liked the sound of his voice much better than my own voice, which I'd always found to be just a touch too low. "I didn't do anything spectacular. I had her drink water and made her puke. That was really miniscule help and, frankly, I got lucky. I could've killed her, with what I did."

He shook his head. "I wouldn't have thought to make her throw up, and neither would anyone else. I'm grateful to you. Everyone is. Plus, you stayed calm, which was really something, too. Thank you." I smiled at him. "Don't thank me for doing so little. I'm glad I could help. I'm shocked you don't have a med machine."

"It's not for lack of trying. Actually, that was the last thing I said to Amias. I even told him, when he had enough of traveling and was ready to come back home, I'd appreciate it if he found a med machine to bring home with him. He needed some space, he said. Said he needed to breathe in the universe, and that he wasn't returning. But I didn't believe him. I don't think any of us did. I thought he would be back, that it was just a matter of time. Only I was wrong. He never came back."

I smiled. "Well, he found med machines. Clarke has more than I can count."

"Figures. Fucking asshole. Sorry, language. I never liked him, though. He wasn't that good at his job, and he endangered lives. But, whatever, I don't suppose it matters anymore. You saved one of the little ones here. It would be hard to explain what children mean to all of us, to anyone outside our planet. They've become a sign for us, I guess. Of life moving on. Of a normalcy we'll never have but we appreciate nonetheless."

I squeezed his hand. "Children are a gift where I'm from, too, even if we know what life they're being born into." I sighed. "How did this even happen? How did we end up trapped in an existence where no one gets to live safely anymore? You guys shouldn't have to stay away from people. I shouldn't have to...do what I do. Kids shouldn't be born into this mess. How did any of this even happen? It's not fair."

I realized what I'd said, and regret flooded me. I never talked about any of it. What was the point? It seemed like whining, because as an adult, I understood life was what it was. Railing against unchangeable facts was a waste of everyone's time.

But Crew nodded, his gaze sympathetic. "We lost. That's how this happened."

It was an answer I hadn't heard before. "Your corporation decided to terminate you, and you guys escaped." Or so it had been explained to me over and over when I dared ask. Afterward, they struggled to find places to hide, so they ultimately disappeared to quiet planets or took over other ones.

Or they'd been forced into some kind of subjugation.

"Yes," Crew agreed easily enough. "That's what happened *after* we *lost*. First, we were sent to the other side of the galaxy, where we fought in a war with the people of planet Earth. We lost that war and got pretty much herded out. When we lost, we came back here. I thought we'd regroup and go again, make a second attack. They were building things that should have made a second attempt easier, more successful. Technologies that eliminated the need to travel through the black hole for such an extensive period of time... But then, some shit happened. Sorry, language."

I waved my hand. "I say *shit* all the time." Or at least I thought it.

He tilted his head in acknowledgement before he continued. "There was some problem with the corporation's intellectual property, so they were forced to shut down. Executives at the top made the decision to terminate us and end the problem, as it was an easy solution for them. Some of us got away, despite their decision. But getting away wasn't the hard part since we weren't exactly welcome anywhere. Some of that is on those of us who behaved like the uncontrollable monsters they thought we were without Evander, the corporation that created us. Some of us came here, and we determined to stay out of the way."

They lost. There was such a tone of sadness when he admitted it. "Earth. Wow. I guess I always thought that was a myth, that it didn't really exist."

"No, it's real, and the people there were fierce enough to beat us, thoroughly. I mean...it was complicated? We were betrayed because some of our own people turned on us and sided with them. I could never figure out why. Some listened to a recording that changed their minds about everything, or so I heard. I listened to it myself, but it didn't have an effect on me. Still, those that were moved by the recording turned on us. Their changing sides made a huge difference, so we lost. First time in my life I lost, still not really over it." He sighed. "Maybe I won't ever be. Anyway, yes, Earth is real. Blue, green, beautiful and not a myth."

I tried to revise everything I knew based on his words, but I'd have been lying if I said I could process it all that fast. "I never heard *any* of that," I said, the only thing I was sure of in that moment.

"Ah, so Amias didn't share *every*thing with you." He winked at me. "I'm not totally without my own stories to share during our time together."

We made our way back toward their bar turned- home and went inside. I took a deep breath, still wrapping my mind around his words. I've always been good at moving forward, at not holding onto thoughts that might drag me down inside, but it was as though I hauled the world behind me. "Well...give me a job," I said finally, flopping my free arm to my side.

"What?" He tilted his head, dropping my hand. "A job?"

"I'm going to be here for weeks, right? I need to be useful. Hopefully, there won't be any more need to treat poisoned children, since I'm sure you will find that man. So...please, tell me how I can make myself useful while I'm here, since I'm going to be eating your food, using your water, and basically draining your resources. A job. I need something, since I can't do what I'd normally do."

He shook his head. "If it wasn't your choice, no one should have to do what you were doing. Unless the credits were going in your pocket by your will, it was despicable."

I swallowed. "I wouldn't...I wouldn't choose it. I normally try not to think about it, because it's just my life. Regardless, my skill set isn't useful here, so I feel like I can finally take a breath about it."

I hadn't thought about it before, but once I said it, I found I meant the words.

"So why don't you take a day or two for relaxation? The idea was impossible to digest when I first came here, and it was a good three years before I truly appreciated downtime. But every so often, we all need a day to ourselves. Take one. Take today. You just saved that girl's life, even if you are going to dismiss it as getting lucky. One day, where you just eat, take a nap, whatever. Then tomorrow, as you requested, I'll see if I can figure out something for you to do. Sound fair?"

I was going to answer him, but his expression suddenly went distant and sharp, as if he heard something I couldn't. "What?"

"You have a visitor coming," he said, nostrils flaring as if he could scent the stranger on the breeze.

What? I touched my chest. "Me?" I didn't know anyone on their planet.

The door hit the wall with a bang, seconds before Mace strode into the room, dragging a non– Super Soldier with him. I recognized the man instantly: Bill, the pilot who failed to mention I wouldn't be able to leave the planet for weeks. He held my bag in his arms and shook like a leaf ready to fall from a tree.

"Raven, Bill has something he'd like to say to you." Mace released the man, who slumped to the floor, and behind me, Crew chuckled quietly. Bill, for his part, didn't seem amused. He looked terrified.

"I...I shouldn't have neglected to tell you about the electricity storms, and I should have explained how they would make it impossible for you to leave. Truthfully, we probably shouldn't have landed. That was...dangerous of me, and it isn't okay that I did it to take your money." He held out my bag, shaking it impatiently for me to take. "Here is all your stuff."

I blinked. He spoke slowly and really enunciated all of his words. It seemed a bit like he'd practiced the speech, or as though he'd said it several times over and over again. I looked up at Mace who stared at Bill intently, one brow raised expectantly.

"And?" Mace said, prodding Bill verbally.

"If there is *anything* I can do for you during your stay here, please don't hesitate to let me know." He squeaked the last bit.

I rocked back on my feet. "Well, what's done is done." I grabbed my bag from him, and he sagged in relief. "Thank you for the apology."

He nodded and then ran from the bar. Crew stared at Mace. "You terrified him. What did you do?"

"Nothing he didn't deserve. I didn't hurt him, if that's what you're asking. I reminded him his job is to take people on and off planet, and how easily we could find someone else for that position, should he fail to fulfill the expectations of his role. I also might have mentioned I didn't find it at all amusing how he stranded a young woman here, and how any further infractions would be considered a failure to fulfill expectations."

Crew laughed. "I'm surprised you didn't have him get on his knees."

Mace shrugged. "Could have, but I thought that might be a bit much. Do you need anything else, Raven?"

I shook my head. "I'm good, thanks."

I didn't have much, but enough clothing to wash it without having to be naked in between outfits.

Mace grinned. "Good. So, everyone volunteered to help. Gunnar is going to stay there until lunch, and then some of Grisham's guys are going to take over. I'm not sure where Ransom went after, as I'm giving him some space, but I'm pretty sure he went with the group seeking out the stranger. Nothing popped up initially, so whoever he is, he must be good at this. I can't even hear any extra heartbeats, can you?"

Was that possible? They could just count so many heartbeats? I supposed it made sense. Crew shook his head. "The exact number there should be, with the addition of Raven's."

Mace touched my arm. "Your heart rate sped up while we were talking. Does it bother you, knowing there's a stranger around? Because I assure you, he's not getting in here."

I shook my head. "Truthfully, I think the idea that you can hear so well that you can count the heartbeats of an entire town horrified me. I'm always in awe of your power, even when the scope of it sounds scary. I wasn't worried about the stranger, since I wouldn't eat the flower if he offered it to me. I'm more worried about the children. How many do you have around here?"

Crew rubbed his face. "About a dozen. She makes a good point, Ransom," he spoke to the man knowing he'd be able to hear him. "Assign some people to all of the kids. Thanks for that. I never think about families and kids. I need to. Sometimes, I think I'm not cut out for this."

5

LAVENDER DAYS

"Seems like you're pretty cut out for it," I said as I stared at Crew. "I mean, you've led hundreds of men, right?"

Mace patted him on the arm. "He was a unit commander, so try *thousands* of men. That's why so many followed him here. I think what my boy here is trying to say is he doesn't like being in charge of women and children. Maybe even men who aren't like us, but basically, he doesn't care for looking out for those weaker than he is, right?"

Crew crossed to the bar and poured something like water into a glass. "I wouldn't mind it at all, if things didn't happen like they did today. I wish I could keep everyone safe, and I don't only mean whatever sicko came here and poisoned a kid. That's never happened before, and it never will again, because I'll never let my guard down. Someone will be on heartbeat duty from now on, so we'll have one former Super Soldier assigned to constantly count heartbeats. If the extra person didn't come on Bill's shuttle, they'll need to be caught and interrogated."

He wasn't talking to me, but I followed along well

enough to ask, "Does anyone want to fill me in on what other things you'd be worried about happening?"

"Oh, we didn't tell you, did we? Sorry." He winced. "We've all known each other so long, sometimes I forget to fill in others. Sorry. I'll be sure to correct that. So, regular people die so easily—a piece of machinery falls on them, something blows up, a kid drowns. Short of having one of us standing over them at all times—which I don't think anyone wants, because that's just weird and unsettling for all parties involved—but, yes, without constant supervision, you guys are at so much risk all of the time."

I put my hand on his arm. "I think everybody understands, as soon as they are old enough to do so, that we have a finite number of years. None of us have any idea what will actually take us out, and you can't have some savior complex. You don't really believe you're responsible for our lives? Well, I say *our*, but I mean people like me, not counting myself. I'm a temporary visitor to your existence."

He furrowed his brow for a second before it smoothed out again, then he shook his head. "If we can't keep them safe, why would they have us here? Why would they let us stay?"

"*Let* you stay?" I gawked at him. Did he really think they existed by the good graces of those less powerful than him? "Crew, no one is *making* you leave anywhere. Few planets could stop you, honestly. Clarke took over our planet. He didn't ask permission."

Crew took my hand in his and squeezed. "Clarke sounds like a megalomaniac now. He was always off, and clearly time worsened his problems. We prefer to think of our place here as a partnership. We came onto their planet, and we share their land. We would leave if they wanted us to go. We don't want to be treated like conquerors. We want to be part of their lives. When we were working for the company that made us, that was how I always imagined things could be— when I actually thought about changes I would like to make, that is, which wasn't often."

"I'm impressed you did at all. " Mace laughed. "I never thought about anything more than the next fight we'd face. Sometimes I might've wondered whether or not the planet we were invading would have any good desserts."

It wasn't funny, but I couldn't help but smile at the way he confessed to his sweet tooth. "Did they? Have good desserts?"

"Not as good as the ones I make now." Mace winked. "Dessert is my specialty. Speaking of which, since you're not working, would you like to come with me to acquire some ingredients for tonight? I thought you might enjoy the walk to the mountains."

Actually, it seemed like a great idea, and I stretched up on my toes, flexing my calves. I wanted to move. "Sure."

"She hasn't eaten anything yet, so why don't you feed her, too, and get her something to drink. Are you a coffee person? We don't have it here—no need for it—but it's easy enough to procure from our neighbors like you." Crew smiled. "And maybe you'd like to use the bathroom?" The last part was directed to me, which was good because Mace had run into the kitchen as if he'd been sent on a mission to get me food.

Since Crew brought it up, I realized I absolutely did need to pee. In fact, thinking about it made the need more urgent. I nodded to him. "Thanks. I'll go do that. Maybe you *are* cut out for these things—the *watching out for people who aren't like you* thing."

As I left the room to head for the bathroom, a smile lit up my face, and I shot a glance over my shoulder to see him return it. I saved a life—even though it likely was more due to luck than skill on my part—and a little bubble of effervescence seemed caught in my throat. I couldn't believe I got to spend the next six weeks doing things with interesting people who absolutely weren't going to want to sleep with me. Even if they did, Clarke wasn't going to tell me I had to in order to continue to live by his good will.

The circumstances that had brought me there were dire. I'd never get over my grief, as it burned like a hot coal in my chest. But maybe Amias sent me to their planet to have a break? He likely knew about the storms, after all. His ultimate intention had been for me to bring them his note, but maybe he'd had a secondary, secret plan. I doubted it as quickly as I thought of it, though. Thinking back, his focus had remained laser sharp on killing Clarke...but maybe he'd thought of the possibility of me having a break there somewhere in the back of his head.

I chose to think he had planned it. *What harm does it do to think so?*

He and Stone were gone. I could imagine whatever I wanted. It harmed no one, and if it gave me peace, perhaps it served a good purpose.

I used the bathroom, brushed my teeth with my newly returned toothbrush, and cleaned as best I could with the products I managed to pack. Quickly, I changed into a pair of mostly clean pants, which at least were an improvement over what I had worn traveling. I snagged a clean shirt, glad one of them remained, then pulled my red hair out of the holder that restrained my braid. Twining my fingers into the locks, I began to un weave the braid, feeling the weight of my curls hitting my shoulders like a burden. Funny—it used to be a sign of wealth and society for a woman to have her hair braided, but on my planet, it came to mean prostitute. The intricate braid and the brand on my forehead—a ragged circle of braided ink that went from the center of my forehead to my scalp, where it vanished into my hair—proved me to be nothing more than the property of Clarke.

Most of the time, I hardly even noticed the brand, but I couldn't take my eyes off it right then. It happened when I was twelve, which seemed awfully long ago. They put me in a chair, and a man with hair on the backs of his hands tattooed me. Despite the so-called numbing ointment, I screamed the entire time. After they gave me the mark, it became clear. I was this person. They taught me how to spread my legs. Someone paid a lot of money for my virginity—not that I ever learned the price—and that would be my life for so long as I lived. At fifteen, they took my ability to have a baby. I never feared sexual diseases or anything of that nature, as the men went through the med machine before they were allowed to touch us. I simply existed.

If I behaved, someday I could petition to have a baby. If my petition was granted, I would go back in the machine to have the process reversed, and Clarke would decide who he would breed me with, if they said yes at all. Stone and Amias could love each other as they saw fit. They could even marry, because they were both men, but my future forever would be determined by whomever owned me, whether that be Clarke or his associates.

Tears flooded my eyes, and I wiped them away. *Wow. Where had that come from?* I sniffled then said, "I'm fine. Just having a moment." I spoke to the walls, knowing they could hear me. I wiped the tears away with the backs of my fists in frustration. It was just that I had so few choices, but I remembered a different world. For the first five years of my life, I thought I would grow into a future I didn't have anymore.

Why should circumstances, like where you're born, determine the rest of your life?

I sighed. The thoughts didn't help, so I splashed water on my face then left the bathroom to meet Mace downstairs. He looked up as I walked toward him and offered me a smile. It was nice that he didn't push me about the *I'm fine* statement, especially since we both knew he heard me lose it.

"We're going to look for fruit?"

"I know just where to find it." He smiled. "So we're not so much looking as gathering." He grabbed a basket off the table. "Then, tonight, I'll make pies and people will buy some. Dessert is my specialty."

It was the second time he'd brought it up, so I decided it must be a real point of pride for him. I nodded, following behind him without further comment. He led me toward a field on the end of the street, through drizzle as light as mist. When we reached the tree line, he stopped walking and blinked at me as if he just thought of something. "Should I have gotten you a raincoat?"

I shrugged. "I don't have one, or an umbrella. Is it going to pour? I don't suppose you have a weather predictor in your brain or something?"

Mace shook his head, his sideways grin revealing a dimple on his left cheek. It was the second time I looked at one of the Super Soldiers and thought the word *adorable*, which seemed particularly odd when it came to people like him.

"Stay here a second," he said.

He ran back to their house then returned carrying a sweatshirt with a hood. "Here," he said as he handed it to me. "It's mine. Just in case, so you won't get soaked. If you got sick because I brought you along today, I'd never forgive myself. Also— " He grinned that sideways smirk again as he opened the basket he carried. "— this is for you."

Inside the basket, neatly tucked in a soft blanket, I found a warm bun spread with some kind of jelly and a bottle filled with an orange fluid. He'd brought me food. I smiled at him, my throat feeling a little bit closed in that minute. Words failed me, and it took me a second to come up with what I wanted to say.

"Thank you." That seemed pivotal. "I...This is so nice." I pulled out the container with the orange liquid. "What is this?"

It was awkward because he held the basket toward me, but when I moved to take it, he tugged it back. *Okay*. I guessed he intended to carry it for me. All of the sweet things he did for me got added to a running tally in my mind. Where I was from, people just didn't have that much time to be nice to each other, and I had to wonder what I would owe for the debt of gratitude. We didn't have to be mean, but the time for kind gestures just wasn't there. Mace was making me feel all kinds of warm inside, and I tried hard not to be moved by the gestures.

"It's orange juice." He blinked. "Don't have it where you're from? I know the plantings were different on all the various planets. No oranges on yours?"

I shook my head. "No oranges."

I removed the lid then took a sip and nearly sighed with contentment. I found the drink sweet, yet tart at the same time. The two tastes warred in my mouth, and I wanted more. And then more. I almost drank all of it at once.

Mace took my arm with his free one and we walked together as I started on the bun. My teeth sank into warm dough with just the right amount of bite. "This is...amazing. All of it. You bake? You did all of this?"

"I squeezed the oranges a few days ago, but the buns were Gunnar. I do dessert, he does breakfasts. Amias used to be dinner, but Ransom took that over after he left. He actually makes the alcohol we sell, too. Crew is the one who hunts, when we need it."

I never considered how Super Soldiers might earn a living, but there it was. *They have to live just like the rest of us. They have to make their way.*

"I never saw Amias cook anything. Not in five years." I took another bite of the bun—it was delicious. "If I'd known he could do this, I would have pestered him. Seriously? This is incredible."

He shrugged. "It's a bun with jelly, but I'm glad you like it so much."

"People don't...that is, I don't really have people help me with things all that often. If I'm hungry, I have to sort it out. Or not eat. I mean, I guess that's not fair. If Stone was cooking, he'd ask me if I wanted something, and I'd do the same. We both fed Amias."

Mace shook his head. "Boy, did he luck out, having others feed him. That man could cook. He didn't like it, but he could do it." He laughed. "Lucky bastard, getting a family that didn't know he should be cooking for them." Mace shrugged. "We've always had to do things for each other, even before we were free in the universe. We had to take care of each other on missions. If we didn't, and someone got hurt, the company would put that person down. So... yeah, we looked out for each other."

I hated to think about the way they'd lived, so I focused on my surroundings. We crossed a grassy clearing toward a small hill that looked like it led to a much bigger mountain.

My home was surrounded by hills and mountains, with the ocean on the opposite side. Our hills were dead, desolate places but these were loaded with trees and flowers. I took a deep breath. There was a scent in the air I didn't recognize but loved. A delicate, sweet smell, like deep forests yet somehow more powdery and with the slightest tinge of woodsmoke.

"What is that?" I took another deep whiff. "That scent?"

He smiled at me. "Lavender."

"I've never heard of it." I heard of oranges but not lavender. So many things I didn't know, all of it starting to compile a big list.

Mace nodded. "Well, then I suppose I'm in luck because I'll get to show it to you for the first time in a few minutes."

Eventually, we stopped in front of a field of purple that stole my breath. It looked almost like I could swim through the violet display, as if the sea of blossoms could lift me like an ocean wave might.

"I...I love this. The color. The *purple*." I wasn't being particularly articulate. Mace set down the basket he held and took my hand in his, tracing his thumb back and forth across my knuckles.

"I think technically it's the color lavender. The color comes from the plant name, right?"

I swallowed, rolling *lavender* through my mind. It felt exotic and somehow lovely. "I've never heard that word before. Isn't that strange? It's a color, you say, and I don't know it. Then again, there are a lot of things I don't know." I couldn't read, a constant pain to my ego. There had to be some women my age on my planet who could read. Maybe their parents had snuck the lessons in, but mine hadn't. I found myself wondering about so many things, and somehow, I figured the answers had to be in books, so it seemed unfair to be unable to ever learn what secrets they held.

"There are a lot of things I don't know, too." He spoke in a low voice, so I turned to look at him. I expected to find him regarding the lavender, but instead found his attention was solely focused on me. "We only have six weeks, but I could try to teach you to read, if you want. Get some basics in before you have to travel back home alone, at least. Although Amias gave you very descriptive cards to get here, he didn't give you ones for the journey home, did he?"

I shook my head. *Fuck.* "I hadn't even thought about that."

Mace made a noise I couldn't decipher as my anxiety rose, making my breath quicken and my head hurt. "Do you think you could do that? Could you make me cards?"

"No. I don't know the trip to your home well enough to do so, and I'm not sure how Amias did it in the first place. I find it interesting that Amias was able to create them, as he never made the journey that way himself. He left here in his own shuttle, but how he created them is a question for another day. I won't let you get lost, that I promise you." He gripped my shoulders then smiled like he heard something. "Ransom won't, either. Oh, and neither will Gunnar." He rolled his eyes. "Crew says he won't, either, so you can relax. *One* of us will get you home. Although..." His voice tapered off, his gaze going distant again.

"What?" I squeezed his hand, my breathing leveling off. "What were you going to say?"

"I wonder why you have to go back at all. You're here. Why not stay?" He nodded to the left, so I headed that way by his side. We moved slowly, and I enjoyed the breeze and the smell of wet.

"I can't stay," I sighed, closing my eyes to feel the wind

kiss my eyelids. "People will get in big trouble if I don't go back. They might already be, but I can't make their pain worse by never coming back. If there is music to face, I have to face it."

Mace scrunched up his nose like what I said smelled bad. "Or, you could say what's done is done. You're here for six weeks. By then, they will have faced whatever music themselves already. You returning might only compound their situation, serving as a reminder to Clarke of what they did wrong. He could choose to punish everyone again. You might not be thanked for your return."

I hadn't thought about that possibility, but he made a fair point. How would I know which would help them more —staying away or returning? I never faced such a choice before and didn't know the right answers.

"Mace, I've been here less than a day. In six weeks, you might be well rid of me. You could be counting the days until you don't have to hear my voice or heartbeat again, so don't suggest my staying. We both know that might not really be an option, or even something you'd want at that point."

He dropped my hand. "Wait here a second."

Without a word, Mace left me standing there and ran into the lavender field. He came back with a piece of the plant and handed it to me. "Smells even better up close."

Had he ignored me or just chosen not to respond? Maybe it was better we didn't broach the topic of the future, instead focusing on the moment. I brought the lavender to my nose. He was right. I closed my eyes and let the sweet floral fragrance move through me.

Why would Amias have ever left their planet? I stared at the beautiful field glistening with raindrops in awe. With so much beauty and freedom at his fingertips, why ever leave?

"Maybe we can convince you to stay and become a part of our community. Maybe you'll be tired of all of us by then. People leave. Even close friends take off and go." I lifted my lids to regard him. "But this place is more than us. That lavender field? It was planted by a group that lives on the outskirts of town, over on the other side. They're like us. You met some of the regular humans today, but there are more of them, about four dozen more. We need to grow that community. You could...live somewhere else with other people." He winced. "It doesn't have to be us, if you'd rather not, is what I'm trying to say."

I stepped toward him—close enough to be considered outside good manners. I invaded his personal space, but he didn't seem to care. I wasn't sure exactly why I wanted to be closer to him, but I did. "You have been nothing but nice to me. Holding me last night? Making me feel welcome to stay with you for six weeks when I showed up out of the blue and invaded your life? I can't imagine *not* liking you. Any of you, so maybe let's shelve this discussion, and see where we are in six weeks." I swallowed my need to keep going. Sometimes saying less was more. "Although I do think I'll go back when the time comes. It's hard for me to imagine living with myself otherwise."

He rubbed his eyes. "You might be surprised what you can live with, but I hear you. Come on."

Mace linked our hands together again, and we walked for a while in companionable silence. It wasn't hard to be quiet with him. Eventually, we reached an orchard, and once again I caught my breath. There were apples every- where, or at least it looked that way. The spicy scent of cider kissed the air, likely from the overripe apples that had fallen from the heavily laden branches.

"Wow." I stared open- mouthed at the scene. "There are so many."

"I planted these trees ten years ago. They're kind of my pet project. We had to go off-world to get them—long story, but I was out on a job and I came back with these beauties. Crew acted like I took forever, but he was glad in the long run that I'd done it." His smile was huge. "Come on. You pick tonight's apples."

I remember thinking their world to be dusty and desolate when I arrived, having landed in a rundown town, but it turned out that I had to look harder at things. Their world was gorgeous. Alive. Vibrant. The most beautiful place I'd ever seen.

I needed to remember that moving forward. I had to learn to look past the cracks in the walls and the way that the buildings were rundown and see the woods around it, see the hills, and the fruit. And the lavender. I needed to open my gaze to the possibility of what could be rather than just what was evident at first glance. Where I was from, they might keep things well maintained and neat, but no beauty lived there. I knew better than to go solely by my first impressions.

We stepped into the orchard, and I noticed the fruit grew in many different colors and sizes. "Which ones do you want?" he asked.

"How do I pick?" I had never seen such a place. "What are the qualifications?"

He put a hand on the small of my back. Somehow the touch seemed more intimate than when he held my hand. I stilled before I got used to the sensation of the heat and warmth of his touch. It was different when I didn't have to do anything, I realized, because I actually wanted him to touch me. It was my choice.

"Apples ripen from the outside, by the trunk. Feel it. If it feels firm, then it's ready for you. Lift it upwards and twist."

Sounds great, but just one problem. "Unlike you...I can't reach them. I'm short." The trees were very, very tall. I didn't know if that was true of all apple trees, but theirs towered far above my head. I smirked, wondering if the trees were enhanced like the man who had brought them there.

"Easy fix." He set down the basket and opened the top of it. Then, in a smooth move, he picked me up and maneuvered me until I was on his shoulders. I gasped, grasping at his wrists before I felt secure. "Now you're tall enough."

A branch hit me in the face—I was a little bit too tall, in fact. The thought made me giggle. "Sure. Almost too tall."

"Just make sure you don't take a branch to the eye and pick your apples. You can drop them into the basket."

I saw one that looked promising and grabbed for it. The firm flesh of the fruit felt warm in my hand, despite the chill rain, and with a twist, it came free just as he'd said. I dropped it into the basket easily with a little peal of laughter. "How many do we need?"

"As many as you want. I don't think there is such a thing as too much pie with these guys." He squeezed my knee. "And you weigh almost nothing, so take as long as you want."

I grinned and eagerly reached for more fruit. Picking fruit, it turned out, would easily rank among the most fun experiences of my *life*.

6

LIGHTNING

M ace set me down and grinned at our harvest. "We're going to be able to make five pies with this much fruit. You're going to be everyone's favorite person. I never make more than two."

"Why did you let me pull so many off, if it's more than you do usually?" Had I taken too many apples? Depleted the trees?

He shrugged. "Most of the time, I do this in a hurry, so I grab the bare minimum. This was fun, and you enjoyed picking the apples. Seemed like a great way to spend our day together, so I saw no need to rush it. Plus, now I can look forward to teaching you to make the pies."

Less than a second after saying he'd teach me to make pies, he turned and pushed me faster than I could even fully process. I hit the tree behind me, hard—hard enough that my head spun for a second. Disorientation hit me, with the smell of ozone and burning, and I realized he'd just gotten hit by lightning.

The loudest boom I'd ever heard echoed around us, until I thought I went deaf from the noise, and even though

I hadn't taken the hit myself, I felt the electricity all over. I buzzed everywhere and rolled over to puke, jolts taking over my body. Even as my stomach emptied itself of the sweet roll and the wonderful orange juice, I knew I hadn't been directly hit by the bolt. *Mace.* He had been struck by lightning. Maybe he even saved me.

I got to my knees and crawled over to him. Every movement was painful, but I got to him despite my tingling fingertips. His skin was singed black, his eyes closed, and his body smoked yet somehow, he breathed. I touched his chest. *How was it possible to survive that?*

"Mace," I said his name. "Mace." He didn't answer, and I didn't expect him to. This was lunacy. I looked up at the sky. The lightning was everywhere, and as I watched, it struck the ground on the other side of the field. *Okay. This is bad.* "Can you guys hear me?" I was on a planet filled with former Super Soldiers. Surely, someone could hear me. "Mace has been struck by lightning, and I'm not okay."

He lifted his hand to grab my arm. "It's okay." His eyes opened. "I'm injured, but I'll recover. I'll always recover. We have to find shelter. Guys, don't try to get out here. Not yet. The lightning. I've never seen it do this before."

Dread filled me when he struggled to get to his knees. It was bad, really the worst possible scenario, if he was this hurt. That lightning, what could it have done to him? Incinerated him right there? *I don't know enough about this stuff.*

"It hit right next to me, not on me, I don't think."

In a random thought, I looked over at the apples in the basket. They were actually on fire, so I didn't know if he was right. I was pretty sure it struck him directly, but it wasn't the time for arguing. It was for getting out of there. *Somehow.*

We crawled, me following him in steady progress, across the field until we ended up inside a small cave. I figured he had to have intentionally picked our destination, since I wouldn't have seen the cave at all if he hadn't led me to it.

"I know— " He struggled to speak. Breathing must be hard for him. "— that it looks like I won't survive this, but I will. We're made to survive. Stay right here with me. When it's safe, they'll come and get you. They want to now, but lightning is striking everywhere. Never happened like this before. Don't know why."

Having delivered that information, he hit the ground on his stomach, fully passed out but still breathing. I put my hand on his back to feel the intake of his lungs, not trusting my eyes in my fear. It was desperately important to me for him to live. There had been too much death, too many people gone already. I might have only met him, but I could already tell Mace would be someone important to me. With his pies. His quick smile. His sad, haunted eyes. And, despite all of it, the way it was clear he tried to find the good in life.

With that thought in mind, I passed out, the dizziness overtaking me.

When I woke up again, my hand still rose and fell on his back, so the first thing I registered was that he still breathed. Night had fallen outside, but I could hear the lightning still striking the ground outside with crackling pops and booms. Had the storm really never behaved in such a way before?

What was going on?

I scooted over a bit and rolled him so that I could see his face. It was hard to tell with darkness dragging long fingers of night into the cave, but he looked a little less singed. *That has to be a good sign.*

"Mace?" I spoke in a low voice. "Can you hear me?"

He didn't reply. The others could probably hear me, but it didn't matter. I wouldn't be able to hear their replies, and I had nothing to report anyway.

I was thirsty, and I'd bet he also needed hydration. My head was a little clearer, though my chest still hurt some from gagging earlier. Despite all the things I knew about healing, I'd never before faced an enhanced person recovering from a lightning strike, but water was always important. It was what I would've done for burns, anyway.

The cave was about the size of a small closet, which meant not much room to move around and no visible water. I poked my head outside, and I could see a river winding a silvery trail through the back of the orchid. It was risky, if I tried to cross the distance to get to it, and I'd have to hope I could find something on the riverbed to even carry the water back to him.

He'd shoved me out of the way and stopped me from dying, I reminded myself, cracking my knuckles in preparation. I could take a risk for him. I'd just have to hope the lightning didn't strike me down. It couldn't really come after me twice in one day, could it? And why was I thinking of it as *coming after* me? Lightning was random, so personifying it seemed silly.

Wasn't it?

I shook out my arms, dancing from foot to foot as I tried to gear myself up for what needed to be done. "I'm trying to get Mace some water," I said aloud. It was possible no one would hear me, but I said the words in case they could. "If I get struck down, that's why. He needs help."

I sprang into motion. Little buzzing jolts still assaulted my body, but once I got out of the cave, I could stand up enough to sort of angle my rear end into the air and half crawl, half walk to the river. Finding a rock with a hollowed-out indent, I decided it would have to do, and then I quickly found two others of a similar shape. I took a quick drink myself and then filled up three rocks, which was all I was going to be able to carry at once. Looking up, I jerked in shock. For just a second, I would have sworn I saw someone standing on the hill, with lightning striking all around him. I could feel his gaze on me where I filled the dented rocks with water.

I blinked and the person was gone, or maybe they'd never been there. *Maybe I'm just half out of my mind, imagining ghosts in the ozone-filled air.*

Putting my attention back to the rocks, I tried my best to fill them with water, despite my hands shaking with each new boom of sound. As soon as I got them filled again, I began to make tedious progress back to the cave. With my head still down, I made it back inside with a relieved sigh. "I'm back," I said, just in case they were listening. Thinking they'd be listening for me when the storm went crazy put me in the narcissistic or selfish category, yet I still hoped they could hear me.

It took some maneuvering, but I set down the water, scooted up to Mace, then lifted his head into my lap. It was tricky, but I managed to get him to swallow some water, even though he stayed out cold the whole time. I hoped it would help.

After that, there was nothing for me to do besides watch the lightning and wonder if the man I saw on the hill was real or a hallucination. Not trusting my own mind was a problem. The circumstances made it seem likely her brain would come up with someone, just so she wasn't alone in that moment, but she knew Johanna met a stranger... Could it be the person who poisoned JoHanna? Or was I really seeing things?

I put my hand in Mace's hair and petted him, combing my fingertips through the strands in distraction. I was out of ways to help him, and my touch sadly couldn't magically make him better. We would have to wait out the night. I watched the lightning, still feeling it nefarious somehow. Of course, what kind of creature could control the weather?

Or who?

I blinked. That wasn't possible, was it?

I woke up, not remembering falling asleep, but sure my dreams were haunted by men with lightning in their gazes and smoke curling out of their nostrils like a dragon. I leaned against the cave wall, my hands still in Mace's hair. The warmth and realness of his scalp against my fingers grounded me in the present, and I sighed.

"Hey," Crew said, and I realized that he was there with us.

I rubbed my eyes. "Hi." My heart tripped a bit at the sight of him. He looked so clean, so normal, so safe. I smiled despite myself, and wondered if they knew what to do for Super Soldiers struck by lightning. "Can you help him?"

"He's going to be fine. His heart is strong, and he's getting better. I'm a little bit more concerned about you." He put his hand on my forehead. "You're burning up."

I blinked. Was I? "I...I didn't realize."

"I know. You were too busy venturing out into a lightning storm the likes of which we've never seen to get Mace water. Thank you for that, but no more. Come on."

I shook my head. "I don't know if we should move him."

Since he'd pointed out the fever, I became really full cognizant of it. Everything ached, and shivers left my limbs trembling. Yeah, I had fever. I winced. People died of fevers all the time; would that be it for me? Crew picked Mace up, sort of dragging him off my lap and out of the cave before he came back in for me. Crew did the same for me, and once I was finally back out in the sunshine, I saw Ransom and

Gunnar nearby. Mace lay over Ransom's shoulder, still unconscious from the look of him.

Once we exited the cave, Crew adjusted me so I was gently cradled in his arms like a child, with my head against his shoulder. I would have complained about the treatment, but the fine trembling quaked through my body, sapping my energy reserves.

"Let's go back home. All will be well."

I shook my head. *Well* wasn't a word I usually applied to my life. Pain? Much more apt. "I have no idea why I'm sick."

"The water," Gunnar looked over to the river. "It's not really fit for human drinking. Mace will be fine, as his digestive system can handle it. Yours can't. Right now, you're just uncomfortable. Later, you're going to feel like hell, but you'll be okay. We boil most of our drinking water."

I groaned. *Just my luck.* I risked my neck to get him the water, yet I made myself sick in the process. "We need to get the apples. He wanted to make pies."

"They burned up." Gunnar touched my leg, drawing my attention. I furrowed my brow. Yes, he was right. I saw it, and I remembered them burning now that he'd mentioned it. *Fuck.* I'd forgotten. "Thank you for trying to save his life. I can't believe this happened. We need to get out of here before it happens again. *If* it happens again. We don't know why it happened the first time."

Mace groaned and Gunnar grinned at him. "Yes, you're in pain. You got fucking hit by lightning, Mace. I mean... who has that happen?"

I shook my head. "There was a man on the hill. I don't know if he was real or if I was hallucinating. Lightning struck all around him. He just stood there staring at me, and then he was gone." I could still see him, in my mind, so I searched their faces to see if they understood.

They all stared at me blankly. Finally, Ransom spoke. "I'll come back after we get Mace and Raven home. I'll see if I can track anyone, or if they left behind any footprints or other evidence. What in the hell is going on?"

"I'm sorry." I buried my face into Crew's shoulder, inhaling the clean scent of him and whatever soap he used. If I could have crawled inside of him to hide from everything, I would have. "I brought all the bad luck with me."

His hand on my back was a comforting feeling, especially when he began to rotate it in big, soothing circles. "You saved JoHanna. You told us what happened with Amias, and you tried to help Mace when you should have hidden in the cave. I think you're rather the opposite of bad luck, Raven. Close your eyes. All will be well."

I knew then why men followed Crew. My heart thumped twice in my chest as I looked up at his eyelashes, dotted with moisture from the still- misting rain. I would have done whatever he asked if he spoke to me like that. I closed my eyes, exhaling on a sigh.

I WOKE up when the bed dipped. Opening my eyes hurt, but I was glad to see Mace crawling in next to me. I'd puked most of the night, until my body felt weak from heaving. It was over though, I thought. Hoped. *Really hoped.* Puking was just the worst. My fever seemed to have abated, too, leaving me feeling weak and beat up.

And I probably smell like hell.

But Mace put his arms around me and drew me against him as if he didn't notice my scent. He gave me a quick squeeze, and I relaxed into his warmth and touch.

"Your skin was singed, " I said through my thick, raw

throat, rubbing my nose against his neck. "So glad you look better."

He pressed my head against his chest. "Go back to sleep. We're both still recovering. We're just going to do it together because...well, just because."

I closed my eyes. "Okay." I didn't have the energy to debate it, anyway.

Time must have passed, because the next time I woke up, I found myself in his arms but starving. I tried to sit up and a strong hand stopped me. Mace obviously didn't want me to move. "I'm hungry," I complained.

He nodded. "Ransom is bringing us food. They didn't care so much about me being hungry, but they are worried about you." He smirked. "Gentle food, Ransom. Like toast. Other than that? How are you feeling, Raven?"

"Confused about what happened to us."

Mace played with a lock of my hair. "Something made the lightning go crazy. It struck us like it was looking for us. Gunnar says you were right, you saw someone where you thought you saw them. I think Ransom intended to do the tracking, but Gunnar is actually a better tracker. He picked up traces and is searching for him , but I have no idea if he was related to what happened to us, or how he could be related to a lightning strike. I mean, we've been here a long time, yet in all those years of living alongside the upper-level electrical issues, we've never had lightning behave in such a strange way. It kept striking between here and where we were, so they couldn't get to us. Then it just stopped. I'm...not sure what to make of it. Crew is working with some others to try to figure it out. Then, you apparently drank some bad water."

"The same water that feeds the trees, so could you explain how that works? Do the apples make you sick?"

He shook his head. "The apple seeds that I planted are special. They naturally filter out the bad water. I guess you could call them enhanced apple trees. By the way, we have *so* many apples now. The guys picked something like three dozen of them, because you mentioned the ones that burned."

Looked like we would be making a lot of pies.

"Hey." He knocked my foot with his own, and I glanced at him again. "You should have stayed in the cave. You shouldn't have gone into the lightning like that. You don't ever have to save me, Raven."

I shook my head then blew out a breath. "I really thought you needed water. I thought it would help your condition, so I needed to get it as quickly as possible. Obviously, if I'd known the water was tainted, I wouldn't have done it. I'm very sorry about that."

He shrugged. "I didn't get sick from it, at least not that I can remember. If I got sick, I was out cold when it happened. We don't tend to get sick, though, so it's likely I didn't. In any case...thank you, but please don't ever do something like that again. You're so fragile. I don't want anything to happen to you."

"It was going to strike me. I saw it. You pushed me out of the way. I'd have been burned up, like the apples we picked."

He made a face, concern knitting his brows. "I threw you hard. Did I hurt you?"

"It hurt, yeah, but that doesn't really matter. I would have been much worse off. Dead. Fried. Cooked like a holiday fowl. " I hated the thought. "And it's amazing you weren't killed. That's some pretty tough skin you have there." I scooted closer. "Thank you for saving my life, Mace . You may not be fragile, but you're important. Lightning can't kill you, but I bet there are things that can." Before I could overthink it, I kissed him lightly on the lips. I almost never kissed, but I intended it as a gift of gratitude. It wasn't what men wanted from me, so I had little reason to ever bestow such tokens, but right then, he seemed to warrant the thank you. "It was such a good day before it...almost blew up."

"You make me want to be..." His gruff voice trailed off. "Ransom is here."

The door flew open, and Ransom strode through it holding a tray covered in food. "Toast. Butter. Tea. Eggs, because you haven't had protein in a bit."

I sat up, stretching. "Thank you. Long night. So glad that it's over. So I wasn't crazy? The man was real?"

"Very real. Gunnar found footprints but no other traces. They're good, whoever they are, at hiding themselves, but he will be found. I assure you of that." Ransom set the tray down over my lap and then grinned. "People have been dropping off things downstairs for you, Raven. I'm not sure what to do with all of it. I didn't want to come traipsing in here while you weren't feeling well with a bunch of stuff, but now that you're up, I'll bring it."

He ran a hand through his hair, like he wanted it out of his eyes.

"I could cut that for you? Your hair, if it's bothering you. That is something I actually know how to do," I explained, pointing at his head.

He grinned, which made Ransom look a lot younger than normal. "I'd love that. Thanks."

"*Please* help him." Mace said dramatically. "The last time he did it himself, it looked like he currently served in a war he was barely surviving." Mace threw a pillow at him, and Ransom grinned, unrepentant.

"I'll go get the stuff," he said as he turned to leave. I stopped him by reaching out to grab his arm. Under my hands, his muscles were huge. I could never forget how big these guys were. It was easy to disregard, because of how gently they treated me, but I remembered what hands like theirs were capable of doing. I shuddered, thinking of the pain.

Focusing on the conversation at hand, I asked, "What stuff? What are people dropping off, and maybe more importantly, why?"

Ransom widened his eyes. "Oh, sorry. Thought you knew why. You saved that little girl and then you almost died with our weird weather. I think they just want to do things for you. Some of it is a little off. I mean, as Super Soldiers, we don't know exactly how to give that sort of gift. I wouldn't, anyway."

Mace laughed, throwing his head into the pillow before he groaned. "You'd probably bring the girl a bomb. A small one, a bomb for ladies, one she could carry in her back pocket and throw if she needed."

"Don't act like you're so much better. " Ransom rolled his eyes. "You'd brew her poison."

He shook his head, which looked funny with his nose in the pillow. "I would make her a pie and it wouldn't be poisoned."

I took a bite of my toast. It really was just what my poor stomach wanted after being so terribly abused the night before. I ate slowly—less was going to be more, that was for sure. "So, I have weapons downstairs? I...I wouldn't have the slightest idea how to use them."

"Some people seem to have brought you things like pillows and decorations. There's a lot of general stuff, and if you don't want the weapons, I'll store them for you someplace else. Behind the bar, maybe? You can get to them there, if you want."

His words reminded me of what I'd forgotten—all of the noise downstairs the night before. I hardly noticed it, because I was so out of it, but they must have had customers while I was upstairs getting sick. Someone had sat with me, despite that, though.

"Last night is a blur. How many people were down there? I mean...you're all enhanc...Super Soldiers." I corrected myself. "That couldn't have been nice to listen to, so I'm sorry."

Mace lifted his head. "Are you actually apologizing for nearly poisoning yourself while you tried to save me?" He put his hand on my leg. "Knock that off. If they didn't like it, they could leave. Besides, most of us have gotten pretty good at ignoring whatever we don't want to see."

"Did you sit with me?" I asked Ransom. I was pretty sure it had been him. "Sorry if I was...really out of it."

He shrugged, his gaze seeming to be on Mace's hand on my leg. "I was glad to be there for you." A second later, he came over and sat down on the bed, scooting over to lie down on my other side. "Maybe we can wait to bring up the stuff? Mace can help me in a few minutes, when he's feeling better. Or he can go get it himself, since I'm pretty sure he feels better already."

There were definitely undercurrents in the conversation, but I couldn't follow any of them, and I wasn't sure I'd want to anyway. Not when my toast and eggs were so delicious. I tucked into the meal with gusto. In between bites, I asked, "Do you think the man on the hill had something to do with the lightning?"

Mace glared at Ransom. "Aren't you due for the US machine? Isn't today your day?"

"I traded with Brenson from down the street. Isn't today your day, too?" He lifted his eyebrows. "Since you're so worried about my calendar."

With a smirk, Mace leaned on his elbow. "Obviously I'm in no condition for it. Raven, to answer your question, I'm sure there's lots of tech we don't know anything about. Our old bosses were always inventing things; however, this would be the first time we encountered something with the ability to control weather. If it isn't some new, unknown tech, then how could someone control the lightning? That's impossible. So, it's either something we need to find about or a very strange coincidence that a man poisoned a child then you saw a stranger while you were trapped in a cave, afraid. I don't know which, as yet."

Ransom yawned. "I'm actually tired."

I finished my breakfast, then Mace picked up the tray one-handed to set it on the floor on his side of the bed. He put his head back where it was, next to mine. "Tired, too. But you see, I've actually been through an ordeal while you're just lazy."

"Okay, I feel like I'm missing something here." I looked back and forth between them. "Or are you both just being mean?"

Ransom shut his eyes and snuggled down next to me. "We're just poking at each other. He's my brother, and I'd die for him. He knows that, but I've got to give him a hard time, too. It's just the way things work."

That made no sense to me, but I supposed I didn't have to fully understand the intricacies of their relationship. I'd have years to process and dissect their behaviors and the strange things I saw while on their planet later, so perhaps it didn't matter if I lived in the moment. The room became quiet, other than the rhythmic sound of their breaths.

They'd both fallen asleep, or at least they lay relaxed next to me with their eyes closed. I wondered what triggered their fussing at each other.

Should I move? Should I extract myself from their embrace to leave them, so I could move around? Would that wake them?

Crew appeared, leaning in the doorway. He observed us, his long lashes framing his lovely eyes while they rested on me before he finally entered the room. When he did, he set something down in front of the bed. It looked like a big, decorative chair, similar to the ones that Clarke had in rooms where I did my work for him.

He winked at me before he sat down in the chair. Well, if we were going to sit in silence, at least I wasn't doing it alone.

7

THE MAN FROM THE MOUNTAINS

Eventually, I had to move, my bladder making it urgent rather than optional. It was convenient that Crew and I were sharing silent time together, because he reached out his hand and lifted me from the bed. He only used one arm, thereby not disturbing either of his friends—really, they were probably more like brothers—from where they slept. I tried, and likely mostly failed, to pretend I wasn't impressed with his strength. As quietly as I could, after a grateful nod to Crew, I dove into the bathroom and turned on the water. It was probably fruitless to have bothered so much with being quiet, I thought, as the sound of the water in the sink practically blasted the room with sound—or so it seemed to my hyper alert senses.

I thought about it, and I realized I didn't envy them that particular superpower. As a regular human, I could tune things out when I slept, but they didn't have that luxury.

All of it had been so strange. Being there, trapped on their planet, was starting to feel like a refuge—even after puking and nearly being struck by lightning. I couldn't let it become that for me, though, since I had to go back. The more I allowed myself to get used to their way of living, the harder it would be for me to leave when the time came.

But, oh, how I enjoyed the attention they gave me. They seemed to light up when I was there, and I was enjoying each of them so much. In some ways, being with them reminded me of being with my brother and Amias, but they never made me shiver just by smiling at me. Then there was the uniqueness of the place—the many things that made their world so different from the one I'd always known . Instead of thinking of the geography, though, as the warm water rushed over my body, my mind strayed back to how handsome they all were.

I rubbed the soap in long strokes up and down my body and closed my eyes, remembering the cockeyed smile with its little dimple, the dark eyelashes fringing gorgeous eyes, and the way their skin felt against my own. I didn't enjoy looking at people usually, not in a sexual way, although some told me a few of my clients were attractive. I gave up caring what men looked like the day I lost my virginity to a man three times my age with bad breath and cruel hands. Did it matter what a man looked like if they all wanted the same things, actions I could perform from rote memory at this point? I didn't think about anyone sexually, male or female, and I certainly never cared about the shape of their hands before.

Maybe it was this place, these guys, or perhaps grief simply made me lose my mind, but I had to admit they were each really gorgeous. Brutal in the way all Super Soldiers, as they'd put it, were.

But gorgeous too.

If I had a kinder life and a real chance at happiness, I

wondered if I'd be able to truly enjoy that aspect of them. To take pleasure in how they looked, and how they looked at me.

Not that any of my considerations mattered, as they were wildly unlikely to be interested in me in a sexual manner. After all, they went into some machine and it turned it off for them. My breath caught in my throat. I'd been curious about it, but maybe I should ask them to use it. That would be great, in fact, as I could make myself stop thinking about them in inappropriate ways entirely, thereby evening out the playing field.

The idea was still on my mind when I got out of the shower and rubbed my skin dry with the pillow-soft towel they left out for me.

Could I just go into the machine? Would it fix my problem, at least temporarily?

When it wore off, it would be fine. I'd never struggled before with such strange urges, as the men at home didn't affect me in any way. Well, sometimes they even caused the opposite reaction, and I shuddered remembering. Of course, my reaction could simply be because they treated me as a person who might break if mishandled, rather than trying to destroy me for fun.

Tears flooded my eyes, and I fought them back with quick blinks and slow breaths. What was the matter with me? My life was *my* life. Thinking about my fate had never brought me to tears before.

A gentle knock came from the door, so I wiped at my face. I was covered in a towel, modest enough to let them enter. "Come in."

The door opened slowly, revealing a gentle- eyed Gunnar. "They sent me up to get you, and I...well, I heard your tears. I could pretend I didn't, but it feels like a lie, so I thought I'd just knock."

"Right. The funniest things keep rolling around in my mind, possibly because it is so quiet here. Usually, I'm so busy, I just go through things. One day to the next, one foot in front of the other, no time for rumination or dissection of my motives. With a sudden wealth of time to consider things, it lets me think about feelings I never considered before."

Gunnar stepped away from the door, so I followed him back into the room. "Boy, do I understand what you're talking about," he admitted, scratching at his chin with one long fingered hand.

"You do?" I sat down on the bed, knowing I should get dressed but not quite ready to.

He leaned against the wall, his strong arms crossed over his chest. "When we were first created, we were so busy fighting and destroying. It was the whole purpose of my life. Then we lost. Badly." A muscle ticked in his jaw when he spoke those words, the frustration of defeat still clear on every tight line of his muscular body. "I never lose, but we did. Then we were running for our lives, trying not to be exterminated. When we arrived here, we really had to work to fix this place up, and our previous skill set left us woefully unprepared for the task at hand. Amias used to say we just had to keep trying, that at some point our luck would change and we'd learn the skills we needed." He smiled at the memory, but then he shrugged. "Then we were done. Mostly. People come and hire us to do things, and we keep this township going. It's always a struggle, and everyone has to get jobs off-planet to keep going. The whole place feels transient sometimes, but we've maintained it for years. And then there is this time of year. Everything goes quiet. We're just here, just going about our lives. The first year, I had a lot of time to think about my life. Well, every year I do, I guess, but that first year, I wasn't sure I would make it out the other end with my mind still intact. We didn't know how long it would last, the lightning time."

"What did you do to get through it?" I couldn't pound on trees or climb to the peaks of barely scalable mountains to deal with my feelings of unrest, which is what I imagined Gunnar did, if he felt edgy.

He shrugged and joined me, sitting next to me on the bed. "I don't know if I did? I think I'm still getting over it, or maybe the pain is just part of it now. Like, it's become part of who I am. Despite that with time, things got easier to bear. It's not that my...discomfort went away or lessened, more like the basket I was carrying it around with got bigger. Maybe that doesn't make sense?"

"Well. " I squeezed his arm then adjusted my towel. "It does, actually. In a big way. Hopefully, I'll understand even more before I leave. Or I'll just go back, fall into my old patterns, and never notice it again."

"Because you have to go back to your version of a corporation? You have to go back to doing what you were doing, so you don't have a permanent break."

I nodded. "That was it exactly."

He made a face. "They want us to go downstairs. It's time to get ready for tonight. You don't have to, of course, because you're our guest, but if you want something to do tonight, we can certainly keep you busy."

I liked the idea. I didn't want to think. "Give me a few minutes to put on some clothes?"

"Sounds good. " He glanced at me over his shoulder one

last time on his way to the door. "Tomorrow I'd like to bring you with me for the day. I'm not on guard duty tomorrow, so you can come with me. I promise to try not to let you get struck by lightning." He smirked. "Mace didn't appreciate my joke."

I shook my head. "It was absolutely not Mace's fault. Hey, question for you before you go? Do you think I could use your sex machine?"

He blinked and then turned fully to regard me. After a second, he tilted his head to the side. Was he listening to the others or just struck silent by my question? "Why would you want to?" he finally asked.

"I...I'm having unusual—for me, anyway—feelings. I just thought your machine might help me get them under control."

I had his full attention, and I experienced the uncomfortable sensation of being a moth on a pin. He stalked over to me, even his gait different than his usual lazy stride. "What kinds of feelings?" He practically sniffed the air around me, he so thoroughly considered me.

"Am I talking to just you or all of you?" I held up my hand. "Never mind. It's *always* all of you, I get that. I do. I just have to...manage my embarrassment. Forgive me."

He shook his head. "You don't have to be embarrassed about whatever it is. We never think about privacy, as it has always been like this for us, but I understand that it is sometimes easier to admit something to one person rather than a group."

I swallowed. "You have a crowd downstairs. They can *all* hear me. In fact, your neighbors can likely hear my every word, probably for blocks." I closed my eyes for just a second, breathing in slowly through my nose and out my mouth. "Can we forget I said anything at all? Can we just pretend I didn't even bring it up?"

He shook his head. "Probably not permanently, but if you want to shelve the discussion until another time which might offer more privacy, I can understand that. I just..." His voice trailed off. "This is just me talking, but not anyone else. Don't get in that machine."

I rubbed my eyes. I'd feel better about the conversation if I was dressed. "Okay."

When Gunnar left, I got dressed quickly. If I was going to be on my feet all night, I wanted to be comfortable. I grabbed a t-shirt and a pair of pants that I wore when I was cleaning up at home, because of their stretchy, comfortable fabric. My shoes would have to do, since they were all I had, but I managed to get my hair up in a ponytail. I absolutely didn't want to braid it.

Despite crying earlier and being sick from the whole lightning event, I actually looked pretty good in the reflection. My eyes seemed somehow brighter, and my skin had an almost eerie glow. Maybe it was from the crying? I laughed at the thought.

Finally, I realized I was wasting time to avoid facing the fact every Super Soldier in the vicinity just heard me announce I wanted to get their sex machine to remove my sexual desires, so I found my way downstairs.

I expected them to turn and look at me like a science experiment gone wrong when I entered. I wasn't disappointed. In less than a heartbeat, their bright, cheery laughter faded until I was silently regarded by everyone.

Shaking my head, I dug deep for my training. What had my teacher said again? *Men are always men.* Her theory was they were fundamentally all the same at their core, a premise I hadn't bought then and didn't buy currently. It didn't mean, however, that none of my skills would be useful with these particular men.

I waved my hand through the air. It was a room filled with men. So they weren't sexually interested in me? If my teacher, long since dead, was right, then a man was a man. "Oh, come on. You *must* have seen a woman totally humiliated before this." I laughed, even though it wasn't funny and despite the sweat on my palms. "Thank you for the gifts, gentlemen. I'll go through them later. Much appreciated."

If I raised my voice so I spoke a little higher-toned than usual, then so be it. I smiled, dipping my lashes to hide my eyes coyly. Within seconds, everyone laughed and went back to what they were doing. A little self-deprecation tended to make people stare less, as with my previous experiences of embarrassment.

Well...*almost* everyone laughed. My current roommates didn't seem to find it funny.

Ransom held out his hand from behind the bar. "Come here."

I walked toward him. "How can I help?"

"Well, you can never do that again, for starters." He motioned for me to come closer. I sighed. *So much for moving on from the earlier conversation. Oh well. I tried.* And, for just a second, it even worked.

I rounded the bar. I wasn't going to address it again, not if I could help it.

Ransom motioned toward a plate he stashed under the bar for me. "That's your dinner. I know it hasn't been that long since lunch, but I figured you'd still be hungry. We can reheat it, if it gets cold."

"Thank you." It really was very sweet that he'd thought

of me. I wasn't used to anyone else putting my needs before their own. "What can I do to help you?"

There wasn't a huge crowd at the bar right then, *but surely, I can help out.* He looked around, scanning the room. "You can polish those glasses." He gestured with a tilt of his chin. "It might seem stupid for a bar in the middle of nowhere, but I really like things to look good around here."

It didn't seem stupid. He took care of what was his. I picked up a glass as well as a towel. "Why did you throw me out when I first came in? That first night? You told me to leave."

"A beautiful woman, traveling alone, arrives at my bar to ask for The Five? When I haven't heard anyone call us The Five for years? I just had this sensation, call it a hunch, that you were bringing trouble with you." He winked and smiled, then he sighed. "Or that we might cause trouble for you, like you seeking us out would hurt you in the long run. I don't know how to explain it, other than calling it a hunch. My brain? It doesn't work like everyone else's. Sometimes it skips a step, and then I can see what will happen next. It's not premonition, exactly, and it's hard to explain. The closest I can get is to say it's as though I've suddenly sped up or something." He shrugged. "It used to help in battle, but not so much now. No real call for it these days, even when I take a job."

I touched his arm, feeling his strong muscles beneath my hand. Yep, I was in so much trouble. I tried to clear my head. "I appreciate you trying to explain. I'm not very bright, or at least I don't know a lot of things that weren't deemed necessary." I passed him a shiny glass. It really was a good distraction, he was right. "But I can understand that there are truths for other people that aren't true for me."

"Hey. " He knocked my foot with his. "Not very bright? Are you crazy? You're obviously very smart. No one taught you to read yet, so that doesn't mean anything. You can't be expected to know what no one took the time to teach you. They only taught me because reading made me a better killing machine. Trust me, if they hadn't deemed it useful for their purposes, I wouldn't have ever been taught, either."

"Hard for me to picture you all as killers." Especially when they'd shown me nothing but kindness.

He winced. "Every man in this room is a killer, whether you can imagine it or not."

An interesting thought, but for some reason, it didn't scare me as much as it likely should.

They all fell quiet again. I looked around, trying to guess at the reason. It couldn't be because of me, as I didn't respond. Besides, they all seemed to be in conversation. Not that it mattered. They seemed perfectly capable of doing more than one thing at once. Even Ransom stared at the door.

"What?" I whispered although it occurred to me, I needn't have bothered after I said it.

The door flew open, and a man appeared in the opening. Like everyone else male in the room, he was huge. His face showed several days' worth of beard growth, and his eyes were bloodshot.

Crew rushed over to him, placing a hand on his shoulder. "Druid, what's going on? What brings you down this way?"

"Here." His voice shook as he spoke, as if speaking words strained him. "Here."

"Who's here?" A man I didn't recognize rose and walked over to him. In fact, soon most of the room surrounded him in some way.

Ransom, by contrast, blocked my exit from behind the bar. Was he trying to keep me behind him? Was Druid somehow dangerous?

"What's going on?" I asked again.

"That's Druid. As is obvious, he's one of us, but they did things to him. Experimented on him, because in some ways he wasn't what they planned. His brain, while brilliant, doesn't work like the rest of ours. He lives on his own most of the time, so we don't often interact. The man on his left is called Wolf. They grew up in the same juvenile hall, before Druid got taken by the corporation. Usually, if Dru wants something, he goes to Wolf. He doesn't usually come here."

Right at that moment, Druid grabbed onto Crew. "Here."

"Who's here?" Everyone was asking, but this time I asked, too.

He turned to look at me, desperation in his eyes. "Girl."

Druid stalked to the bar, and Ransom glared at him. "There are lots of women around. I know it's odd. Back when, there weren't, but there are a lot more born now. You can't have this one, if that's what you're here for. She's ours."

I blinked. I was theirs? What was that supposed to mean?

"No," he slammed his hand on the table. Finally, he took a long, audible breath. "You saw him."

His words threw the image of the man by the cave into my mind as though Druid showed him to me again, pushing that memory forward somehow, so I could see it again. Maybe that was something he could actually do? My voice was gruff, from the shock of having someone ruffle through my mind like a junk drawer, but I managed to answer, "Yes, I saw him."

"He's here." He visibly swallowed. "And he's like me. But he's...wrong."

Having delivered that speech, Druid stalked back out of the bar. As he left, pressure seemed to fill my head, making it feel as though it would explode in his absence. I grabbed onto my forehead, nearly falling forward, crying out at the sensation.

Ransom grabbed me. "Damn it. He pushed at her mind. Hold on. It'll pass."

I laughed, even though nothing was funny about the pain bringing me to my knees. "I wondered if he was doing that. If he showed me the man."

"That's one of the things they did to him," Mace explained as he jumped over the bar to my other side. "The corporation was trying to recreate something someone did on the other side of the universe. They messed up a whole lot of the people they used for their experiments. He can do that now, to non– Super Soldiers. I've never seen him do it here before, though. Only once, on another planet, before we were free." He put his hand on my forehead. "Maybe you were right about us being bad for her. She keeps getting hurt."

The pain passed. "I think he only wanted me to understand."

Crew caught my attention. "Okay, Raven?"

"Okay." I nodded.

Gunnar leaned over the bar and handed me a glass of water. "Here."

I took a long sip. "So someone like him is here? That's the point? He wanted us to know that. Like him, but bad."

Wolf rocked back on his feet. "Do you think it's possible one of Evander Corporation's experiments are here, and that they can somehow fuck with lightning? Like a person can *do* that?"

I opened and closed my mouth. I wouldn't have thought

it possible, but there were so many things I didn't understand, despite what I saw with my own eyes. The whole place continued to confuse me. I expected an uncivilized wilderness, since that was how Amias described it...but I wasn't sure anymore that Amias understood it when he lived there.

It had only been days for me, yet I could tell these people were huge hearted and trying to do their best.

It was more than I could say for almost everyone else that I had ever known.

"So we have a big situation. We can't hear his heartbeat, and we know they messed with him. It's possible he can control the lightning, of which he currently has an unending supply, and he might be able to call it down on our heads." Crew ran a hand through his hair. "This is a total fucked up set of circumstances." He looked at Wolf, clicking his fingers with the command. "Get your people together. Get everyone. We're going on a mission, like the old days. We'll find him. He's a danger if he can't be contained, so we deal with him."

Anyone who showed up at the bar right then would have no clue they were drinking and reveling only moments before, because everyone surged into motion. In seconds, they were all out the door and attending to various tasks.

Crew was still speaking. "Ransom I need you for this. Gunnar will stay with Raven. Gunnar, I might need you, too, but if so, Mace or Ransom will come back to stay with her. Worst case scenario, Raven, I'm going to ask you to go hang out with the other regular humans. And then we'll just station someone outside of there."

Ransom shot Crew a look but continued with whatever task he'd been assigned. Gunnar placed his warm palm on the center of my back, drawing my attention back. "Don't worry. No one is hurting you with me here."

Crew nodded, his gaze stern. "You're tasked with her safety. Nothing happens to her."

Having delivered that statement, they all left, following the crowd of super and regular humans searching for their foe.

Why would something happen to me? I hadn't been particularly threatened by the man, and he saw me alone and unarmed in any way. Was I in jeopardy? "Am I in some kind of danger I don't understand?"

Gunnar didn't meet my gaze, instead picking up the chairs by the tables and turning them over so they were upside and on top of the table, being held by their bases. "You're always at risk. You could fall down those stairs or drown in the tub." They sure seemed preoccupied with those two possibilities—falling and drowning. Had that happened to many people there? "Anything could happen. He hurt a little girl, and if Mace hadn't shoved you, he would've electrocuted you, so, yeah, I think you're in danger. There's a possibility he has a problem with the regular humans, so we'll watch all the regular people a bit closer. And I'm personally going to take care of you." He met my gaze finally. "Because you're ours. I saw you react when Ransom said that. I just want to reiterate that we all feel that way, so you're clear."

I walked toward him. We were close. Not so near that I could touch him, but if I took one more step, I could. "I know what it means when Clarke says people like me are his. What does it mean to you?"

He winced. "Not that."

"So then explain, because I don't understand it." I swallowed. "Does it mean that I must open my legs for people when it suits you? Does it mean I must always obey you? What does it mean to you? You already know I'm a prostitute, so I feel that my question is quite clear."

I couldn't have explained why I demanded the answers from Gunnar in that moment, but I needed them, and I knew he'd answer me.

"Prostitutes get paid." He shook his head. "I think what you're describing sounds like you're being held captive. All of you."

I looked away from him. "So, if not a captive, what do those words mean to you? Define what you mean when you say I'm yours?"

He swallowed, his throat straining. His voice sounded a bit gruff when he spoke, but he said, "It means that we will always take care of you. We'd like you to stay here with us, because you want to, not because you're forced. It means we get to be yours, too. It means that you would also take care of us. You'd stay with us, and maybe you'll let us...feel like men. Maybe that doesn't make sense to you, but most of the time, we just feel like some sort of machine. Not like men, because we only serve a purpose. I want to feel like a man with you. It's what we all want. As for you, Raven, you could have whatever you want. You could be free to be whatever you want, just knowing it was under our constant care."

I took that step toward him, stretching my hand to touch the place over his heart. "Would that include having sex with you?" I searched his eyes, sure I'd spot it if he tried to lie to me.

He put his hand over mine. It felt warm, and I trembled, but not from the cold. "Only if that's what you want. I can't feel those things yet, but I'm sure I would want to. I'm one hundred percent sure of it, but it's your choice, I promise.

For the first time, your choice. If you don't want it, then we'll just be a family."

I took a moment because his words seemed to bang around in my head without making sense. I could hardly understand them. When I finally found words, I simply said, "I won't get in the machine."

8

READING THE SIGNS

Thunder rumbled through the air like a constant, distant growl, and lightning kept the sky strobing above us in ripples of blue and iridescent light. Despite the fact I was inside, dry, and safe—*well, safe-ish*—I shuddered with every new rumbling growl of crackling atmosphere.

"Did they get him?" I leaned against Gunnar as the two of us watched what essentially amounted to a light show outside.

"Not yet. Close twice, now. Don't worry; they will." He tugged on the end of my hair. "We've only ever lost once, and we don't intend to repeat that performance."

I looked at him, finding him more pleasant to gaze at than the scene outside. "You act like you lost that war all by yourself. Weren't there hundreds and hundreds of you guys?"

He smirked at me. "Yes, for sure, there were. Still, it feels like I personally lost the war."

"Well, if you hadn't, then we wouldn't be sitting here

today." I winced again with another particularly furious boom.

"I never touch people the way I want to touch you." He shook his head. "It's nice to have these kinds of moments, so in this hypothetical, where I haven't lost, I'm not sitting here thinking about touching you right now. I'm a killer. You should stay away from me in this real life. And you should never be made to do what you were made to do in life."

I swallowed, but I couldn't disagree with him. "It's never bothered me before. I just accepted my fate, but sitting here? It feels different. Like a dark, twisted pain I'm afraid I'll have to live with now. Space, like what we were talking about before, gives us a little bit too much time to think."

"There is nothing dark and twisted in you, only in what has been done to you. Trust me, I'm dark and twisted. We can recognize our own."

I rolled my eyes at him, which made him grin. "Yes, you're *so* dark and twisted as you snuggle with me, all tangled up like we've known each other for years. Both of us are totally not the type to do this." Other than my brother, I never hugged anyone on purpose before. Not even Amias. "Yet here we are, as though we've done this a million times."

He leaned his head closer, rubbing the slope of his nose against mine. "Mmm, it does feel kind of normal, but also just extremely nice. Do people live like this? Do they just get to hold each other whenever they want? They just get to be this way?"

I nodded. "I think they must, in other places. Where things just went better, you know?" Someplace else. I had to believe that. "Gunnar, will you teach me to read right now? Or start to?"

He lifted his head, his gaze momentarily confused.

"Mace might be better for that. He's sort of a natural teacher. I don't know that I am."

I took his hands in mine and squeezed. "Well, Gunnar, I'm desperate to learn to read. I always have been, but no one has ever taught me. I feel like there's a world I'm missing. We're here waiting, anyway. It might be a good chance to take my mind off that." As if on cue, the thunder boomed again, and the night lit up. "I won't force you, not if you don't want to, but..."

He waved his hand. "Sure. I'll do it. I mean I have no idea whatsoever how but we'll muddle through. By the way, that conversation we had earlier? What we talked about? I'm pretty sure that no one was listening. Everyone was a little busy."

I smiled at him. "I guess that's good, unless I have to figure out how to have that conversation in near privacy with three other people now?"

He shook his head. "We'll work it out. All right, well, let's see if we can make some headway. If this goes badly, then that's on me, not you."

Gunnar grabbed a piece of paper and started to show me some letters. We started with vowels, and while I wished I could say I grasped the concepts instantly, I suspected there was a reason most people learned when they were young. I stumbled more than I would have liked, and after an hour I was done with it.

Still, he remained patient without being patronizing. At some point, I forgot to listen to every strike of noise and to twitch at every flash of light outside, as if they meant a battle approached.

After a bit, Gunnar stopped, rose and reheated my food. I found the meal delicious, despite being reheated, and I dug into the chicken-like substance they roasted with gusto.

I lifted my fork toward Gunnar. "Want some? I can share?"

For a second, I thought he'd refuse, but then he opened his mouth and took the chicken right off my fork. We watched each other chew and swallow, an unfamiliar intimacy drawing us both closer somehow. I shivered again, but I didn't want the moment to end. I held up my fork with chicken again, offering it while leaning a bit closer to him. "More?"

"I should absolutely not eat your food, especially since I'm not particularly hungry." He leaned closer, too, his breath stirring my hair. "But I like this."

I squirmed in my seat, enjoying the way the low rumble of his voice stroked across my nerves like a touch. "I like it, too."

When he would have taken another bite, he stopped and lifted his eyebrows. His expression told me something was wrong before his words. "Someone is hurt. Not one of us, but someone from one of the other groups. They're bringing him here, because they hope you can help him."

My appetite fled. "Sure. I can try."

He nodded once then leaned over to take my plate. "This fucker. I can't understand why he's so good."

I took his arm. "Trade with someone. You want to be out there. Or just trust me to stay inside on my own. I swear, I have no strange desire to get fried by this guy. I'll stay inside. Ask Crew, then go. I'm sure they can use you."

He shook his head. "I'm right where I need to be, and absolutely where I want to be."

I tilted my head. "Or maybe you'd like to be in two places at once?"

"Why does it feel like we already know each other, when we've really only recently met?" He asked the obvious question, and I caught my breath, surprised he said the words aloud. I didn't deny his question, as it explained how I felt about him. And not just about him, but with *all* of them. Was it because I knew Amias for so long? Did being close to him explain why I immediately felt connected to them?

Or maybe it was the opposite? Maybe they trusted me because Amias trusted me.

Did it really matter why?

The door burst open, slamming into the wall, and Wolf entered with a gust of rainy wind. He carried two men with him, one across each arm.

"I thought it was one," Gunnar shouted. "You said one, not two."

Wolf shook his head. "It's rough out there. It was one; now it's two. Out of them, I think Grey is worse off than Panther."

He set both men down on the floor, and I rushed over to assess their situations. They looked like Mace when he got hit by the lightning, with their singed skin and smoking clothing.

I looked up at Gunnar. "I wasn't able to help Mace. I fed him contaminated water. He got better because you guys are amazing, but not because I did anything to help him."

It was Wolf who answered me. "Leave Panther. He was struck, but yes, he'll probably get better on his own. Something else happened with Grey. Something blew up around him before he got struck."

Panther moaned but Grey was silent. I ran over to Grey. I really wasn't a doctor, but with no other choice, I tried to assess his injuries. There was blood, wet and sticky against my hand. Where was it coming from? I...

The door flew open again, causing Wolf and Gunnar to jump forward.

"Stop." It was the man from the storm, the lightning man. He held up his hand. "Take another step, and I will fry her just enough to knock her out. I'll fry all of you to get to her, and there won't be anything you can do to stop me. Get in my way, I fry you, and then I fry her. I don't have anything to lose, so don't test me."

They both stopped moving. He'd spoken so people not here would hear it, which meant that everyone else had to be somehow detained or hurt. I looked at Gunnar, but his attention was solely focused on Lightning Man.

I stood up straighter, standing between him and my patient. "What do you want from me?"

"You are going to come with me right now."

I was absolutely not going anywhere with him. "No."

"*Now*." He raised his hand and with precision, like he was slicing into a piece of meat, he zapped every conscious person in the room all at once except for me. I cried out, but when I would've rushed forward, the intensity of the other blasts knocked me on my rear end. My body buzzed, the feeling—now familiar—still agonizing. I stroked my hand over my chest as he hauled me off the floor and dragged me with him. "You're coming with me."

I wrenched out of his grasp just long enough to see Gunnar out cold before I was dragged away, nearly stumbling several times.

"What do you want with me?"

His silence was my only answer.

WE WALKED until I couldn't anymore, and then he carried me. It was a day and a half before we finally came to a cabin. The landscape changed so many times, I couldn't keep up with it anymore. Desert. Forest. Hills. Mountains. Plains. We charged through it all. I passed out, woke up, and he let me get down long enough to relieve myself a few times.

Then we went back to it.

The cabin was old, rustic, and had seen better days, but I suspected that could be said about me at the moment if I looked in the mirror. It hadn't rained on me since we'd left the town, which made me wonder how much of the weather had been the man's fault.

I didn't know his name, which was fine by me. As far as I was concerned, while I had known a lot of bad men in my life, this one ranked highest on my hate list.

Of course, my hate list was just created in the last few minutes. I needed to start adding people to it. Like Clarke.

"Help," a woman called out from somewhere in the cabin. "Someone, please, help me."

Her voice rang out, and I wanted to help her. When I struggled, the asshat carrying me didn't put up a fight. In fact, he all but threw me down onto the hard ground. I stumbled but righted myself, despite my wobbly legs. I ran inside, fast.

I figured Lightning Asshole must have brought me there to help the woman, as it seemed the only logical reason why he'd want me, specifically.

Opening the door, I made it inside before I stopped abruptly to take in the cabin. Heavy with pregnancy, likely full term, a woman lay chained to the fireplace by her wrists. I found the source of the cries, at least.

"Hello." It seemed a stupid thing to say, but I didn't know what else to do.

She lifted her tear-soaked face, shaking her head before it drooped. "Oh no. He got you. I'm so sorry."

I swung around. The man who'd brought me there stood

behind me, but I decided to ignore him, turning back to her. "What happened to you? Did he do this to you?" I rushed to her and began to struggle with her restraints.

She stared past me at the man behind me. "He's evil. You need to get away before he does this to you, too."

"Help. Her." Lightning Man growled before unhooking her wrists in a single motion. She flinched at his touch, but I was glad she was finally free. She collapsed into my arms before she cried out, a low moan of pain.

I swallowed. "Your wrists?"

With no handle yet on what exactly was going on, I struggled to keep up second by second. Lightning Man ran out of the cabin, leaving us alone.

"They hurt," she panted. "But I went into labor this morning. That's what really hurts."

"I see." And I did. He'd brought me there to help her. On the upside, I could help her with this particular issue, assuming it was a normal delivery. If things got complicated, we'd be out of luck. I wasn't a doctor, but hopefully we wouldn't need one. "I'll do my best to help you. What's your name?"

I took her by the arm and moved her over toward a bed in the corner. It had makeshift sheets, but not much else. Lightning Man's cabin was barebones at best, but it was going to have to work as a delivery room.

"What is your name?" I repeated and squeezed her hand. It seemed important to know that before we got started.

She visibly swallowed, her hands shaking. "Raine. I'm Raine Ezra. He took me from my home. He hurt me. Got me pregnant. He's had me with him ever since."

That sounded like hell. I'd only spent one day with him, and it was more than enough. "I'm Raven, no last name. I'm a healer, sometimes. Well, a semi-adequate one, not the best. But he found me and brought me here. He's been trying to kill everyone. Me. A little girl. He tried to poison her. He tried to hit me with lightning. I think he might have killed all my companions."

Raine moaned again, her long black hair falling into her face. She blew at it, and it moved away. "He probably thought he was saving that girl and you. He's not well. Don't get me wrong. He's evil." Her voice shook. "The worst. He did this to me." She pointed at her stomach. It was the second time she told me, but I wouldn't blame her if she said it a hundred times over and over again. "And then was so horrified by it. He wants all women to die now, so none have to go through childbirth."

I squeezed her hand in mine. "So I understand...this wasn't consensual?"

If he was her boyfriend, and she was just mad at him for the moment, I would treat the situation quite differently.

She gaped at me. "Of course it wasn't. He took me from my planet. I didn't have a family, but I was making do. It wasn't great, but it was better than this. I've been with him ever since he brought me here. I tried to get away but..." Tears flooded her brown eyes. "Now I'm here. Pregnant and alone. Giving birth in this place."

Instead of squeezing her hand, I hugged her. "You're not alone. We're going to get this baby out." *And then I'll kill the fucker who did this to you.* He was enhanced, which would make it harder. Harder, but not impossible. Lightning came at his beckoning, which was even worse, but so help me, he could die. I just had to figure out how.

Despite everything she had been through, Raine instantly fell in love with her daughter. I wouldn't wish her situation on anyone, and I wouldn't have blamed her if she didn't want to see the child, but her daughter looked up at her moments after delivery, and the new mom was hooked.

Lightning Man visiting the baby hadn't gone well. He was back outside in seconds, seeming agitated by the sound of her crying.

I stared at him as the sun rose on the horizon. He was huge, but I wasn't afraid of him. We were outside the cabin together, an unlit fire pit next to us. I didn't know what was next, so I closed my eyes and let the breeze toy with my hair.

Finally, I asked, "Does it hurt? When the lightning comes into your hands, does it hurt?" I didn't know why I was asking, but I was curious. Since I was stuck there with him, as his captive, anything I learned might be pivotal in beating him.

He side-eyed me. "Yes. Why is the baby crying?"

"That's what babies do." I was sure she was hungry, and it could be hard for new mothers to nurse. Unfortunately, I had very little training in that area. I wasn't an expert on getting babies to latch. *They didn't deem it needed information for an infertile prostitute to learn about childcare.*

It was amazing watching Raine bring new life into the world, and the child's tiny fists fascinated me.

I was glad the lightning hurt him. *He hurt so many others...* "Are they all dead? All of them, back where you took me from?"

"Don't know." He stared off into the horizon.

I needed to formulate a plan. I had the start of one, but no idea how to execute it. I fiddled with a loose string on my shirt, and said, "I need boiling water. To get the baby very clean." Truthfully, I could have used hot water an hour ago, but we made do without it. I assumed he wouldn't know what babies or mothers needed, or he wouldn't have bothered to collect me. He left the poor woman chained up for days. She could have given birth like that, and the ramifications of what could have gone wrong were staggering. I wasn't even going to let myself think about them.

He turned to regard me. "I can make fire."

I walked toward him. "Good. Do that. Now. How about a fire pit, so I can keep doing whatever I need for as long as I need. And I need something to hold the boiling water. Can you get me those things? So I can take care of your child?"

He blinked. "Yes," he said, and he took off running, likely in search of a pot somewhere. He had plenty of firewood, and I knew he could summon fire from his fingertips, if he so desired, so the kettle was the only thing I could think of him running off to acquire. I closed my eyes for just a second. I hated the Lightning dude. He was evil. He'd raped that girl in there, held her prisoner, and gotten her pregnant, then tied her up like an abused animal at the end of her pregnancy. Whatever happened to him to make him different from the other Super Soldiers, I hardened my heart against him. I would feel no sympathy for his circumstances, since he didn't deserve my sympathy. There were people who deserved none.

Lightning returned in a whoosh of movement, a giant pot in one hand. The thing resembled a cauldron out of fairytales, and I watched him slosh it full of water before he set it down on a hook over his firepit. I watched, not saying a word, as he made a fire. Sometimes he'd dart into the woods and come back, but he remained completely focused on his task at hand.

Maybe he was so focused that I could try something? Worst case scenario, it wouldn't work.

"How do you hide your heartbeat from them?" I stepped toward him. "Is that just something they did to you when they put lightning in your hands?"

He shot me a look that told me he didn't appreciate the question. Still, he answered me. "This." He pulled out a device from his pocket. "We had them way back when we were with Evander. I stole it on my way out."

I pointed to the device. "I'm not very smart. I can't read, and I don't know how to do a lot of things." I just delivered his baby, but I had a feeling he'd buy into my act of stupidity despite that. I wasn't lying, after all, because I didn't think I was particularly smart.

But even I was capable of figuring out what he did with that device. "You hit that button? That small one right there and it just works?"

He rolled his eyes and held out the device in front of him. "Click. They can hear me now. Click." He demonstrated as he spoke. *Asshole.* "Now they can't."

Good. I was pretty sure he wouldn't see me coming now. And I had to figure out how to save that device. I had no idea if anyone back in the town was alive, and I had no expectation they'd be looking for me, since they had to be horribly hurt. Despite that, when I got Raine out of there, I wanted our heartbeats very evident. *Click.*

He can kiss my clickin' ass.

I smiled internally at my joke.

"Can you boil the water in there for me?" I pointed at the cauldron. "Please?"

He nodded. "Sure."

With lightning dancing across his fingers, he set fire to the wood he'd brought then placed the cauldron on top of the rocks he'd stacked to support it. I twisted my hands together nervously. "Why did you try to poison that little girl?"

"To see if you could save her." He shook his head. "I heard you say you were a healer sometimes. I needed to see what you could do, so I'd know you were the one who could save Raine."

I opened and closed my mouth. "Then why shoot lightning out of the sky at me?"

"Well, then I wanted to see if you could save *him*, the man you were with. I knew he'd save you, but could *you* save *him*?"

"So this whole thing, this whole lunatic plan, was to see what I could do? Why didn't you just ask me?"

He shook his head. "People lie."

"And if I'd failed, people would also have died." Did he not see the problem? The absurdity of testing me by risking lives?

He shrugged. "Most humans are expendable."

I took a deep breath. Arguing with him wasn't going to get me anywhere. Instead, I waited for the water to boil. It always seemed to take such a long time when I wanted it quickly, and this wasn't different. Beneath the pot, the fire raged. He'd taken no care to see that it stayed small, and I appreciated it.

Finally, after what seemed like a year, the water boiled.

"Can you carry that in for me?" I was about to scald the crap out of my hands, and I might be permanently damaged going forward. *Some things are worth the pain.*

9

BURN MARKS

I couldn't successfully shove a Super Soldier, not with him at full power, and I wasn't going to pretend that I could. Instead, I launched myself at the bottom of the very hot pot. With a burst of motion, I pushed it over. He was surprised, which was the only reason it worked. In his abundance of ego, he actually thought I would just wait for him to kill me while I took care of Raine.

Knowing it would hurt and experiencing it were two different things, though. The pain wasn't delayed, and the agony hit, sudden and intense, but I didn't hesitate. I pushed the water right onto his body. The boiling water scalded him, immediately scorching his skin pink. He cried out, and my lips curled in sick pleasure. Super Soldiers could burn, too.

Now, to get him into the flames themselves. *I have to...*

I never got the chance to try. One second, I was alone, and the next, I absolutely wasn't. Crew appeared, a blur of light and motion my eyes couldn't entirely track. He grabbed onto Lightning Man and shoved him into the fire, face first. He wasn't alone, as another Super Soldier helped to pin Lightning Man in the flames. The two of them—the stranger and Crew—held him down as he fought to free himself.

Backing up to give them room, I couldn't get over how quiet the area around us seemed to be as they burned him to death. He didn't cry out, and at some point, he even stopped fighting them. He went limp, and they dropped him on the ground. That was when the man I didn't know lifted what looked like some kind of sword and took off Lightning's head. It rolled to the side, fully burning in the fire.

They both panted, and so did I. Shock, I thought, noticing my whole body trembled.

Crew swung around to regard me. He looked incredibly disheveled, covered in dirt, and smudged with mud. The man with him did, too.

I don't know what he saw on my face, but he was next to me in a second, cupping my cheeks. "Did he hurt you?"

I shook my head, clutching at his hands with my own just for something to hold. "Not me. No. He needed me to deliver his baby. There is a woman in that cabin. She's been his prisoner—he hurt her, raped her, and she's just had his baby."

"That fucker," the stranger said in a low voice just as Raine rushed outside, the baby in her arms.

"Raven," she threw an arm around me. "You're okay. I saw what you did. That was so brave. I wasn't brave, not once. What you did..."

"Would have gotten me killed," I finished for her. "If these two hadn't shown up. I wasn't going to be able to do what they just did."

It was as if Raine realized we weren't alone in that moment. She widened her eyes, her gaze darting between the two men. I didn't blame her when she stepped back behind me, blocking herself and the baby from their view. She was a new mother, wearing a makeshift nightgown he must have given her, and she'd been brutally abused by someone who was physically just like them.

"I think you're plenty brave, Raine. I don't know if I would've survived the way you did. This is Crew and...I'm sorry, I don't know your name." I motioned to the red-headed man with him.

He visibly swallowed. "I'm Gator."

"This is Gator. And I was staying with Crew when I was brought here. They won't hurt you." I was sure Crew wouldn't, but I shot Gator a look that said he'd better not. He visibly swallowed again. If anything, he seemed more nervous than Raine. "Raine has been through hell. She needs rest and to get out of here."

Crew grabbed my wrist, staring at the bottom of my left hand before turning his attention to the right. "You're very injured."

I was. The burning was awful, now that he mentioned it, and I might be in some kind of shock because I should be feeling it more. Right then, it was more like my heart raced and I couldn't really think past what we had to do next.

"We need to do something about this." Crew looked at Gator. "Suggestions?"

Raine cleared her throat. "He kept burn cream on his ship. Sometimes the lightning would burn him. He had a cream there."

Gator raised his eyebrows. "Where is this ship?"

She pointed left. "We walked about three hours."

"I'll find it." Gator met my gaze and then Raine's. "I can find anything."

I would love relief from the pain, but Raine's needs came first. "She needs to get to town. Bring her to the others who have kids. I'm not a midwife or a doctor. I can only do what I can do."

"We'll all go to the ship," Crew announced, still looking at my hands. "And then we'll fly it back to town. Be back a lot faster that way, and Raine can get what she needs." He met her gaze. "We're talking about you like you're not here. We can take you back that way."

But that made no sense. "Ships can't take off because of the lightning. The electrical storm." Wow. My hand had really started to throb. Badly. I needed to get it under some water soon. Like right that second.

"We won't try to go up that high. Low flying should be fine," Gator supplied, walking over to Raine. "I realize I might be scary, but if I could carry you and your baby to the ship, it would be my honor to do so."

Despite the immense pain threatening to steal my breath, I had to smile. Gator spoke a little differently than everyone else. It must have been perfect because Raine, after a long moment, stepped toward him. Her baby made a small sound, and she rocked back and forth to offer the child comfort.

"Raven seems to trust you. She was wonderful to me. She saved me. I'll trust you because she does. I guess if it won't be too much to handle, you can carry me. Otherwise, we're going to have to wait, because as much as I'd love to be super powerful, I'm not, and I don't think I can walk to the ship right now." She looked down. "As I've proven for over a year by doing nothing to defend myself, I'm not strong."

I shook my head. "You survived. That was all you needed to do."

Gator nodded. "Nothing will happen to you anymore, I promise you that. My men and I, we live here now. For so many years, we were on the wrong side of things with no chance to do better. Now, it's all we want to do."

Crew side-eyed him. "That's a lot more rolling around in morality issues than my guys do. We're just trying to get through the day."

"These are conversations we have." Gator ran a hand through his hair. "With your permission?"

She nodded, and he scooped her and the baby up, heading in the direction that she'd pointed. Crew didn't move toward doing the same for me. "Other than your hands, which is bad enough, did he hurt you?"

I shook my head. "He hauled me around but that was it. I got here just in time to deliver her baby. If we'd been any longer, I hate to think of what might have happened."

He cupped the side of my face. "Forgive me."

"Forgive you?" Maybe the burns had addled my brain, but I didn't have a clue what he could apologize to me for, considering he rescued me. "Why?"

He sighed. "For letting you get taken. You're mine. Ours. We were sidelined. He set fire to so many things, we couldn't get through without putting them out, so they didn't risk the human population. By the time we got through, you were gone, and I couldn't hear him." He looked away. "So I grabbed Gator. As he'd be glad to tell anyone who would listen, he's a great tracker, so we came."

That reminds me... I rushed over to the dead body and tried to grab the device before it burned, but my hands wouldn't allow it. Crew rushed past me to scoop it out of the flames. "That's how he did it. How he hid his heartbeat."

He shook his head, flipping the device over in his hand. "I didn't know any of these still existed."

"You've seen them before?"

Crew nodded and put it in his pocket. "But it feels like

something from another life. Come on, let's get to that ship. We'll fix those hands."

"There are things in that cabin that might be useful to you," I told him as he lifted me up as though I weighed nothing at all. I was tiny, compared to him, but not weightless. It was impressive and although I'd spent my life with people like him, I'd never been carried around before.

My hands throbbed and I closed my eyes, leaning my head against his chest.

"You got hurt trying to save a stranger from someone who could have broken you in half with one hand. You were smart and creative about it. I'll send someone up here to go through the house. Ransom gets wanderlust sometimes. It'll be great for him, and it doesn't have to be this very second. Stop thinking about everyone else and try to just rest until I can take care of you."

Stop thinking of others? That might be next to impossible. I liked thinking of others. First, because I liked knowing I helped them and second because it was easier than thinking about myself. I wasn't going to explain my logic to Crew, though, not when my hands burned like I still held onto the bowl.

"Good job getting him to click the device like that. It got us to you even faster, although we would have found you anyway. The baby being born was enough of a noise for us to hear, so we tracked you. I can't believe how completely egotistical that was of him." He laughed. "But then again, it seems he's gotten away with doing things all over the universe that he shouldn't have."

I could hear his heartbeat. Despite carrying me and walking faster than I could, his heart sounded slow and steady, as if it didn't exert him at all. I thought about what he said, imagining people like him scattered across the universe. "It's almost like they need people to police the enhanced— sorry, Super Soldiers— to keep others safe."

"Call us whatever you want. We're just glad you found us. You're ours."

I would dwell on what his possessive tone meant another time. *Ours*. I liked the sound of it but had no idea if I should or not. I knew they talked about going off the machine. I liked the thought of that too, which surprised me more than anything. Still, I had no idea if it would be one of the things that wound up being bad for me despite me wanting them.

The pain throbbed, so I forced my mind to focus on something else. Instead, I thought about Raine. She would need cloth to make diapers for the baby. She also needed time and a safe place to rest and get better. Time to just be with her baby. Could any of that happen?

"Gunnar? Grey? Panther? Wolf?" I hadn't let myself think about them, but fear for them had my hands shaking again.

"All recovering. The lightning puts us down hard, but they're all going to be okay."

I don't know if I fainted from the pain, but I jerked awake as another stab of pain sliced through me. A lot of time must have passed, based on our surroundings, because we were suddenly at the ship.

"Raven." Crew ran a hand through my hair. "We're here."

The ship buzzed nearby, an almost insect- like hum that wasn't quite noise, but it vibrated my skull nonetheless. I tried to clear my mind and focus. It had to be...what was his name...Gator. He likely started the ship, because Crew still held me. Unless Raine knew how to work a ship. Or perhaps the baby?

I giggled at the ridiculous notion despite the pain. Then

I blinked. Damn. My head was foggy. I wasn't thinking clearly.

"Crew...?"

He touched the side of my cheek. "You have an infection. Fuck."

How did he know?

"I can hear the strain," he answered as if he could hear my thoughts, too. More likely, he probably guessed, but maybe he could hear me...

"There's a broken med machine," Gator—yes, that was for certain his name—called out. "And I might be able to fix it."

The baby cried, a tiny plaintive wail that gave voice to the sound of the pain still flaming up my arms. What was she going to call the baby? Did they have a custom here regarding naming children? Some cultures did...

There was a lot of scrambling, and eventually I was set down on a bed. Raine dipped onto the small mattress next to me.

"It feels different in here," she said in a low voice. "Sounds stupid, but it's like the energy of the ship knows he's dead, so I can breathe in here again." She shook her head, her baby asleep on her shoulder. "You can't care very much about any of this right now, huh? The pain must be awful."

A loud buzz suddenly filled the space, louder than anything else. Raine gasped, and I jerked then cried out from the pain. Raine settled her hand on my thigh in a comforting touch. "They fixed it."

"Easy fix." Gator said then shook his head. "Asshat must not have wanted to do it. He wanted to make you suffer, Raine."

I lifted my head. "We have a working med machine?"

Crew came over and lifted me. "We do, and you're getting into it. I'm not a doctor. So we're just going to hit power, and let it fix you. When you wake up, we should have made it back to town. See you in a little bit. Try not to worry for five minutes."

That was, as I was quickly realizing more and more, easier said than done.

He placed me in the bed of a machine. I hardly remembered my first trip through a med machine to get sterilized, and I never warranted another visit. I didn't earn enough to garner time in one even if I got sick. As Clarke had let my brother die, it became clear none of us mattered to him outside of what we could bring him financially. I swallowed. Why did I deserve to use a med machine, when so many others who needed one went without? I wasn't special. Tears leaked from my eyes as I thought about all of the people who had loved ones waiting for them, yet didn't have access to a machine, while I didn't have anyone waiting for me.

"Hey," Crew looked down at me. "Whatever you're thinking, don't. This is going to be fine. I promise."

I shook my head. "It isn't that. Maybe I don't deserve it."

He scrunched up his eyebrows, shaking his head. "I say you do, and I'm in charge here. That's all there is to it, so get some rest."

Crew shut the lid without another word, and after a brief second of confusion, I fell asleep, darkness moving through and then over me like a warm blanket as the buzzing swallowed my world.

～

IT WAS the lack of noise that woke me. Crickets sounded somewhere in the distance, but other than that, no noise filtered to me wherever I lay. I struggled to wake, and a gentle hand stroked my hair away from my forehead. "Easy, beautiful. You were in there a lot longer than I expected, but you're healed now. It might take a few seconds for you to reorient from the machine, so move slow and take it easy."

Finally, with more struggle than I could ever remember having before waking up, I blinked awake. My head was on Crew's lap. He ran a casual hand through my hair as he regarded me quietly.

"I feel funny," I said, because I did, and I couldn't quite define it.

He nodded. "That's the drugs. They even hit people like me, sometimes even harder than they hit you. But you've been asleep for a few hours. Just rest. There's no rush to get out of here."

"Raine?" I managed to ask. My throat was dry, but he produced some juice from nearby and offered it to me. First, he helped me sit up, and then he gave me some to drink. I swallowed it down, the cool sensation pushing away the parched, dry feeling.

"She's fine, " he finally said. "Gator brought her to some other families. She'll stay with one of them, and they'll help her and the baby."

I never found out what she decided to name the baby. In that moment, I didn't really think I'd remember it anyway, if he did know it. I rubbed my eyes. "Everyone else is okay?"

"As far as I know, they are. Gator told them where we are, if they need us. We're just far enough outside of town for me not to be able to hear them and they can't hear us. I figured I'd give us all a little privacy while you recover. There are too many ears interested in you right now. You've become a local celebrity overnight. That can't be fun, especially when you're not feeling well." He sighed.

"And obviously we have to start working on privacy issues."

I was sure he was right, but it was too much for me to think about right then. Instead, I leaned back against the wall and closed my eyes. I decided to take his advice and just let my body wake up, since lethargy weighted my limbs.

Eventually, I opened my lids. Everything was sharper, brighter. I could see again and the dizzy, off feeling had passed, thankfully. Crew leaned against the wall next to me, his eyes closed and his breathing steady. After a second, he opened them to regard me. "Feeling better?"

"I am." *Much, much better actually.* My hands didn't hurt, my body felt cool. A crick in my neck I'd forgotten I had was gone. I noticed the absence, having grown so used to the pain. "Thank you. How were you able to fix it so fast?"

"That was Gator. He's really capable with a lot of technologies. We were the same rank way back when, but he followed me here, and now it's like I've somehow become everyone's de facto leader. I didn't ask for the role, in case you're curious. Anyway, it was just a spliced wire problem. Net could have fixed it, but he didn't want to. The more I learn about him, the worse it gets."

I blinked. "His name was Net? Lightning Man, you called him Net?"

"That's who we think he was, at least. He never introduced himself, but from what everyone can remember, that was his name." He shook his head. "He had a lot to answer for, and maybe he met death too quickly."

I leaned my head on his arm. "Maybe he did, but I'm glad he's gone, and I'm sure Raine is, too."

"Raven. " His voice sounded more like a sigh. "I need you to know...I never did any of those things. Not ever. I was ordered to do some bad things, but not like what he did.

And I'd like to think, if they had ordered me to do terrible things, I wouldn't have done them. I would've taken my death from them and said no."

"I do know." I guessed I shouldn't have sounded so sure, but I felt sure. None of the people hanging out with Crew shared Lightning Man's level of evil.

I was sticking with that name for him, too. I preferred it.

I lifted my head to look at Crew, only to find he'd closed his eyes again and seemed to be resting. "Are you okay?"

He seemed sort of...off. Tired. Granted, he'd run after me at high speeds, so he was entitled to get tired. It's just I knew it took more than that to wear him out. These men showed me so much kindness, and I didn't feel like I was at risk in their presence at all. Just the opposite. They kept protecting me.

I'd never had so many people solely focused on me before, as I'd been more of a peripheral person. I'd gotten very comfortable by myself, in fact, and used the time to observe others. Being their focus now, well, it struck me as more than unique.

Swallowing, I ran a hand through his hair when he didn't answer me. "Crew?"

"I have a pretty bad headache."

I hadn't expected that. "Does that happen to you usually? I know you guys are almost never sick."

He winced. "First headache ever that didn't come from banging it really hard."

Amazing. What would it be like to never have a headache? I couldn't fathom it. "Then you should go get in the machine. It'll help you."

Crew shook his head. "I don't want any more medicine right now, thanks. I think I need to just give it time. They always told us, if we missed our treatments, we'd feel like hell. But don't you worry, because it's going to be okay. Maybe I just need to rest for a bit? It'll pass. I'm not being clear, sorry, Raven. I've stopped going in the machine that takes away sexual feelings."

It was news to me, and although the idea should have frightened me, it didn't. He suffered through pain simply because he wanted to be with me? Or at least I hoped that was why he did it.

"Is there food?" I rose. I could feed us while he wasn't feeling well.

He made a sound I decided was an affirmation, and I spotted what looked like a fridge unit nearby. I didn't find much food inside, but a few small, wrapped packages lay on the shelves. I didn't know if it was from Lightning Man or if Crew and Gator had brought fresh food. Either way, I wasn't starving right then, but it was good to know it was there.

We were out of the earshot of others. The idea sizzled through me, full of possibilities, but it also seemed a strange thought on a planet filled with Super Soldiers. The sound of Crew's deep, even breathing caught my attention. He was where I had left him, but his relaxed posture suggested deep sleep. His face, however, wasn't restful. Pain clenched the muscles of his jaw, rippling across his expression like lightning.

I wished I could fix it for him, but he said no more machines. I wondered if he kept me on the ship not solely for privacy but also to hide his own pain. Amias told me stories about what happened if you seemed weak but were one of their kind.

I discarded the thought quickly, though, as Crew stayed honest with me to a fault. Although it might suit him to give himself some privacy, I honestly believed his motive was for my sake.

I sat down next to him, smoothing my hand across his brow. He started to open his lids, but I shushed him, drawing him down so his head was on my lap. Stone had headaches when we were kids, and I used to rub his forehead. It helped some, he claimed. If I could offer Crew some relief, I wanted to give it freely.

It didn't hurt that I liked to touch him. He always smelled clean and male at the same time. He never touched me without my consent, and when he did touch me, his skin sent shivers through mine. He led these men, and the best leaders led by example.

The beautiful man, with his soft skin and long fingers, was nothing like Clarke or his associates. Nothing like any of the other men I knew before, if I were being entirely honest.

I ran my fingers through his hair, feeling the soft strands streak like silk across my palms. My hair wasn't so soft, and I wondered if it was a product he used or just another trait of their superior genes.

Long moments passed, while shadows from nearby trees stretched slim, dark fingers to slice across the room. His even breaths continued, his face nuzzling tighter against my stomach with a sigh as the breeze teased the leaves outside the window. After a time, his arms slid around my waist, holding me in his arms even as he continued to sleep. Outside, the light started to dim, as the afternoon waned.

My stomach growled, reminding me I hadn't eaten. Although I could go without food if the need arose, I didn't have to at the moment. I moved slowly, gently reorienting him on the bed before I snuck back to the small fridge. The packets of food turned out to be dried meats, familiar to me as Amias taught us to make them, and we often ate them as snacks on long walks. I wondered if the making of the cured meat was a lesson Amias learned from Crew or perhaps just part of their standard training. Since I learned he could cook the whole time and never told us, Amias' meat seemed somehow less impressive.

I took a bite and tears flooded my eyes, surprising me. The taste was a little bit like having Amias back, and I choked on a startled sob. I wiped the tears away and pushed away the memories. Crew might be out of it, but he'd hear my distress if I didn't calm down. The last thing I wanted was to wake him up because I was crying over dried meat. I scrubbed my face with my palms then finished my food.

Cleaning myself up was harder, because I wasn't sure how everything worked on board their ships. Luckily, the med pod seemed to have somehow refreshed me, so I wiped down with a towel and felt much better.

A sound from Crew jerked me around, as I recognized it as meaning pain. I quickly rejoined him on the bed, and he gratefully wrapped his arms around me, as if finding a life-line in a storm.

We all need someone sometimes. Even Super Soldiers.

10

TURNING THE PAGE

I must have fallen asleep. Morning light shone through the windows of the shuttle when I next opened my eyes. Behind me, with his arms still around my middle, and his breath on my neck, Crew still slept. I wondered if any other Super Soldier slept so long before undrugged, but then noticed another change since we'd fallen asleep.

Crew was hard, and his cock—his large and very hot cock which pressed up against the seam of my ass—seemed very happy this morning.

A man awakening hard wasn't something new for me. Although I chose not to rest around clients, men frequently dozed off afterward then awakened wanting another round of the play from the night before. But Crew was different, somehow. For one, I wanted to know him intimately. I bit my lip, imagining how it would feel if I pushed myself back to feel his hardness press even harder against me, or even better, if I rocked just a bit...

I moaned, because imagining the sensation had my body clenching in need. Was this desire, the emotion so many talked about, but I never truly experienced? I pushed away the thought, irritated with myself.

He wasn't feeling well, and he never agreed to be the object of my fantasies. Crew's cock might be hard, but the response could be sheerly biological. Maybe he was having a great dream. Maybe he was thinking about somebody else. I gulped at that thought, because it bothered me more than it should.

Maybe he was just hard because his body was waking up after basically being chemically castrated his whole life?

Crew made a sound in the back of his throat, a little bit like a moan, then shifted his hips a smidge before tightening his arms around me.

"Is it really morning?" he whispered, his voice all gruff from being unused. "I fell asleep around lunch time."

I ran my hand over his, the knuckles still scraped from his battles. "I know. You needed the rest. How are you feeling?"

His breath washed against my neck so evenly, for a moment I wondered if he'd fallen back asleep. I startled when his deep voice growled over my skin again. "Well, a little bit in awe. They stuck me in that machine when I was sixteen. I—it's been a long time, and I think I forgot what this felt like. Never before have I awakened to find myself pressed up against the most beautiful woman I've ever seen, so between the two sensations, it's rather incredible."

I almost rolled my eyes at the compliment but stopped myself. Men didn't usually bother to flatter me or say sweet things to get what they wanted. Still, Crew never lied to me before, so although I was hardly the most beautiful woman anyone had ever seen, who was I to dissuade him of my own charms?

He thought I was the most beautiful woman he'd ever

seen? I blew out a quick breath. How completely amazing was that—even if it was absolutely crazy at the same time? The feeling whooshed through me like a river finding a crack in a dam, so I rolled over to face him, and to feel that hard cock even closer to where I wanted it to be.

For the first time ever.

I actually knew how to pretend to seduce someone. I could lower my voice, lift my eyebrows, stick out my breasts, sound breathy and excited...all of the things I knew men enjoyed. But I wasn't at all sure what to do, suddenly. I didn't want to pretend with him, but I didn't know how to do any of it without using my skills.

"Crew..." I lost steam after I said his name, staring at him in silence. What was I going to say? As though they moved of their own accord, I put my hands on his chest, his rock-solid torso warm beneath his shirt. He didn't move, and I leaned closer, until our breaths mingled.

I kissed him. I'd never had the ability to decide who I wanted to kiss solely because I wanted to do it before recently. My heart raced as though it was the first time my mouth met another, and although it was ridiculous, it absolutely felt as though it was. He didn't move, allowing my lips to play across his for long seconds, but then he kissed me back. Maybe he was amazed by this, too? I didn't ask, but I reveled in our gentle exploration of each other.

His mouth was firm but soft, and he tasted somehow sweet. I pressed closer to him, and he did the same until we clung to one another. I knew moves I should make, practiced things I could do to amplify his pleasure, but instead, I focused on getting lost in the trace of his mouth against mine.

He didn't seem to notice or particularly care that I suddenly became inept at the art of seduction. Crew ran his hand up and down my arm, strong movements that sent shivers through my body.

I pulled away to catch my breath. He took longer to catch his than I did, and I tried not to let my lips curl in pleasure at the thought.

"Wow," his voice was low.

I agreed completely, but I blushed. "I hope that was okay. We never talked. I mean…I just assumed."

He ran a hand through my hair, once and then twice. "Do you somehow think I wouldn't want your kiss?"

"No." I ran a fingertip down the slope of his nose, and he nipped at it then smiled. "I feel like I don't know what I'm doing. Like I've never done this before. We both know that I have, and…"

He interrupted me by kissing me. Then he pulled back, staring into my eyes. "Maybe you haven't, not like this, anyway. Nothing has to happen, Raven. We can just stay here and kiss. All I wanted was to hold you. Just because I'm going through withdrawal from that machine, it doesn't mean you owe me any sort of relief."

I leaned up on my elbow, smirking at him. "Nothing about this feels like obligation to me. It's more like…for the first time I want it…for me? That is, if you want it. You're also not required to…"

He kissed me, effectively shutting down my awkward babbling. I was more than okay with him shutting me up. Maybe what I said spurred him on, because he pressed down on me, kissing me over and over again. A heat sizzled in his embrace that hadn't been there before.

That had been Crew keeping it easy going. This was Crew really concentrating on me.

I sighed against his mouth and gave in to the heat that

he created inside of me. It grew with every press of his mouth and lick of his tongue against my own.

Crew lifted himself up and over me like he was going to do a pushup before he propped himself on his elbows. "Not going to hurt you. Not for anything."

His voice was barely a caress against me. I caught my breath. He'd never know what his soft promise meant to me. Not ever. I didn't know that anyone had ever cared before. Crew caught his breath, his eyes widening.

"I just remembered."

I tilted my head to see a range of emotions flicker across his face. What was he thinking? "What did you remember?"

"What I used to like in the machine."

I blinked. That was completely unexpected. "Do you usually forget?"

"It's mostly like a blur. Never mind. I don't want to think about that. What I want to think about is giving you pleasure. That's what I like, Raven. I like to give pleasure, even more than I like to receive it."

I opened and closed my mouth. Was this really happening? Or was I still out cold and hallucinating? I was going to go with the first one. *This is real.* "I...ah..."

He scooted down, and in a swift movement, removed my pants. With a flick of his wrist, they flew across the room. I didn't know what to do or how to behave, as I never— Men didn't want to...

"Crew?"

He kissed the top of both my knees before he slid my panties down my legs. I shivered. Anticipation had never been so sweet. Or terrifying. But I wanted him. I craved Crew's attention like a drug, and I was afraid I'd happily become addicted to him.

"This okay, sweetness?"

That's a new name. Although some men liked using nicknames, no one had ever called me that one before. "If you want to. You know you don't have to do this."

"The most beautiful woman I've ever seen is offering herself to me, and you think I would pass up on the feast? It's the stuff of dreams, Raven, and I lived a long time without dreams."

He pushed my knees aside and kissed his way down my legs, caressing each of my thighs. I watched his face, surprised by the nearly worshipful expression I saw there. I swallowed. We had to stay bare, hairless all the time, but without the products we used at home, I had a little growth. Would he like it? Did it matter?

It was such new territory to me. I didn't know what the rules were, or how to behave.

Crew touched the small curls between my legs reverently before he raised his eyes to find my gaze. "You're red everywhere."

"I think that's normal." I'd never thought about it before, but he wasn't wrong. Redheads did tend to be red everywhere. I had opened my mouth to ask about his opinions when Crew touched his lips to those curls, frying my every thought.

His voice was low, so low I could barely hear him, but I could feel his words there, between my legs. "I want to taste you everywhere."

Moisture flooded my core. *Damn.* I hadn't known talking could be seductive, but it was—it really, really was. He moved lower, licking me, and I squirmed, almost coming off the bed before his hand on my knee held me still.

I closed my eyes. It was too much to look right then, too much to see. I could only feel what was happening, only let myself exist on that plane and no other.

Finally, and too soon, he found my clit. With the smallest nip, he used his tongue to torture me in the sweetest ways. Crew took silent direction really well. If I moved or caught my breath, he gave me more of that sensation.

I wanted to cry out, wanted to let go from the pleasure he gave me, but I couldn't. I never orgasmed, never made a sound during sex that hadn't been put on or used to make the other person feel good. It was like I couldn't find my own voice, only gasping in need.

The vulnerability of noise, it seemed, wasn't available to me, not when he gave me so much and my body ached for him. But Crew was there, he was giving me these moments, and he was strong, big enough to take on just about anything.

I let go. With a shout so loud I was sure that not only could everyone on this planet hear me but all the ones in the galaxy, too, I exploded around his tongue. Gripping the bed, I panted and held on for dear life while he wrung every ounce of pleasure out of me.

When he was done, my body twitched like an electric current fed it and every so often, despite the fact the switch was off, it jolted me.

Crew pulled me against him to hold me tightly. "That was amazing. Thank you for that."

Thank *me*? I hadn't done a thing. Despite the lack of application of my seductive skills, he shook against me as if he'd been the one to shatter somewhere in the stars. I began to move, intending to remedy that situation, but his hand gripped me closer to him.

"Need to hold you for a few more minutes, sweetness," he grumbled, nuzzling my neck.

I lifted my brow to regard him. "I want to make you feel good now."

"You did." He stroked my back, his head on my shoulder. "Trust me, you did. That was more than I could have dreamed of. If you'd let me, I'd make you feel good that way every day forever."

I stroked my finger down the side of his face. "We're not finished."

I enjoyed the taste, but I wanted more. I wasn't done, not even close to being done. I wanted him to shatter for me, too.

His face fell. "I'm terrified of hurting you. You're so tiny, and I'm so much bigger than you. I..."

"Sshh," I said and kissed both of his cheeks, smirking. "I promise. This will be great. You won't hurt me. Just the opposite."

I pulled my shirt off and let it fall to the ground. My bra was next. I dropped it to the floor. Now, I had his total attention, his gaze fixated on my breasts. Although I couldn't read minds, I was sure that he wasn't thinking with his nerves anymore.

In a swift move, I pulled his shirt off, which required him to help, but he still hadn't taken his gaze from my breasts. *Looks like Crew is a boob man.* I smiled. Most men were, but I never reveled in the attention as much as I did right then.

"Do you want to suck on my nipples?" I asked, biting my lip.

He nodded, still hypnotized. "If that's something you'd like."

"From you, I would." I scooted closer to him. "But I want us both undressed before we do that."

I wanted my hands on his skin everywhere, and to feel

his cock jump when I stroked him. To harden. To be mine for just a little while. It should have been awkward, undressing him, since we were lying down, it always seemed more awkward that way. But nothing other than anticipation filled me, even as we practically switched sides of the bed to get his pants off.

Crew was huge, and I reveled in looking at all of his flesh bared to me. I let my gaze pass down his body—over his defined abs and huge muscles to the way that his calves flexed with his movements, and finally to his very erect, waiting-for-me, cock.

"You on top, I think," he said. Crew's voice was low. "That way you can't be hurt in any way. You'll determine how things fit, what you like and don't like."

He was really sweet, but I hated him worrying when he should be enjoying. I climbed onto his lap, wrapping my legs around him when I did. "I'm not worried, and I'm not fragile. We were made to do this together."

Whatever he would have said, I didn't let him finish. Instead, I lifted my knees enough that I could take hold of his cock and I pressed down on him, taking him inside of me inches at a time. He sucked in air, his eyes closing on pleasure. "Fuck."

I watched him, his whole body wire taut for me. In the middle of this moment, there was something so beautiful about him succumbing to sensation. His lids lifted, slowly, his gaze heated and focused entirely on me. "I didn't know it would feel like this. I didn't know anything *could*. It's you, Raven. From the moment you...Fuck."

I leaned down and kissed him, moving my body to rub against him. Warmth flooded me. Yes, up and down. Vibrant sensation zinged through me with each movement, unlike anything I'd ever experienced. Instead of nothing or discomfort, little fireworks of pleasure shot through me, arching upward and building somehow.

Giving in to instinct, I squeezed my breasts, tweaking the nipples between my fingertips. Another jolt of pleasure moved through me, and Crew moaned, so I reached down and squeezed his nipple on my next thrust onto his shaft. I didn't imagine it was easy to bring the beautiful man to such unrivaled want. He was mine right then, and I loved the sensation, and the power of it.

Then I more than loved it. Pleasure warmed me from the inside, traveling outside until I swore I could feel it in my toes. Heat like lava. It traveled my body. I moved faster, chasing the sensation, and the more I did, the more Crew responded. He grew even impossibly harder, grasping onto my hips, driving me down on top of him. It seemed as though he knew what he was doing, all of a sudden, and I didn't, lost to my needs. *It's amazing how quickly the tables can turn.*

I knew the mechanics, but I'd never experienced anything like Crew before. Hadn't known it was possible. He had. And, oh yes, I needed him, didn't know how I'd ever done without him. Was it…was it…?

I exploded, finally making it over the impossible crest and shattering into a million tiny pieces. He cried out, jerking inside of me, his fingertips tight against my hips. My muscles clenched around him, the orgasm dragging impossibly onward. Again and again, until I quaked with pleasure. He pulled me to him, our bodies becoming even more tangled, but I melted into him. Crew kissed me, all over my face. I closed my eyes, just trying to breathe.

It wrecked me. Pleasure, so much it bordered on painful, yet I loved every second of it.

Confusion ran over me. What did any of it mean?

I swallowed, my breath still wheezing out of me as tiny aftershocks shook my body. How was I supposed to go back to letting men rut on top of me after that? I shook my head. Maybe I didn't have to? Except I did. No, I needed my head to shut down. Tomorrow's problems could wait for tomorrow. I wanted to be there, in the moment with the beautiful man kissing me and stroking my back. *Yes, that's nice.*

Really nice. My thoughts settled. In fact, they seemed to float away.

He rubbed my back, kissing me, his lips dragging little sparks of pleasure along my skin. Maybe he'd keep doing that forever?

I must have drifted off, because when I opened my eyes again, I was sprawled over his chest. Outside, a bird's shrill call grated my ears, which was probably what had woken me. I yawned and thought about how much I'd been sleeping since I got to their planet. Granted, I'd been injured, but still, it seemed like a lot. I lifted my head and Crew grinned at me.

"Hey, sweetness," he whispered. "You okay?"

I would always be okay if he continued to look at me with kindness, adoration, and the light of the universe illuminating from his gaze. I blinked. *Okay, dramatic?*

I didn't live in a world where *the light from the universe* did anything, let alone *blaze from his mind*. I wasn't the kind of girl who got lost in ridiculousness after sex. Yes, it felt incredible. *The best ever.* I hadn't known it could be like that, but I knew better than most how sex had little to do with emotions. Most of the time, it was just a business transaction.

I met his gaze again, and my good sense fled as my lips curled in a silly grin. *Damn it.* I was hooked on this guy. Not just him, either. I was sure, if the others were there, I'd be equally willing to do it with them. It wasn't even about the sex, although it did confirm what I already suspected.

I fell for them because they were being kind to me. Because they seemed to care.

Because they saved me. More than once.

Plus, they're gorgeous and smart and...

I shook my head at Crew. "My head is all over the place."

"So is mine." He ran a hand through my hair. "A million different thoughts. One to the next. I thought maybe it was normal. Maybe I don't know how to do this—how to live without some kind of chemical lobotomy fucking with my mind. Maybe I just don't know how to control my thoughts now."

I scooted up a little bit, so we could be forehead to forehead. "I've never been lobotomized, but this is not how I normally am. I feel different, and I don't know yet if it's a good thing or a bad thing."

He closed his eyes and took a long breath. "Just taking you inside of me for a second. Letting the scent of you into my cells."

I grinned, amusement flooding me. "Like that! You probably don't say things like that normally, right?"

He opened his lids. We were so close, we were pretty much breathing the same air. "I don't. I'm not some kind of poet. I'm barely a man. I'm a monster created to lead monsters. I had one chance to change my life, to be better, to fix it for all of them, and I didn't take it. They would've followed me to a better life on the other side of the galaxy, but I chose to stay with Evander. That makes me a pretty bad monster leader, when it comes down to it."

"Crew, you saved them. That's what they all say. You saved them. You did that. Maybe that time on earth when you didn't change sides, it just means you're loyal. Right or wrong, you don't abandon who brought you to the party. And hindsight is always clearer, right? Like we know what to say days later, after someone insults us."

He smirked at me. "If someone insults me, I don't usually let them live long enough to repeat the performance. If they insulted you, they'd be dead in a very painful way. I'm your monster now, too, beautiful."

I lifted an eyebrow. He moved through two nicknames for me, back and forth. "You need to pick a nickname for me and stick with it. How will I know when you're addressing me versus someone else?"

His laugh surprised me. We were moving through so many emotions; it was hard to keep up. "I don't use nicknames for other people, so they're all you. Like I wouldn't ever call Mace sweetheart, just to be clear."

I tilted my head, then raised a brow. "Why not?"

"Well...he might kick my ass."

I could stay like this all day, every day. I never needed to move. I would stay tucked against him forever and ever, laughing, and saying terribly important things that might not actually have any meaning at all. It would be a constant dichotomy of confusion that I somehow loved. I smiled at the idea before asking, "Could he? Kick your ass?"

"If I let him." His breath caught for a second. "We have company, speaking of Mace. He's headed toward us. Guess he really didn't want to wait until I brought you back. He couldn't possibly believe you were fine without seeing it himself." He smirked. Crew wasn't really talking to me right then, he was talking to Mace. "Yeah? I've had you to myself long enough."

Mace's intrusion didn't actually bother me, and I didn't think it bothered Crew either. He could come and lie here too, talking nonsense with us. He could be part of the golden moment. In fact, they all could. Having them around would multiply our happiness, not deflate it.

Crew kissed me, his caress a promise of more to come, if not at the moment. *Soon*, his kiss promised.

I squirmed to get off him and put on some clothes, only to discover my body ached from our time together. By the time I grabbed my shirt, I full-on winced.

Crew touched my arm. "How badly did I hurt you?"

"I'm not hurt." I leaned over to kiss his chin. "I'm sore in the best possible way. Don't obsess, okay?"

He sighed. "But I'm so *good* at it."

We had that in common.

11

FEVER DREAMS

I t took Mace about a half an hour to reach us, which raised Crew's eyebrows. We were both dressed and waiting when he arrived, and I didn't have to be a Super Soldier with enhanced everything to tell Mace wasn't feeling well. I rose when he appeared, but Crew shook his head.

"You shouldn't have come if you were feeling like hell." He sighed. "I can hear you struggling. We could've come back, and you could've been resting."

Mace ignored him, staring at the ship instead. "Amazing to see one in this good of condition. And there's really a med machine?"

"There is one, yes. We could put you in it."

Mace shrugged. "Only if you want to fight first. I'm done with machines messing with my insides."

Crew didn't move, yet the tilt of his head made Mace drop his gaze for a second. There were obviously really long-term unspoken conversations between these two. I'd never really thought about it, but it did seem Mace was his number two, the one he looked to in order to get things done. Maybe it had always been that way.

Mace wasn't in charge, but he was high up for sure. Did Crew deliver a set down without saying a word? I put my hand on Mace's forehead, judging his condition. Under my touch, his brow burned, proving he ran a fever.

"I've never seen a Super Soldier with a fever before," I admitted then tugged on his hand. "Crew's right. You shouldn't have made this trek right now."

He sighed and sank on the stairs next to Crew. "I've always been defective."

"What does that mean? Hold that thought." I rushed into the ship and came back outside with a cloth and some water. Combining the two, I wet the cloth. I always liked the sensation of a cool cloth when I was sick. "Go on. Defective?"

He shook his head. "I always got sick when the others didn't. The bosses didn't know about it because Crew hid it from them. Otherwise, they would've put me down. This isn't sick, though. This is the result of stopping that machine."

I winced and sat next to him. "I'm sure Crew had a good reason for not telling anyone." Placing the cloth on the back of his neck must have been the right thing to do, because the second I did, he closed his eyes and sighed.

"I did." Crew stretched out his legs. "No one was putting him down just because he could catch a flu. Mace is my family, and he was the best at what he did. No, fuck that."

I continued to rub the back of his neck. "The med machine would probably help."

He shook his head. "No. No more machines. Don't people get better? Don't regular people get sick or have a reaction and then their own bodies fix it? Sure, we need the intervention when it's serious, but shouldn't I be able to just get better?"

Mace put his head on his knees. Crew side-eyed him then turned to me. "He tends to get a little belligerent when he doesn't feel well or if he gets injured. He'll go in the machine if I tell him to go in the machine, but what his body is telling me is that he needs a nap. I'd bet, if he got some rest, his fever would go down and he'd be fine. Meantime, I'll fly us home."

"No." Mace opened his eyes. "I don't want to go home right now. I don't want to be this sick with everyone knowing it. I want to be able to fall apart a little bit with only you, Ransom, and Gunnar knowing. And Raven. I don't want the entire contingent of Super Soldiers here to know my business."

Maybe the lack of privacy could be an issue for them on occasion and wasn't just my concern? "We can stay here a little bit longer, can't we?" I asked Crew, and he nodded before he got to his feet. "My headache is long gone. I'm going to go hunt us some dinner. I won't be very far. Minutes at most, and I can be back even faster, if needs be. Just call my name. In the meantime, Mace, you try to rest. Raven speaks for

me until I get back. If she gets too worried about you, she's going to tell you to get into the machine, and you're going to do it."

With that, he nodded at me before he bent over to kiss me. The quick brush was light but full of heat. "I'll hear if he gives you any trouble, but I don't think he will, because he's as crazy about you as I am."

Crew went back into the ship and came out with a weapon I hadn't seen before—likely his tool for hunting.

"You can't be comfortable on the stairs. There's a bed inside."

Mace leaned his head against my shoulder, closing his eyes. "I like it out here. Sunshine and Raven. That's all I need."

If he felt as bad as I imagined, he would need more than my shoulder and the sunshine to recover, but within seconds, I heard his snore. I didn't blame him for not wanting to get in the med machine if the sex depriving machine made him so sick upon cessation.

Time ticked by, marked by the buzzing of insects and the gentle stir of the breeze as he snored on my shoulder. I reveled in the few stolen moments of quiet. I never had much time to myself before, which made the entire trip feel like a vacation of sorts, even if Mace felt poorly.

"Could you?" He lifted his head, his gaze not clear when he spoke to me. His eyes were all kinds of hazy in that moment. I touched his cheek. He didn't feel hotter, but he must be having some kind of fever dream. I might not be able to tell. My fingertips weren't an exact science.

I tilted my head. "Could I what?"

"Could you love me like you love Crew?" He blinked. "Like what we talked about?"

I shook my head. We'd had no such conversation, and no one had ever used the L word when talking about or to me. I loved Stone and Amias, but I never said it and neither did they. I hoped they said it to each other. The big L was a dream.

Touching his cheek, I smiled at him. "When did we talk about such things?"

"On the big blue cloud." He blinked rapidly, and I smiled at him. His words confirmed my thoughts about his delirium—he wasn't awake.

Mace leaned over as if he intended to snuggle into deeper sleep. I didn't mind, but not on the steps. Especially not if he needed as much rest to recover as Crew needed. "No," I took his hand. "Inside. Come on."

He didn't fight me, so I led him to the bed. When I would have backed off, he drew me to him, pulling me against his chest as he sprawled across the mattress. I wasn't tired, but I lay there until he was settled and snoring again. Then, as gently as I could manage, I slipped out of his hold. He didn't budge and kept dreaming. I hoped the deep sleep meant he was detoxing from the years in that machine.

Why did they stop these men from feeling sexual urges? Were they so afraid they couldn't control themselves? Or were they easier to control if they were contained? Or were they afraid they'd hurt others? From what I knew of the worlds, few would care if they hurt women regularly like Lightning Man . In our society, it would be accepted rather than abhorrent behavior.

No, it had to have been about control.

So why did the men continue to take the meds once they were free? Maybe they didn't trust themselves?

Well, I trusted them. I'd seen the worst of the worst. Whatever they did before, it wasn't who they were anymore. They were trying to keep babies safe, to help people have comfortable, safe lives. No way did they need the machine to make them good people.

Without anything to do to occupy myself while Mace slept and Crew hunted, I began making an inventory of all of the belongings we "inherited" from Lightning Man. Although Crew went out to obtain food, some here would suffice as well. Besides that, I also identified clothing, medicines of some kind, and papers I couldn't read. I made the items into piles, sorting, straightening and otherwise picking up the space to make it more comfortable.

Mace made a sound, and it wasn't a good one. *Pain.* I knew it well because I'd heard it many times when I tried to help people in the past. He moaned again. And again. I put my hand on his forehead. Actually, he was cooler than before, implying his fever had abated. That was a good thing.

Faster than I could have imagined, Mace thrashed on the bed. He swung his arm back and I would have taken a fist right in the face if he hadn't been grabbed before he could make contact.

Ransom stood next to me. How had he gotten there without me noticing and so fast? His dark eyes were serious, his beard slightly longer and thicker than the last time I'd seen him. He held Mace's arm easily, smiling a half smile down at Mace. "Easy, brother, you don't want to hit our girl. Not even in sleep. I know you'd never forgive yourself."

Mace continued to roll around and then darted up, launching forward. I was right in the way until I got swung aside—this time by Gunnar, who yanked us both backward to avoid the blow. In the meantime, and as fast as Gunnar moved, Ransom pushed Mace down on the bed.

"Easy, Brother. Come on. Just dreaming. You're safe here. And you don't want to hurt anyone. Don't make us tie you down." Ransom positioned himself on the bed until he was behind Mace, holding him against his chest, like he spooned him from behind. It really was very sweet. Ransom lifted his head to regard me. "He'll hate this, but it's the safest way to keep him here without tying him up, which I think he'd hate more. He's always convinced he's too dangerous and too broken, so we're just going to lie here and never mention it again."

Gunnar nodded. "Not a word. Just glad we got here before he did something he'd regret. Who knows what battle he's fighting right now?" Gunnar let me go, running his hand down my arm with a soothing stroke of heat as he did. "I am so sorry I let you get taken."

"You got zapped with lightning. I'm just glad you didn't die. Don't think of it again." I hugged him. "Thanks for showing up just in time." I turned toward Ransom on the bed. "Both of you. Crew is hunting."

"We know," Ransom yawned. "I've had a headache all day and this asshat didn't tell us he was leaving. We had a good scare for a few minutes before we figured it out and came after him." He patted the bed next to him. "And Gunnar is hurting, so we're a great trio. How the fuck did Crew get through his so much faster?"

Gunnar limped over and got on Mace's other side. "I think he went off the machine the day she got here. He's always ahead of us. Like he just knew that this would happen. I don't know. But I'd guess."

"He'll never tell us." Ransom put his head down.

I stood watching them for a second as they settled down around Mace. Their presence seemed to calm him down. Every once in a while, he muttered something. Eventually, he settled, his breathing evening out—not snoring anymore, just even. Right about when I noticed he'd fallen asleep, I noticed the other two were out, too.

It was sort of adorable. They didn't regularly sleep together, as they told me as much, but they were willing to keep each other safe. Without hesitation or qualms, they climbed into bed with Mace because he needed them, no questions asked.

My heart turned over. What would it be like to have someone care so much about you, they willingly risked themselves for your good? But thinking them adorable wasn't the only emotion my shattered thoughts considered. Little sparks of desire still pooled in my belly for Mace. What would it be like, I wondered? To have all their hard bodies against me, or at least two of them? Then maybe one could...

I shook my head. What was the matter with me? One good sexual encounter and my brain stopped working. I didn't even know if the three of them actually wanted me. They were just going through withdrawal, so they could change their minds, right? For that matter, I could change my mind.

Scratch that, I realized. If they all wanted to, I would gladly be game. It might be very fun, in fact. I swallowed. *Perhaps more than fun, too.* That was the scary part. What was I supposed to do with any of this?

Crew made a noise. It had to be purposeful , because I knew just how quiet they could be if they tried. A second later, his hand touched my waist, followed fast by his chin on my shoulder. He kissed my neck, and I gasped as the warmth moved through me again. Apparently, Crew would only have to remind my body about what we shared for it to be ready for him again.

"I'd do anything for them, " he whispered in my ear. "They'd do anything for me, for each other. And for you. Anything. I don't know how it happened, Raven, but you're one of us. It might not be something you want. Amias ran off because he didn't want to be here anymore. It killed me a little bit to lose him, and to know he felt that way. You're ours now, too. We will always see to it that you have what-ever you need. Always. Almost instantly, you became someone we need." He stepped back. "Come outside with me? Let them sleep. I'm going to cook, since they'll likely wake up hungry. It won't take them as long as me. I always pass out longer. They're faster to recover, and always have been. Even Mace, who has, as he told you, more human reactions—even he gets better faster than me."

I followed him outside where two dead animals waited to be skinned and cooked. They looked similar to pigs from my planet, but not exactly the same. Amias once told me about adaptations, and how different animals changed to suit the environments of the planets where they were introduced. I understood a little bit about it, enough to assume the animals would taste very similar to the pigs that we kept at home. Cooking wasn't my main job, since everyone had a different role to fulfill to keep Clarke's empire strong...

It was ridiculous, really. *Why didn't we poison his food?* I shook my head. He was enhanced, which meant he would've smelled it, but no one even *tried*.

"What can I do to help?" I asked, deciding I didn't want to think about things at the moment.

He pointed to a comfortable- looking seat next to his fire pit. "Sit and keep me company. This is going to take some time."

"I'll keep you company, but I'd like to help." I joined him by the fire. "Might be nice to know how to do something useful, since my previous skill set isn't helpful on this planet." I paused, shaking my head. I wasn't sure anymore how I'd go back to letting people handle my body against my will. I admitted, "I think...something has changed big time in me. And I'm not sure at all what the future will hold."

Crew didn't argue with me about my future being off kilter, he only squeezed my knee companionably. Instead of meaningless promises, he spent the next few hours showing me how to cook the animal—a *visayan*, he called it. It was a long process, and we actually didn't speak very much, which was comfortable with Crew.

Sometimes I'd catch him staring at me. When he knew he'd been caught, he'd wink at me. About the third time, I winked back, and he laughed. It was just the easiest thing in the world to be together with him.

Eventually, he used sticks to suspend the pig over the flames. His timing struck me as flawless, since the sun dipped low over the horizon. *Just in time for dinner.*

The pork sizzled and popped over the flames for a few minutes, making tantalizing scents warm the air, when he lifted his head and grinned at me. "The food smell is rousing them."

"Is that okay? Shouldn't they sleep longer?"

He shook his head. "If they were really sick, they'd be still out of it. I mean, I'm not an expert, but that's what I think."

"Why did it move through you so much faster? Is it really just how things work for you?"

He smirked at me. "Smart girl asking what they won't. I stopped going in the machine the day I met you. You arrived on my scheduled night, so I didn't go in. Due to that, I'm a bit ahead. I guess, technically, it means it moved through me slower."

I squeezed his knee again. Gunnar had been right. "That fast, you wanted out of the machine?"

"I wanted..." He caught his breath and then steeled his shoulders. "I wanted the chance to really love you, the way a man loves a woman, if that's how it ended up feeling. Amias met and loved your brother, you said. When you told us that, it struck me like someone plunged a knife into my stomach. A man who was my brother ran away to have a life because he didn't feel free to have one here with us. I have to believe it's because of that machine. I'm so glad he found Stone, and I'm so glad he sent you to find us. I knew you might not have anywhere close to that kind of interest in me, and I understood the possibility you'd like someone else, but I wanted the chance, if it ever came. Plus. You're just so fucking pretty. I knew that right off the bat. It turns out you are so many other amazing things too. I just thought, maybe if I stopped, there might be a chance."

I caught my breath, tears flooding my eyes. I didn't let them spill. His words moved through me like a gift from the universe to squeeze beauty into my soul. "Crew."

He leaned over and kissed me. "I'm not pushing you. I just hope we can both be on that path. If you never get there, that's fine, too. I'm just so happy to be near you. I get to feel like this, to feel real. To feel like a man should feel when he's around the most special, beautiful woman he's ever seen."

It was hard to talk past the lump in my throat. "If I start crying, know they're happy tears."

"There are happy tears?"

He no sooner asked than Mace sort of stumbled out of the ship. He missed the bottom step and winced but kept walking toward us before he threw himself down on the other side of me. "I'm so sorry, Raven. So fucking sorry."

I rubbed his back. "You're okay. I'm okay. Nothing happened, thanks to Ransom and Gunnar. You don't need to make apologies for fever dreams."

I put my hand on his cheek. He was nice and cool, and although he was stumbling a bit like he'd slept hard, his gaze was clear.

"It was like I knew what was happening, but I also didn't. I...I would never hurt you for anything in the world."

His gaze was so pained, I acted without giving it any

more thought. I kissed him, squarely and gently on the lips. "I know that. Okay? I do. I've seen and experienced pain from others. That isn't who you are."

He closed his eyes, pushing our foreheads together. "Give me their names. They'll no longer breathe."

"Dinner before death, okay?" Crew laughed. "And don't plan any murders without consulting with me. I want in on that."

12

BACK TO BEFORE

The visayan was the best thing I ever ate. Or maybe it was the company? Although Ransom stumbled out first, Gunnar quickly followed suit, and we soon sat around the fire sharing the meal I helped prepare. Their easy banter and laughter didn't make me feel excluded; rather I felt like part of a happy group. The novelty of the sensation—one I hadn't experienced since Amias and my brother passed—filled me with satisfaction almost as quickly as the food.

The pain of loss wasn't gone, I realized, feeling the familiar little stab and breathing through it. I still grieved Stone and Amias, but it was almost like I was learning to appreciate everything else more with the loss so sharp and jagged in my chest.

I wasn't over it, by any means. I might never be. I just didn't want to cry right then, though, which was unusual for me when it came to thinking of Stone and Amias. I set my plate aside with a small smile, and Ransom caught my gaze from across the fire. "It's okay, you know. I'm doing it, too," he admitted softly.

"Doing it?" I wasn't sure what he meant, and I certainly wasn't bringing my grief to the happy moment together.

He tilted his head, his gaze seeming to see more than I thought I revealed. "Missing Amias. I'm sure you miss your brother. I keep thinking Amias should be here, too, and it's been five years since I saw him. This is raw stuff, especially for you, but I think it's okay. We can be happy. He'd want that, I think. Or at least that's what I decided. For me, anyway."

I swallowed. "This is the best meal I've ever had, and I think it's because I'm having it with all of you. I'm happy, and I'm glad I'm here with you...and then...I just...I remember."

Mace put his arm around me while Gunnar came to sit behind me. In a move I didn't expect, he put his legs around me then dragged me against his chest. Crew touched my knee, his gaze warm when it met my own. In that moment, three of them touched me, and Ransom held eye contact like I was the most important person he'd ever seen. I sucked in my breath. I'd never felt like people were so attuned to me before, like I mattered more, not ever before.

"I'm sorry. " I shook my head. "I'm turning the best night ever into..."

"Into what it needs to be," Gunnar supplied. "We can feel all kinds of ways at the same time. That's what makes us human, right? We don't have to be just one way. I mean...I don't know. That's just what I've learned all these years watching. We can feel happy. We can think the food is outstanding. We can...know that the girl sitting with us is like a gift from the universe we never expected to find. We can think about the fact we miss our friend, who should be here with us. We can be sick to our stomach because we never met his husband. I don't know. All those things, all at once."

I nodded. "I think you're right. I know I got to live a life that you didn't have, but please know—I also haven't exactly lived a traditional life. I'm a prostitute, and that shaped my experiences. Look at my head and…"

"No." Crew squeezed my leg. "You're not a prostitute. You're a woman who was held captive and forced to do things for years. There are words for all of that. We can use them, if you'd prefer."

I held up my hand to stop him. I knew what he meant, but I wasn't ready to think about my life under any other terms. I rubbed the back of my neck. Sometimes things were just too…*much*.

That is okay. Maybe. What did I know? Between the lack of education due to my status and gender and my own inability to pay attention, I missed way too much.

I leaned back against Gunnar. These guys were all wide awake. Super Soldiers hardly ever slept, and they'd all had a good knock out from their detox hours. Despite my healing sleep and my rest afterward, nighttime made me tired. It wasn't how I was built. On evenings that I didn't have to work, I always fell asleep easily—like my brain had a shut-off valve, forcing me to sleep despite my responsibilities to Clarke's clients.

I yawned, knowing I could fight it if I had to, and Gunnar squeezed me tighter.

He said, "You can sleep, if you want. Or we can take you inside to the ship. In the morning, unless Crew says other-wise, we'll fly back home. We can't be away too much longer. They might need us."

It was really sweet how they looked out for everyone

else, despite sneaking me away for a bit of privacy. They had to go home, and I liked the idea of going back, too. It was nice there, and I hadn't really had time to fall into any kind of routine with them. *What will that be like?*

"I'll move. If I fall asleep, you're going to be stuck with me leaning against you." The fire kept the area warm, and it wasn't raining on us. The thought tilted my head up, and I searched for the stars, but I couldn't see them through the electricity putting on a show above us.

Without Lightning Man , we weren't in danger sitting out there, and we could safely watch the colors swirling in the unsettled sky.

"I like it, " Gunnar whispered in my ear. Everyone could hear him, but it was sweet nonetheless. "I've got nowhere to be. It's nice right now. If you fall asleep and it gets cold for you, I'll carry you inside to that awful bed. I'll even cover you up in blankets."

I smiled. Despite my tiredness, I very much doubted I could fall asleep on Gunnar outside on the ground.

"Do you remember the game Amias used to play?" Mace asked with a smile, as he threw a piece of wood into the fire. It popped before it exploded in brilliant sparks. He grinned and did it again.

"I used to play a lot of games with him," I answered, yawning. Was this something new? I looked between them.

Mace smiled at me. "Well, I think he probably didn't play *this* game with you, not unless he wanted you to pass out. It was the *hold your breath* game. We used to hold our breaths, figuring out which one of us could do it the longest."

"No, you're right, we didn't do that." I smiled. Gunnar stroked a hand up and down my arm. Every so often Mace and Crew would squeeze my legs somewhere. Ransom never looked away from me. The night grew very dark, but the fire offered some light, enough so that we could see each other. I told him, "We used to play *What If.* Like he'd say, *What if suddenly this room spontaneously burst into flames?* Then we'd all have to give an answer and vote on who gave the best response. Some of the responses were ridiculous, and that was sort of the point. Those who got the most out there with it tended to win. I'm a little bit dull. What if this room caught on fire? I'd say, well...I'm going to run." I shook my head at the memory. "Stone would have said something like he'd use the flames to find a secret passageway that led to Earth. Or something."

They were quiet as I spoke, their attention focused intensely on me. It wasn't much of a memory, but a way we used to pass time sometimes at night. I shrugged, suddenly self-conscious.

"What did Amias say?" Ransom asked quietly.

I snorted, thinking back. "He said..." It took me a second to answer him. What *had* Amias said? All at once, I remembered. "He said he'd go find who set the fire and see to it they never had hands to set anything again."

Behind me, I could feel Gunnar shift, nodding his head. "Sounds like him."

"What would you guys say?" I asked the night, not looking at any one of them in particular. Whoever wanted to answer was fine by me. Or they didn't have to. It was probably just a stupid game that was only fun because I remembered it.

Mace sighed. "I would get everyone out, figure out who set the fire, and then set a bigger fire on them."

"I would," Crew said, then cleared his throat, "get

everyone out and then ask one of you to take care of the person who caused the problem. While you took care of that, I'd take care of their boss."

I was seeing a real pattern developing in what they were all willing to do, a trend. Lots of *kill the fire starter*.

Gunnar made circles on my back with his long fingers. "I'd...I would make sure everyone was okay. I'd try to put the fire out, then make sure my people were safe. If that meant killing, fine. If that meant getting the fuck out of the area where people were starting fires, that's what I'd do. I don't care about revenge anymore. Or killing people, if it comes to that. I just want my people safe and sound, so that's what I'd do. I would make sure you were all out."

"Brother. " Ransom laughed. "You make sure we're all fine. I'll kill the ass that put our girl in danger."

I shook my head. "Why am I the one in danger? Maybe you're all the ones in danger."

Ransom stretched out his legs. "Because you are so spectacular, it is a for- sure thing that someone would try to take you from us by setting that fire."

I sighed. "I'm not so spectacular. I'm just a girl, like any other girl. There are hundreds like me where I'm from." I ran my hand over my marking just to illustrate the point, lest they forget. "I'm lucky I got here. Lucky I get to have this night with you."

Ransom shook his head. "No, sweetheart. We're the lucky ones. Much more so than any of us deserve, too, I'll promise you that."

"Well, none of us would have won Amias' game. The winner should have said that little green monsters would come and eat the fire or something."

"Guess we all live too much in reality." Gunnar laughed and then they all joined him.

I yawned again. He was just as warm as the fire that lit up the night in front of us. I knew for a fact they'd all protect me from the flames, if everything suddenly went to hell. Maybe that was why I closed my eyes right that second.

Waking up in the middle of the night, I realized I'd fallen asleep. I rubbed my eyes. The fire was low, a blanket covered my body, and I was pressed up against Gunnar. He leaned against a log someone must have dragged over, and we were alone. I glanced around, not sure where everyone else went.

"Hey," Gunnar's voice was low, and my gaze snapped back to his handsome face. "What woke you up?"

I shook my head, blowing out a breath that only came out a little wobbly. "Didn't mean to fall asleep at all. Sorry."

"Why are you sorry?" He ran a hand through my hair.

I sighed, sitting up. "Because I basically pinned you to the ground while I lay on you like a mattress."

"That's not how it felt. Don't make light of it. What it said to me was that you trusted me to sleep on me, to know I'd keep you safe. For my part, I got to hold you, which it turns out is really all I want in the world. I love the idea of holding you. It's...apparently what I want most of all. So don't say sorry, I'd like to be your mattress. I'd do it every night, all night, always."

I turned to face him. Wrapped in a blanket on his lap almost felt like we were alone in the world, even though the sensible part of my brain knew that wasn't the case. Still, I liked the thought of it.

"If I started...to kiss you right now, and maybe do other things, would it embarrass you? I mean...I know that we're not really alone."

He put his hands on my cheeks. "We've made each other

a deal to try to be better about privacy. I don't know how it'll work, but no, it doesn't embarrass me. Does it bother you?"

As a response, I kissed him. It really didn't bother me. Not in the least, in fact. As long as it was the right people listening, I was pretty sure I might even like it. I'd deal with what that meant another time. I discovered there were physical things I wanted out of life and, right then, I wanted them with Gunnar.

People watched me have sex for years on a stream to make sure I behaved. This wasn't really different. Feelings I had a hard time digesting in front of others. I'd decided I wanted these guys.

I rocked against him, and his cock hardened. I smiled. Yes, that was what I wanted. "Do you want to go inside?"

He shook his head. "Only if you want to."

"What I want is you and me right now." I kissed his chin, loving the feel of his scruff against my softer skin.

"Me too." He cupped my face. "Raven, you make me feel human. Like I really am what I always wanted to be. Like I was born to do this with you. Like I'm not just something badly created in a petri dish."

His words didn't make sense at first, but then I gathered the gist past my needs. "You are absolutely a man. A human man, everything you should be and more. You take my breath away with your kindness and..."

He stole mine in that second, kissing me so soundly, I forgot I needed air at all. It became just the two of us in the night to me. We touched one another in exploration until my breath wheezed out in desperation, reveling in the unique sensations we could cause in each other. He pulled my shirt over my head and discarded it, gazing at my body as if he'd waited a lifetime for the view.

My breasts ached, so when he palmed them in his

callused hands, I cried out. He stopped and stared at me. "That okay?"

I leaned into his touch, nipping at his bottom lip. "Very okay. Good noises."

He grinned at me, looking down at his hands as he clenched them, causing a firestorm of sensations to cascade through me. "I don't want to assume."

"Feel free to do just that."

I was shirtless, he wasn't. I tugged on his until he took it off. *That's better. Much, much more so.* He really was beautiful.

My hands slid and dipped over his curves as I explored his chest, all golden skin in the warm crackle of firelight. His fingertips closed over my nipple, tugging slightly, and making me gasp for him. "Your body is like a piece of art. Raven, there has never been a woman as beautiful as you. I've been everywhere—across the galaxy, through black holes. Trust me. No one has ever been as beautiful as you."

I shook my head. He was too much. The galaxy was too broad, too expansive, for me to be the most beautiful woman in it, but arguing wasn't sexy. His chest was, so I licked it. Although they taught me men liked to be tasted, I never felt the need to nibble my way across anyone's flesh before. With him, it seemed natural, so I dragged kisses and nips across his skin, pleasing myself with the taste of him as much as I pleased him with my caresses.

He gasped and gripped me tighter, pulling my face to his so that he could kiss and kiss me. Our tongues danced together, his in my mouth, mine in his. I tried to show him what I wanted to do to him with my tongue, then I smiled, deciding showing him to be my best course of action.

I pulled away, slightly. "Lean back."

He tilted his head in question but obeyed me without hesitation. I pulled his pants down fast, before he could focus too much on what I was doing, and then rid him of his underwear.

"Raven?" The slight unsteadiness in his tone—the uncertainty—would vanish the moment he took my body, so I decided to revel in these moments before he claimed his power. Before he drove me wild, I could torment him a bit.

I took him in mouth. Usually I looked at the act as a task to be fulfilled, like any other in my work, something else to just get through. But my mouth watered as I considered his hardened length, twitching slightly in the cool night air. It was so nice to crave it, so nice to be able to say it was my choice. I moaned as I took him deeper down my throat, covering him with my mouth in one long pull. The flavor of him on my tongue seemed warm, spicy, and just like I somehow knew Gunnar would taste. The more I took him, the wetter I got, so I squeezed my legs together as I rolled my eyes up to see his reactions.

He threw his head back, clutching onto the ground, anywhere, as though he were looking to hold onto the planet for dear life. "Raven, fuck. Fuck."

I ignored him and kept at it, redoubling my efforts as his hips jerked helplessly. What I wanted—no, craved—was Gunnar coming undone in my mouth. That would be heaven. That would be just what I needed.

"No," his one word got through to me. "Inside of you for the first time."

I let go of him with a pop of noise and a small smile. If that was what he wanted, I could afford to be cooperative. Quickly, I took off my pants. He panted heavily, as if he'd run a race as I climbed on top of him.

"You're so fucking amazing." He took my mouth then in what could only be called a kiss to claim me. I might be slightly bruised from it later, but I loved the open- mouthed need and gave him back the same attention. With as much finesse as I could while still basically seated on his lap, I took him inside of me. He was large, erect, and ready, but I was wet for him. I had to really breathe to make the first pass but then he was there, deep inside of me, filling me until I sighed around the sensation. I stopped moving just so I could meet his eyes for a long second.

He said I was beautiful, but he's the beautiful one.

"I never..." His voice faded off before he kissed me again.

I hoped he was as lost as me, because I was flying. I moved then. Slowly riding him, I'd lift myself up and then slide back down quickly. It gave me control, and I found an easy rhythm. I could rub against him in steady pulses, then jolt myself with pleasure by plunging down hard. He squeezed against me, lifting his hips. We groaned together. I did it again, over and over until he stopped me, grabbing my hips and changing our movements. Oh yes, Gunnar had quickly caught the knack, and he wanted to control it.

I grinned at him. That didn't surprise me at all.

His movements were stronger, demanding, and I loved it. Pleasure mounted inside of me, growing with each stroke. He learned my body, my movements, and he was giving me just what I needed. I dug my fingernails into his shoulders and held on for the ride, grinding down into him.

Finally, I exploded, throwing my head back, my muscles clenching around him. With a shout he followed me. We panted, gripping each other as if we might fall over any second. The sounds of the world rushed back at me—the crackling of the fire, the crickets' song, the whisper of the wind, and the fact that it hit my bare back.

I lifted my head. "Are you okay?"

"Am I okay?" His voice was low, rough. "I feel like for the first time in my life, I really am okay. Better than okay.

Happy." He kissed my shoulder. "Just where I am supposed to be and why I am here. Is that too much?"

I smiled at him. "No, it's not. Always say whatever you want to me. I'll do the same with you."

"Good."

Content to stay cuddled in his embrace, I waited longer than I usually would to move off him. It gave me the minutes to feel him start to soften inside of me. I kissed his lips before I pulled myself away. "Thank you, Gunnar."

"Thank me? Should be the opposite of that, Raven." He hugged my body to his and leaned us both back again. "I'm totally devoted to you. I always will be. I knew that before this, and I'm more sure now. Don't ever leave. Spend your life here with us. Give up the idea of going back. Just be here, with us."

I touched the side of his face. "If that's what you all want." My heart raced, imagining it.

"It is. It's what we all want. I can speak for them on this. Trust me." His smile was slow. "Stay forever."

I brushed a strand of his blond hair out of his eyes. "I will."

"Good."

Even as I spoke the words, I could hear the laughter of the universe reverberating in my head. Did I really think I had a say over what happened to me? I never had before. Could it actually be possible that could change?

THE NEXT MORNING, Crew finally flew us back home. If the others overheard the time between Gunnar and me, there was no indication of it, just their usual banter back and forth. The weather was nice, despite the lightning show, so after storing the shuttle, we walked together back to their bar.

"Do you think there are others on the planet that you don't know about?" I asked Mace as we stepped inside. "Like, other Lightning Men hiding out in a cave someplace or something? Waiting?"

He shrugged. "Honestly, I'm not sure. There was a time I would have tried to find out, but at this point, if they're here and not bothering our people, then I'm going to leave them alone. If they become an issue, they'll be handled."

It made sense. Without Clarke's death squad killing anyone on the planet who fell out of line, it wasn't like they could police the entirety of their world. Clarke could—which was why my father and so many others died when he first showed up.

I shook away the cobwebs of the past and smiled brilliantly at him. "Is there anything I can do to help today?"

He pointed at the kitchen. "Let's get started on the pies, after we clean up."

I loved that idea. "Are you guys open every night or are there some nights that you're closed?"

He blinked. "We've been off because we were obviously in the woods and what not, but usually we're open every day. It might be a good idea to start closing a bit, like every Monday. Then we could all spend time together, just us. We could go into the woods or the mountains or take that shuttle and go somewhere else—we could even visit the coast. Just to be together. A day off every week for family time, what do you think?"

What a beautiful idea. *A day off.* Of course, since I was staying, I should find work to occupy myself, so I could earn my day off with the rest of them.

"What are you thinking?" He tugged on the end of my hair, so I met his gaze.

"Lots of things. I'll go get that shower."

I never had to consider my life before, since its course seemed predestined. If I got to make choices, I wanted to make good ones.

13

THE WEAPONS ARE BEHIND
THE BAR

The Frog and The Bull got really busy that night. The door seemed to practically remain open all night as people came and no one wanted to leave. The regular humans mixed with the enhanced, which would have made my head spin at home, where only Amias would deign speak to us normal humans. There were more of each crowd than I would've imagined, though no children arrived, just adults, and the regular folks were getting really drunk. The former Super Soldiers drank too, but it didn't seem to make them drunk, which fell in line with what I knew about them. They couldn't get drunk.

I never drank alcohol back home. I wasn't opposed or anything, but it was against the rules, and I mostly followed rules. But Ransom poured all night, and I kept cleaning glasses. In the kitchen, Mace would cook up food to order while Gunnar served their many customers. I wasn't sure what Crew did exactly, except it seemed a bit like crowd control. Everyone talked to him, and he wandered around eyeing all of them.

Ransom nodded to me. "It'll clear out soon. Anytime now. I think this crowd was mostly to see you."

I waved my hand. "I'm not that interesting. They could see me on the street."

"Raven," a young woman approached me. I hadn't noticed her before, but a man I guessed was her husband stood behind her. "I hoped I could say hi and welcome. My name is Chanel. This is my brother, Jova." She smiled. *Okay, I read that wrong.* "We were hoping we could invite you to dinner sometime. There aren't a lot of new people in this area, and we'd love to get to know you."

Her smile was bright, but I gaped for a few seconds, completely at a loss. "Sure, I'd love that," I sputtered.

"Great." She smiled at me again. "It's nice to meet you. I'll come by when you're less busy, and we can make plans. Have a good night."

Well...that happened. I turned to Ransom but he wasn't smiling. "What's wrong?"

"I don't like how Jova looked at you."

I blinked. "For real? He didn't look at me any particular way, and I notice those things. It was my job for a long time to notice them, if you remember correctly. I promise, they were just being friendly."

He leaned on the bar. "Butterfly, I can hear things you can't. I promise you, he likes you."

Well, that's neither here nor there. I shrugged. "A lot of men have liked me. I really only like you guys."

It must have been the right answer, because he leaned over and kissed me roughly, his lips both possessive and claiming. "Good," he said once I was breathless.

I picked up another glass, preparing to dry it to keep my hands busy as heat flooded my cheeks. "Butterfly?"

"It fits for you, so I've decided to use it as a nickname. I hope you like it, since it's what I'm going to call you." He lifted an eyebrow. "Unless you don't like it."

The intimacy of having a secret shared name that only he could use for me somehow pleased me. "Amias used to call me sister, as if I was his sister just because I was Stone's sister. My brother called me Little Sis. Those are the only nicknames I've ever been given before. Butterfly sounds nice. Do I have wings I don't know about?"

I mock looked at my back and he winked at me. "You do. You just can't see them. I can. It's part of my Super Soldier powers."

"I see. I'll add that to what I know about you guys. *Can see invisible wings.*" I patted his arm, his muscles stretching his shirt out under my touch making me smile.

"Do that."

Mace joined us and set down glasses fresh from the dishwasher. The tech they owned sometimes startled me, since wilderness surrounded us, but I reminded myself they brought in what they wanted when they took over the planet. Amias had called their world uncivilized, but I thought it just the opposite. The longer I stayed, the more clearly I could see it. At home, the ones in power maintained access to all the tech in the known universe. Sure, only certain people of their selection got to use that tech, but they had access to it nonetheless. Conversely, on their planet, they did without most things, yet they lived like they were the people with everything because they shared their resources. They were grateful, happy, and kind.

Will I someday think of this place as home?

"Thank you." I took the glasses from Mace then scanned over his body with my gaze. "I like you in that color."

He looked down like he wasn't sure what he wore. The soft blue shirt flattered his coloring, bringing out warmth in his skin tone and his darkly fringed eyes. His smile was huge. "Thank you, Raven. Your words mean a lot to me. I...I like that you think I look good in this color." His cheeks reddened just a bit. It was so sweet; I had to lean over and kiss him—right there on the spot that turned red.

He stared at me for a long second before he kissed me back. "Please keep doing that forever."

My heart turned over, bottoming out in my stomach somewhere. It was so easy to make them happy, and I wanted to do it over and over.

"What does it feel like?" One of the Super Soldiers—I had to get used to calling them that instead of enhanced, since they preferred it—that I didn't know spoke to us. Despite the ambient noise of all the people in the room, I felt absolutely sure he spoke directly to me as he stared us down. "To have that kind of thing? Kissing? Affection?"

Mace and Ransom made eye contact, and finally Mace spoke. 'Like we're human. Like we're real."

"You okay, Scotch?" Ranson lifted an eyebrow "Dark night? Where are your people?"

"Going home to them." He said with a nod as he rose from his chair. "If I found the kind of jewel you have, I'd go off the machine, too. We all would." He smiled, but there was no mirth in it. "But I doubt that's going to happen for the rest of us."

With that statement, he disappeared into the night. Mace grimaced, and it was like some of the warmth of the night leaked out with the other man's departure. "Shit. I'll go make sure he gets home okay. I know he can go to bad places in his head, with what happened."

"What happened?" Maybe it wasn't my business, but he brought it up. Mace turned and ran out the door after Scotch instead of answering. The movement seemed to spur others to follow. With mostly laughter, and some of the regular people singing, customers started to exit the bar.

Ransom sighed, waving at departing guests. "It's a sad story. Goes back to our Earth battles, but it's not really our story to tell."

I shook my head, touching his arm again. "Don't worry about it. I shouldn't have asked. You're okay?"

His eyes shone for a second. "I'm better than okay, butterfly. I'm alive, maybe for the first time in my life, and that's because of you."

I snorted. "I'm just a girl from nowhere. Anything that happened to you is because you're wonderful."

Crew leaned on the bar, stopping our conversation. "Are you two okay to close up for the night? Gunnar wants to make sure everyone gets home safely, and quite a few drank more than normal. Also, I'd like to find out why Scotch was alone tonight. I'm going to go see Tango and the others. Maybe he took off and they don't know where to find him. I'll be gone until maybe two in the morning, but I'll hustle. I have no desire, none, to be running around when I could be home, tucked in next to Raven."

Had anyone ever been so lucky as me? Gunnar bumped into him gently. "I'm guessing Ransom gets one side of her tonight. If I beat you back, I'm taking the other side. In case you're curious, I'm *going* to beat you back." He sighed, dramatically. "But Mace might beat both of us."

"We're going to make a schedule." Crew winked at me. "Assuming Raven wouldn't prefer to sleep alone. We don't know, she could prefer to have a bedroom to herself."

They got so still, I scanned their faces quickly, looking for clues. It was like they'd all braced for a blow, and I crumpled my brow at the thought of my words having that much power over them. "No, I liked the company. Please keep joining me. I feel...steadier when you're with me. I feel more alive, too. Like I'm not about to blow away into the universe where no one will ever remember I existed."

I spoke the words before I let myself even really think them. They hit me as I said them, and I instantly regretted my honesty. *I have to find a way not to be too much. I have to...*

Ransom's arms came around me and he drew me against his chest. His heart beat strong and steady in my ear, and I relaxed into him with a sigh. "We will never let you blow away anywhere. And we will always know who you are. Want to know why that is?"

I swallowed, blinking fast. "Why is that?"

"Because you're ours."

Crew stroked a hand down the side of my face, drawing my gaze to his handsome face. "That's right. You're ours. So whatever you're worrying about—and I can see that you're worrying by your expression, and I can hear it in the speed of your heartbeat—don't. You're with us. I wonder sometimes, too, if anything about me matters. But then you came and suddenly I can see the point of my existing at all."

Maybe I wasn't the only one who could say big things. His statement didn't make me want to run away. If anything, it just made me feel seen. I smiled at him in gratitude.

"Okay." I pulled back from Ransom. "Yes, please make a schedule. I want to sleep with everyone as much as I can."

"I will." He laughed then kissed my lips again.

Mace leaned over and brushed his lips against mine, causing another little rush of heat. "I'll be back. Got to get these drunk people home safely. Can't let them hurt themselves."

I smiled at all of them. "So you run the bar, take care of the patrons, and make sure people you know are okay. You're all amazing."

I watched as they left, feeling full, but not with food... with happiness. Ransom handed me a glass and I started drying them again. We had a routine, and although he could probably work faster without my help, he didn't indicate impatience. Instead, he synced with me, and we found a rhythm.

After a time, he raised his head and winced. I considered him with a furrowed brow. "Something the matter?"

The door swung open seconds before a man entered— obviously a Super Soldier, and from Ransom's reaction to his arrival, he wasn't happy to see him.

"Evans?" He sighed. "What is it tonight?" He drummed his fingers on the bar. "What's tonight's complaint?"

He pointed at Ransom. The sober, enhanced man — whoops, Super Soldier—looked angry. "I want my gold."

"You were paid." Ransom sounded bored, as though he'd heard it before. "Actually, you were paid more than you were owed, because Crew felt bad for you. He's kinder than me, because I would've told you to shove the gold down your throat until you choked on it. Mace almost died on that operation, because your fucking intel was bad. Despite that, you got paid. So, if that is all you want to discuss—and I'm sick of this shit—get the fuck out of here."

He jerked his head toward the door once, as if implying Evans should find his way that direction. Rather than leaving, Evans took a seat at the table nearest to us. "How about a drink first? Considering all the gold you owe me—that you know you owe me, even if you're being an ass about it—I'll take a drink." He stared at me then, as though he only just really noticed me. "Actually, make it a drink and a roll around with your whore, and I'll call it even. She can pay me in pussy."

Everything moved so fast, I could hardly track it with my

eyes. I touched my skin, where the marks indicated my status on Clarke's planet, and—that fast, Ransom was on Evans. He ripped Evans from his chair. "You don't talk to my girl like that. Not about her. Not to her. You'll never speak to our girl, or about her, again." Ransom pounded on his face, one sharp punch and then another.

Evans laughed. They were both Super Soldiers, so punching him wasn't going to be enough. Ransom knew it, so he lifted him up and then they ripped at each other with claw and tooth. I gasped. Were they going to tear each other to actual pieces?

Pieces of clothing went flying. They went for each other's chests. I wasn't wrong—they intended to rip each other apart limb from limb.

I rushed around the side of the bar, not sure what to do to stop them "Ransom, stop!" I didn't dare get too close, as one stray punch from them that hit me could literally cave in my chest. "Stop. It's not worth it. It's nothing. I'm fine. I swear I am."

He didn't or couldn't hear me. Or maybe he just disagreed? Regardless, the fight continued. Chairs flew everywhere, so I ducked out of the way of flying debris. That was when I saw it. Evans reached into his pocket and pulled something else out. It looked small, like a patch of something. I recognized it instantly, as I saw them used back home by Clarke and his goons to punish the enhanced.

"No!" I knew what he intended to do, and knew I needed to stop him. Knowing and being able to act fast enough turned out to be two different challenges, as I no sooner said no than he slammed the patch down on Ransom's face. For just a second, I saw realization strike my guy before he fell to the floor, silent in his agony.

Oh, this isn't good. I couldn't help Ransom until I took

down Evans, but I was just one person, and I wasn't special. Suddenly, I remembered the townspeople gifted me with weapons, and Ransom put them behind the bar. I grabbed for one, pleased when my hand closed on something solid in the box. I recognized it, since Amias had one and he'd shown me how to work it, despite the rules.

Easy, I remembered him saying. *Just point and click.* I lifted it and fired it straight into Evans' back, just like Amias showed me. Evans froze mid-movement before his body seized and he fell to the floor, still twitching. I dropped my weapon, my hands shaking and my knees going weak . Had I killed him? I really had no idea, but I couldn't look, not then. I rushed to Ransom, ripping the pain patch off his beautiful face.

Shit. My hand spasmed and I dropped it. Yep, I shouldn't have touched it with my fingers. Oh that was stupid. But it would pass.

At least it was off Ransom.

He groaned and reached for me. "Butterfly."

"I'm okay." I wasn't but I would be, I knew, and I gritted my teeth as fear tangled with the gel off the patch in my system.

The door flung open and Crew rushed into the room. He grabbed both Ransom and myself in his arms, burying his face in my neck. "Are you okay? Are you both okay?"

"They're not." Mace touched us both. *When did he show up?* "But they will be. The effects of the patch pass , as long as we get it off them."

"It passes us." Gunnar was there, too? "But she touched it, and she's fragile."

Already, the pain fled my body, my head clearing. "I'm okay. It's going away. I swear it is."

"Okay." Crew set me down before he placed Ransom in a

chair. The latter held his head in his hands. How badly was he hurt? It had been on him so much longer. "Where did he get that fucking patch? Why are all of these old weapons showing up? He shouldn't have had that."

Past tense. "Is he dead?"

Ransom lifted his head and extended his hand, pulling me to him. "Don't you ever do that again. Don't you ever risk yourself for me again. You run. Do you understand me? If there's danger, you run."

"Nothing had to happen." My voice shook. "You were going to kill each other. It didn't have to happen. He only called me a name. I don't even care about it, and he's not even wrong. You called me that yourself, since it was literally my job title, just...how long ago was it? A week? And..."

Ransom dropped to the floor. In a flash, his head pressed against my stomach as my arms came around him, instinctively holding him to me. "I'm sorry, butterfly. I'm so sorry. I should never have said that. It was mean, and I was grief stricken, but it's absolutely not okay. Forgive me. I should never have used that word, especially not with you. That is not what you are."

I kissed the top of his head. "It's okay, Ransom. It really is, but that's my point. It's only a word. It doesn't matter. And, look at me. Maybe you don't see it anymore, but the tattoos on my head have always—and will always—tell people I'm a whore. For some people, I'll never be more than that tattoo. I'm sorry, but if you want to be part of my life for the long run, you're going to have to get used to hearing that sometimes without reacting to *facts*. I can't have anything happening to you because of me." My voice broke, and I scrubbed at my wet cheeks. I was crying and I didn't even realize it. I blinked up at them, searching their faces. "Is he dead? I killed him?"

"You did." Gunnar kissed my cheek, letting my tears fall against his mouth. "And you were perfect as far as I can tell. You aimed and you shot. You didn't miss. You did just as you should have."

I closed my eyes. "Who will come to arrest me?"

"What?" Mace waited until I opened my eyes to regard him before he spoke again. "What do you mean, sweetie?"

"I killed a man. There are laws, I'm sure. Someone will arrest me, and someone else will decide what happens to me."

Ransom rose from the floor, pressing our foreheads together. "Butterfly, half the town heard what happened. They were all rushing here but stopped when the guys arrived. I could hear them distantly. It all happened very fast."

"Felt slow." Not that it mattered.

Crew continued speaking when Ransom stopped. "Everyone heard what happened. No one would dare arrest you, not that we have an agency set up to manage that sort of thing. We tend to...handle each other, and no one would want to do anything but give you a hug."

I blinked. Considering his words, I turned to Ransom. "I shot some mean words at you that night, too, Ransom. I told you I had no blood on my hands and accused you of basically being a killer. Tables sure have turned now, right? I've killed someone. I'm the one with blood on my hands." I looked at my hands, as if to show him, and noticed they shook.

I was in Ransom's arms then. He carried me like I weighed nothing, and he pressed my head down on his shoulder. "There's no blood on your hands. Evans was mean as hell, a bully. He did shit work, and he demanded payment for things he didn't earn. We've been dealing with endless problems with him. We tried to get along, but you saw! He came carrying that patch, which meant he intended to kill one of us. It was him or me. If you hadn't stopped him, I'd be a lot more hurt, and who knows if he would've gotten you before the guys got here? No, that was self-defense. You did everything just right." He swung around. "I'm going to take her upstairs and help her get ready for bed. This has been too long of a day."

I should have argued, but I was tired. Shaky. And also wide awake, practically vibrating with adrenaline. How could all of those things be true at the same time? But they were. Ransom carried me upstairs, hardly jarring me the whole way.

"Sit here." He set me on the edge of the bed and vanished into the bathroom. The sound of water greeted my ears, and I realized he must be warming up the shower for me. I stood up to follow him, but my legs shook. He came back out, regarding me for a second, but I couldn't make out what he thought. "Sit," he repeated. He gently pushed my shoulder back down. "Don't get up right now, okay?"

I obviously couldn't anyway, since my legs shook like leaves in the wind. "Why do I feel like this?"

"Little bit of shock, I think. Totally normal. You've never been through anything like this, nor should you have." He lifted one shoulder in a shrug, as if it made enough sense to him.

But he wasn't exactly right. "I've seen lots of violence. So much I can't even speak about it." Blood, running down faces or hands...I saw pain.

"You've never had to do what you had to do to save me," he replied gently, and I wondered if he was right about the shock. He might be, since I heard the word he didn't say —*killed*. I killed *someone*—and jerked in reaction anyway. He took off my shoes, setting them aside, before he continued to meticulously undress me, one garment at a time. "Another time, I want you to tell me about the violence you've seen. I'll do my best to eliminate the people who made you see things you didn't want to see."

I believed him. I'd never doubt that Ransom could be lethal. "You can't be okay," I said, remembering the patch. I reached out to stroke his brow, and his lips lifted in a half smile.

He undid my buttons and placed my shirt aside. "I've been worse. I'll be fine. I'm more worried about you."

My head was loopy. I might fall asleep sitting up. I also felt like I could run a marathon—very confusing altogether. I smiled at Ransom, remembering something I hadn't shared yet. "Amias called you his little brother," I said, twining my fingers in his hair.

He smirked. I was totally naked, and the blanket felt surprisingly cool against my thighs. *When did he take off my underwear?*

Ransom replied, "He was, what? Three years older than me? They all acted like I was a baby for the longest time. Had to prove myself over and over." He shook his head, but his expression seemed more amused than annoyed.

"Did you?"

He sighed. "Better than I did today, that's for damn sure. I placed you in danger with my reaction. I just saw red. I can't and won't listen to you be insulted. You have become my reason."

Ransom carried me to the shower. When he would've stepped in fully clothed, I stopped him. "Goes better if you're not wearing clothes."

"True, but I didn't want to assume..."

He was funny. "Let's bathe each other," I said with a chuckle.

Ransom took me at my word. After he undressed, we got busy with the soap, rinsing the few moments that had been life changing for me down the drain in a coordinated effort. We were going to smell exactly alike to my non-enhanced nose, and I didn't mind whatsoever.

Internally, I winced. "Can't stop thinking enhanced when I think of you guys. I know you don't like it."

"Call me whatever you want. I just like being in your head at all." The water was warm. I could snuggle right there. "No." He turned off the water. "Don't fall asleep until I get you in the bed—nice, dry, and safe."

I wasn't sure I was going to be able to obey.

I closed my eyes, snuggling my nose into the curve of his neck.

"You HAVE to control your temper. We're all feeling the anger. It comes from the lack of the machine. They were controlling more than our sexual urges." Crew spoke low, but his words carried clearly to my ears. "If I'd known, I would've stopped using it years ago. But all the things you're feeling—the desire to protect her, to take care of her for the rest of your days—it also means you're suddenly more lethal than you've ever been before. You should have killed Evans. After she went to bed, like a civilized assassin."

I smiled against Ransom's shoulder. "The rules of death dealing," I murmured against his skin.

"You woke her." Ransom kissed my forehead while the bed dipped as Crew climbed in it. I guessed he decided he was taking tonight? "Sleep, Butterfly. You're okay. The shock will be gone by the morning."

Crew pressed against my other side, his warmth familiar and comforting. "He's right. I'm sorry I woke you. Just correcting my little brother here."

Ransom groaned. "Just in case you wondered if he was listening earlier."

"All of you are always listening," I said on a yawn. "I learned that growing up. Somehow Amias knew if others could hear him."

Crew sighed. "We all have our talents. He was good at that. Ransom here could get in and out of places totally undetected."

"Crew can lead hordes of men through hell."

I closed my eyes, amused. "I have no great talents."

"That's not true. You're amazing in a million ways." Ransom sighed. "Time to sleep, Butterfly. Tomorrow will come way too soon, and I want you to be rested."

I closed my eyes, smiling as their hearts beat in my ears. Maybe I could sleep a little bit more...

14

RANSOM UNDONE

"Time to wake up. I miss you." Ransom's voice drew me from darkness, and I blinked open my eyes. My body creaked, stiff and clunky. I smiled at him, despite my slow ability to move. His rumpled hair and pinkened cheeks showed he'd been in the bed with me the whole time. If I felt like I'd slept for too long, he must be really out of sorts. Super Soldiers needed almost no sleep.

I stretched, rolling my neck before I sat up. "Sorry. I passed out and then I guess I stayed that way? I can get right up and..."

Ransom put his hand on my knee and squeezed it. "You passed out because you had to kill someone to save me. You're entitled to rest, but I'm being selfish. I missed you." He kissed both my cheeks, coming down on top of me. "If any of the rest of them were home, they'd come in here and tell me off, since I was given specific instructions to leave you alone. If only I was any good at following directions." He shook his head as if in apology, yet his expression seemed more playful than repentant.

I loved seeing him like that, so relaxed and unburdened.

He was happy to be a little bit edgy most of the time, and I appreciated that about him. And sexy? The carved look of his face stretched down to his broad, strong shoulders. A thrum of anticipation electrified my senses, making me aware of where our bodies touched. I cupped the side of his face. "I'm glad you woke me. I don't know if anyone has ever missed me before." I bit my lower lip. "Thank you for saying that."

"Butterfly..." He kissed my forehead again before he moved his attention to my mouth. "Let me show you how much I missed you."

I kissed him back, our tongues tangling until he left me breathless. "I'd love that, actually. Go ahead and show me, Ransom. How much did you miss me?"

I never would've dared to speak to Clarke's clients that way. No, I kept my tone low and easy with them. Push at them with defiance? That wasn't me. Except apparently it was...with Ransom. He called me butterfly. Did that mean that he thought I was going through that kind of change and would transform into some more majestic form?

I shook my head, pulling out of his kiss to admit, "You make me talk like I'm not myself. I'm changing with you."

He smiled down at me before he kissed my neck, his lips traveling until he could nibble my earlobe. "You've changed me so much, I'm practically unrecognizable. The guy that you met your first day here? That's who I was."

I kissed his chin. "Maybe we don't need to worry about who we were. Maybe we just focus on who we'd like to become?"

Ransom must have liked that idea, because his light, drugging kisses changed. Suddenly at the center of his laser sharp focus, I found every bit of his enhanced abilities focused on my mouth, and I arched into him with a moan.

Despite the fire of his attention, I didn't have to struggle to keep up with him. As though he learned the rhythms I liked, or understood how fast I wanted to move, and when I needed to take a breath. Ransom fit himself to me, perfectly.

"Before this gets too urgent, I just want to be clear," he said, his voice husky as he whispered to me. "I want to be with you. I think some people call it making love or other words. I wish I had done more of a study about how people talk about passion, but I never thought it would be part of my life. So...is that what you want as well?"

I took both his cheeks in my hands before rubbing my nose along his. "Very much. I want to have sex with you. Absolutely."

"Good." He nodded. "I didn't want to assume that you..."

I kissed him, the hunger in my caress effectively cutting off whatever he was going to say. I tugged at his shirt. "Let me take care of you for a while?"

He furrowed his brow. "What do you mean?"

I smiled at him. Oh, the things I could teach him... "Roll over."

He nodded. "Okay." When he swallowed, my lips curled into a smile.

As if he saw my expression and somehow felt at a disadvantage, he flipped me over easily to straddle him. I didn't doubt for a moment his dominance.

His eyes widened as he looked up my body, so I stroked my hand down over my breasts, molding their shape while he watched. I leaned over him. "You've seen me naked several times now." I stroked a finger down his cheek, feeling his beard and the highness of his cheekbones beneath the pads of my fingertips.

"Different now. It just is." A muscle in his jaw ticked, a metronome of his tension.

I nodded. "I know."

I tugged at his shirt again, and he took it off for me, throwing it across the room with abandon.

His muscles were well- defined and beautiful in the morning light streaming through the window. I ran my fingers over them, loving the way they jumped as I stroked him. With a scoot I was closer to him, nuzzling on his neck to breathe him in.

It seemed like a good place to start kissing him, so I did. And then lower, all over his chest, anywhere I could reach, stopping to tongue his nipples before I lightly bit his left one.

"Fuck." He bucked beneath me on a groan. "Fuck, *Raven*."

The nickname vanished, which was fine by me. I loved when he called me Butterfly, but him losing control was fine by me as well. *We've hardly gotten started.*

He gripped the back of my hair, running his fingers through it. "Watch how much of that you do. I want to come inside of you."

I heard him, but I only paused long enough to make eye contact with him and wink. He lifted his head and groaned, a fake sound since he accompanied it with a laugh. "You might be trying to kill me. You're so fucking sexy. That red hair. Those eyes. How did I ever do without you?"

I continued my quest to kiss my way down his body. I slid his briefs down his long, strong thighs, reveling in the texture of the chestnut brown hair growing there.

His cock was as erect as I could imagine it getting, and a quick glance proved he gripped the sheets on the bed as if they kept him grounded. I quickly moved, hoping he wouldn't guess my intention.

I took the tip of his cock in my mouth, humming as I did.

His whole body jerked, and he spoke my name on a shout. I smiled around my mouthful and focused on my work. Although I never liked it before, I loved knowing I could make him feel good. I bent further, taking him as far down my throat as I could manage. Where I couldn't fit him, I stroked the remainder with my hand. Over and over again, until I found a motion that had him panting on the bed.

I never heard so many curses in my life as Ransom spewed but he never once asked me to stop. The way that he throbbed in my mouth told me it wouldn't be long until he was right where I wanted him to be.

Minutes passed. He tasted salty and like a man. I relished the taste, wanting more, wishing I could always feel this gloriously feminine, every day. *This wanted. This...*

He came all at once, his moan filling the room as Ransom let himself go. I sucked him down, every drop, until he went soft in my hands.

Finally, when I would have pulled away, Ransom snagged me under the armpits and dragged me upward, swapping our positions until I lay beneath him in moments.

He kissed me, a hard and claiming slash of his mouth against mine, and I let myself get lost in it. "That was... beyond my imagination," he admitted.

I grinned at him. "Then I'm very glad that I did it."

His slow smile held heat that made my toes curl. He practically growled, "But we're not done. We're not even close to done."

We weren't? "Ransom, you're probably going to need some recovery time."

"Am I?" He lifted an eyebrow. "Or did you forget that I'm...enhanced?"

I laughed, throwing my head back. "Oh, the ego. I think even you..."

But I was wrong. In seconds, he sheathed himself inside of me. I cried out, both from surprise and the pleasure that surged through me. Yes, having him go wild beneath me turned me on, and he was exactly what I needed, even if I thought it would be a while until I could have it.

I dug my fingers into his back, arching into the sensations. "Remind me to never question your prowess. Ever."

"That's right." He slowed down his movements, nuzzling at my jawline. "I'm not hurting you, right?"

Lines appeared next to his eyes when he met my gaze. *He's really worried.* "You can't hurt me, Ransom. Take me. Make me yours, any way you want."

He did just as I asked. Soon, I found myself pressed against the headboard of the bed, his hand behind my head to protect me from hitting the wood as he pressed himself into me. Over and over, he moved in and out of me. We cried out together, animalistic moans and grunts as we climbed ever higher. Maybe I moaned, maybe he did. It didn't matter. I lost all sense of time. I just needed him to keep doing what he was doing. Then, suddenly, with one final jerk, I came apart in his arms. Thank goodness he had his hand where he did because I lost the ability to hold up my head, and all my muscles gave out as he spilled inside of me.

Ransom held onto me, eventually pulling me against his shoulder. I breathed heavily and so did he.

"Butterfly..." He finally managed to speak, and I lifted my head, somehow, to regard him. "There are those eyes."

I shook my heavy head, smiling despite my body being utterly languid. "You are the one with the eyes, Ransom. Those blue ones. They're almost unreal, they're so beautiful."

"Everything about you is unreal." He kissed the end of my nose. "Every little thing."

I kissed him and we both closed our eyes. It wasn't time to sleep but I just needed to breathe, right there, with Ransom holding me like I was the most precious thing in the world.

~

"I NEED TO SEE RAINE." I turned to Ransom as I walked out of the bathroom. "Can you tell me where I can find her? She was going to someone's home who has a baby."

My hair was wet, and I quickly braided it. Despite disliking the hairstyle due to it being one of Clarke's rules for us, it was still one of the easiest ways to ensure it wouldn't get in my way, and I'd be damned if I let him dictate my hairstyles, including what I wouldn't wear.

It was easy to braid it, so screw you, Clarke.

"She started off at one of the human s' houses, one with five children. The Millers, if I remember correctly, but when they all got croup, we thought it best to move her and the infant. She's staying with Gator and his group, at the moment—Gator, Seven, Darkness, and Shade. She's living with them, and everyone seems happy enough. We can go see her."

I stared at him. "Raine was okay with staying with a bunch of men? After what happened with Net..."

He nodded. "She seems to be. Gator offered to put her anywhere she wanted, and she asked to stay with them. For whatever reason, she likes them. I can't blame her. They were and are very nice people." He walked over and whispered in my ear. "I think they've gotten protective of her and the baby very quickly."

Well…that was a good thing. As long as Raine was happy.

"Oh. " He stepped back. " Hold on. The townspeople dropped off clothes for you. You don't have to keep wearing the same two outfits. Be right back."

He returned faster than I expected. I hardly stepped into the room when he reappeared holding bags. "The women think this stuff will fit."

"Thank you. I've never had so many pieces of clothing. The two outfits I brought and the one I wear with clients are about it for me." I winced. I really didn't want to talk about my former employment in the same hour that I'd been with Ransom, with his body deep within mine.

He drew me to him. "Are you struggling with talking about it in general or is it because you're talking about it with me…who gave you such a hard time about it?"

It took me a moment to realize what he meant. "Don't worry about it. We've worked through that. I think. Right? Don't hold onto worrying about any awkwardness over things you said before you knew me. You didn't say anything that wasn't…"

He held up his hand. "Butterfly, please. Don't tell me what I said was true, because I can assure you it wasn't. Okay? What do you have to wear when you have to take abuse from Clarke and his associates?"

I lifted one shoulder, picturing the tiny nothing clothes, since it was little more than that. "It's hardly an outfit at all. I'd rather not think about it. I wish I could pretend none of it ever happened, but obviously, I can't. And…" I struggled to find the right words. "I'm so worried about what happened to the people who helped me. I'm being selfish, you get that, right? I'm going to stay here in your safe arms and not care about whatever repercussions they face on my behalf. What kind of human does that make *me*?"

His eyes flared with emotion. "If they can get women out and they're not regularly doing it? If they're not emptying Clarke's bunks, where he kept all of you, then I don't think they're much better than Clarke to begin with. If I could, I'd grab Amias—obviously I can't—and beg him to explain why I shouldn't hate him for the role he played in helping the man."

I wrapped my arms around his neck and held onto him. "Don't be angry at him. Never at him. Okay? If not for him, then we wouldn't have met, right?"

He put his forehead on my shoulder. "One thing you said was true. You're going to stay here in my safe arms. I'm never letting you go."

I loved the thought of that.

We walked together to Gator's cabin, but I spotted no vehicles over the twenty minute or so walk. Maybe they didn't have them, just shuttles or walking to take them places.

Ransom grinned at me, bumping my shoulder with his own. "I can feel you all over me. I'll never be better than I am right now."

My cheeks heated up, so I pulled his face down and kissed him as we walked. "The things you say. All the way out here, can they hear us above the bar?"

"Maybe." He shrugged. "In general, we don't share all that info or compare who hears better or sees better or whatever than who. In some ways, we'll always be in competition to see who is strongest. But not within our group. That we know." He smirked. "Obviously, I'm the strongest."

I laughed, but a second later, he groaned. "I have just

been challenged by all three of my brothers to see if I can live up to my claim."

"Can you?"

He didn't get to answer, as we arrived at Gator's cabin, if I could call it that. They'd built themselves quite a house, unlike anything I'd ever seen before. Sure, it looked a little bit like a cabin, but it was really the biggest house that I'd ever seen. I stopped and stared at it.

Ransom laughed. "It's impressive. Darkness had a real knack for carpentry. I'll build you one, if you want. Anything to make you happy."

"I'm not staring because I want it. I love our...sorry, *your* house over the bar." I really did.

He whispered in my ear again. "I liked the *our*. It's ours. If you ever change your mind, we'll build you a house, though."

A man I didn't know stepped onto the porch to consider us with crossed arms. His white-blond hair flashed in the lightning from above as he leaned against one of the pillars. "You couldn't build this house. Don't flatter yourself, Ransom."

My guy groaned. "Raven, meet Darkness."

He went by Darkness with white-blond hair? I jarred at the dissonance but quickly recovered my manners and smiled. "Hi, I'm here to see Raine, if she's available."

He motioned toward the door with his chin. "She's happy to see you. We're glad you're here. She's only been here a few days, but we want her to stay. We all feel...well, that we're supposed to take care of her and the baby. It is the right thing to do, and maybe it's our way to make things better in the universe."

Darkness sounded like Gator. He'd been all about

redemption, too. I looked at Ransom, but I couldn't tell from his expression what he thought about it.

"This way," Darkness indicated, and Ransom nodded.

Just then, the sky opened up. In seconds, water soaked through every article of clothes and my hair dripped into my eyes. I laughed at the sheer ridiculousness of the situation. I couldn't seem to stop getting wet on their planet.

Ransom scooped me up and we rushed to the door. Darkness grabbed two towels and handed them to us as we entered. "The weather this year. I thought it was Net, but no, it's just nasty. The others are with Crew trying to figure out where all this tech is coming from, but I'm not leaving Raine or Kitty."

"Is that the baby's name? Kitty? I never remembered to ask Raine what she decided to name her."

The blond Super Soldier nodded. "You were too busy delivering the baby, nearly dying, and still making sure she was okay, so you did your part. She named the baby two days ago, anyway. Kitty. Katherine, I guess, but Kitty is what she's calling her. Come on."

They obviously cared about her, because they'd put her in a huge room with an enormous bed. A lovely hand-carved wooden crib stood in the corner, the baby's soft blankets visible from the entranceway. They couldn't have just made the room for Kitty and Raine, could they? Was every room in their home so intricately designed? It was nicer than Clarke's room, which I had seen once from down a hallway.

Raine rocked her baby and grinned when we entered. "Raven!"

"Hi." I smiled at her. "This is Ransom. Darkness said we could come see you and the baby for a little while."

"I'm so glad that you came. This is Kitty. I was hoping to

introduce you. If you didn't find me soon, I was going to figure out how to come find you." She rose. "I wasn't staying here at first. This lovely family took us in, but—long story— I needed to leave. Since then, they've been so nice to me. Darkness and the others. They didn't have to do this."

I looked between them. He was silent, but he gazed at her as if she'd just created the world. *Oh yeah, I bet they're being nice.*

And as long as she was happy, it was great. Still, I needed to verify, or it would bug me. "We could bring you home when this lightning is over. We could take you back to where you were before you were held captive."

She cleared her throat. "My family disowned me five years ago. I don't have anyone to go home to anymore, so I need to figure out how to be independent. I'm grateful to have a few days before I have to figure things out for me and Kitty."

"You can stay as long as you like." Darkness said with a nod then exited the room. Ransom shook his head but didn't comment.

Okay. Well, that is the last I'll say about that.

"I'll leave you two to talk. I'll be outside with Darkness."

Yep, like they can't hear everything in here anyway.

15

THE CABIN PROBLEM

Raine nodded, her pretty face flushed. "I know. Trust me, I know, but these guys try to be polite, which I appreciate." She held up Kitty. "Do you want to hold her?"

I smiled at her. "I have very little experience with babies. I haven't been around many after they're born, unless they're sick."

She nodded. "That's okay. You delivered her. I trust you."

She was right, but it wasn't like I had any alternatives at the time. Still, the birth had beautiful moments we shared, and then we saved them both from Net. I took the baby and held her to my chest. "She's so beautiful."

New life never ceased to amaze me, but Kitty was particularly beautiful. She looked just like her mother, with her lovely eyes and rosebud lips. I could maybe see Net's chin, but I couldn't see much of her father in her. I stroked my finger down her cheek, finding it petal soft to my touch. "I've helped with the deliveries at home sometimes. I'm glad I could help you. I wasn't exactly prepared to do anything, if it had been very difficult. I'm not a doctor. I can't even read. You did all the work, and you were amazing."

She sank on the bed and sighed. "I'm trying to see it as a joyful day. I'm trying. I love the baby, and I'm so relieved that he's dead and can't be near her, not ever."

Raine had been through so much. "I think you're amazing. I want you to know that."

"I'd like for us to be friends." She dropped her head slightly, and I could see that she had dark circles under her eyes. No way had she gotten any sleep with Net, and with a newborn to take care of, she likely still wasn't getting much. "I don't have friends. Not usually."

That was quite a confession. I knew what she meant, but people didn't usually say it aloud. "I didn't really have people, either. My brother did. He was a social butterfly. Everyone loved him. I was his sister, so I was tolerated, but they weren't my friends. They were his, and his husband was my friend, but first and foremost he was my brother-in-law. They're all dead now, though." It still hurt to say it. It seemed impossible to live in a world where I'd never hear them laugh again.

The baby made a noise, and I rocked a little bit, cooing at her. Raine explained, "I didn't have that. I was born into a rich family, but when they died very suddenly in an accident, I didn't have anyone to take me. I ended up becoming a ward of our town." She sighed. "I was pretty alone. People treated me like my condition—not having family—was infectious and they might catch it. Now Kitty has that same situation ahead of her, if anything happens to me."

I took her hand, squeezing her fingers gently. "Then let's be friends, so we'll both be able to say we have friends. I mean, you're staying here, right? They're your friends, now, too, right?"

"They're on a quest to make up for what they did in the past. Taking care of me fulfills their quest for the moment, but I can't live on their good graces forever." She chewed on her fingertip; her gaze full of worries.

I sat down next to her. "Do you want to go home? When the lightning goes away, they could take you home. Well, someone could, I'm sure. I'm not sure exactly who does that, and I sincerely don't recommend the pilot I used."

"There's no point in going home. I don't have anyone there or anyplace to go. I could stay here, but I don't want to be trouble for anyone. I'm a teacher, or I was becoming one, when this happened. I could teach, except I don't even know if they have openings for that." She rubbed her eyes again. "I could teach you to read."

Well, that was a jump, but my interest piqued. "I'd be so grateful. I don't have any money to pay you, so we'd have to wait until I can figure out something to do to earn my own keep."

"You think I'd ever charge you for anything?" Her voice broke. "You saved our lives. It would be the least I could do."

I put my arm around her. Some of her initial *I'm great* façade was coming off, which was okay. I was always a mess; I understood struggling more than having it all together. "Well, I want to compensate you somehow."

"No. I insist. We can start next week, okay? I was also thinking last night about that cabin where I gave birth. Is anyone living there? Like, maybe I could teach somewhere, if someone wanted me to, and we could live there. I just have to figure out what to do with Kitty when I work." She blinked rapidly. "You live with the guys over the bar, right? If you don't like it there, you could live with me, too. I don't know what it's like living over a bar, but we could make that cabin a home, right?"

Wow. Her anxiety had her scrabbling for answers, but I was safe, and I wanted to be sure she understood that. "I like it there. I want to stay, and I think they want me to stay with them."

"Yes, of course." She sighed. "I think I'm really tired."

"One thing at a time. Thank you for the reading lessons, and I'll try not to be the worst student ever."

Her smile was huge. "Don't be silly. You'd be no such thing."

Ransom appeared in the doorway. "Hey, sorry to interrupt. Let's go see the guys. They're going through Evans' cabin right now. Maybe we could go help them?"

There was a desperation in his tone that I'd never heard before. He *really* wanted to go help the guys at the cabin. I gently handed the baby to Raine. "I'll come see you soon, okay? Not for lessons but just to see you two again. One thing at a time. Maybe it'll all work out soon. Answers or a road you can take, I don't know. I pretty much get thrown around from one thing to the next."

She nodded and blew out a breath. "Same, and please, come see me. I swear, I can be better than this."

I knelt in front of her. "I will, and there isn't a thing about yourself you have to change. Let me know if you need something."

She side-hugged me for a second and then I turned to leave. Ransom put out his hand, and when I took it, he squeezed my fingers hard. I stared at him. "You okay?"

His nod was all I got before he whirled me around and placed me on his back. "It's a long walk. I want to carry you."

I hadn't seen the piggyback ride coming, and I sputtered a bit. "Well...I could probably walk."

"Humor me?"

Darkness leaned against the wall outside of the room.

He nodded to us and then stared at Raine's door without saying anything. I couldn't read him, but I picked up on undertones I couldn't explain or even understand. *What did I miss?*

But rather than argue, I held onto Ransom's back and let him carry me from that house at a speed I couldn't even track with my eyes. I pressed my head against his shoulder, my eyes closed because the blur made me dizzy. "Did something go wrong?" I shouted into his shoulder.

Ransom skidded to a stop and gently set me down. His gaze had gone frantic. "Please don't move to that cabin with her."

"So, you were listening?" It wasn't a surprise, but I at least asked it like it was a question.

"I really try not to, and I don't listen to our neighbors. I don't know what's going on with their lives behind closed doors. I'm not interested in invading anyone's privacy, but you're ours. And I can't quite keep my ears off what you're doing yet. I never thought to have this...what we have, okay? I was made in a petri dish. I'm nothing but a killer, yet somehow, you seem to think that I'm worth it. Except maybe you're going to leave. If you go to that cabin, I have to warn you, I'll build a tent to be nearby. Unless that will drive you away further, in which case..."

"Stop." I took his cheeks in my hands. I'm not sure why, but his panic calmed me—like it humanized him by showing he had vulnerabilities, which made me oddly more secure. "I told her no. If you were listening, you heard that. I said I like you guys, and I told her you seemed to like me."

He visibly swallowed. "*Like* you? I..."

A bang caught our attention, then Crew appeared. He was actually out of breath. "Is she leaving? What happened?"

We were close enough to all of them for them to over-hear the conversation, while they likely couldn't have heard the conversation with Raine. "No, I'm not going anywhere. I promise you."

He nodded, then clapped a hand down on Ransom's shoulder. "Okay. Good job talking her out of it, Ransom."

This was getting ridiculous. He didn't talk me out of anything. "I was never considering it. Raine is going through a lot, so she asked me if I would—" I was cut off by the others arriving. They all panted like they'd run hard, even for them. How far did they go in a short period of time? "And I told her no right away. I don't want to move to a cabin with her."

"Good." Crew pulled me into a hug. "We'd miss you so much."

I would miss them, too. I let Crew hold me for a second, then he passed me to Mace who eventually passed me to Gunnar and then back to Ransom. I couldn't find a reason to think it wasn't okay. It was so much more than I ever expected to have. They ran headlong through the woods to get to me because of the possibility I might consider leaving. *I told Raine I didn't have people. I absolutely do.*

THE CABIN WAS A MESS—THINGS strewn everywhere, weapons, more of the patches Evans used on Ransom, clothes, discarded plates with molding food remains. He lived like a person in distress. I was messy, but Evans' cabin hit a different level.

"See what I mean?" Mace asked Ransom. "This is bad shit. Where did he get all of it? I haven't seen this stuff since Evander fell. Some of it, not even then. What about you?

When was the last time you saw a cellular disrupter? I don't even have ear plugs to block one anymore. If I used it, I'd go down with it, and I hated doing it anyway. It didn't feel like a fair fight."

Gunnar sighed. "When did we have a fair fight? We were built to win, not play fair."

Ransom nodded at Mace's question. "I don't want this stuff just sitting here. I don't want it available for someone on the edge to just take and use. What do we do with this? Crew?"

He remained silent for so long, I wasn't sure he would answer. With nothing to contribute except awe, I stayed quiet and watched.

Crew finally said, "I'm of two minds. The former me says let's keep them. We never know when we'll need weapons to kick ass. The recent me would like them destroyed, but I don't know if that's the smart call. I don't want to be caught unawares, if everyone else has them. Well, everyone *not* with us." He side-eyed me. "Would you be comfortable if they were stored where we live, Raven?"

I hadn't expected his question. *Does it matter what I think?* I guessed it did. If Crew asked, he had a reason. "I trust you guys to keep them stored where they can't accidently blow up or anything."

"Then we'll keep them." He nodded. "Ransom, go through all of this. I want an accounting, then keep what could be useful. Make a full inventory."

"On it." He smiled and rubbed his hands together. "I love sorting, I just do."

The clutter seemed to be getting to me. I stepped outside of the cabin, the walls suddenly feeling like they might come in on me. It was cooler outside. I lifted my head to the sun, closed my eyes to keep from going blind, and breathed.

"Hey..." Gunnar tugged on my hair, getting my attention. "What made you upset? We can get rid of the stuff, if it bothers you."

Crew pointed at me. "Don't lie. It hurts my ears."

"What happens if you all get sick of me? Do I move here? Do I leave the planet?" I swallowed. It was easier to just say the words, not dwell on whether or not to say them.

"We won't get sick of you." All four of them echoed the words pretty much in unison. I smiled. *At least they're in sync.*

Which was sweet, but not what I wanted. "I understand it's unlikely all four of you will get sick of me at once, but what about if Crew does?"

"Why specifically me?" He stepped toward me; his brow furrowed in concern. "I think I might be the least likely to get sick of you. I'm head over heels, not going to have that happen."

They all grumbled something, but I forced myself to press onward. "Because you're in charge. They ultimately defer to you, so if you get sick of me, they'll get rid of me. Right?"

"Where is this coming from?" Gunnar looked at Ransom.

He shook his head. "She was with Raine, who is understandably loaded with anxiety. Maybe it stirred hers."

"Or yours did." I shook my head. "Is it a completely unreasonable question?"

"No," Crew said and drew me to him. "But I'm totally devoted to you. Always will be. And I think they'd vote to throw me out if I even suggested such a thing." He kissed my head. "Maybe we could make the upstairs in the bar more of a home? We didn't care before, but it makes sense in a way I hadn't considered. We could make it an actual home."

Gunnar laughed. "I love that idea. I'll do that. Let's make

it more like an apartment. Bar is one thing; home is another. I mean, we've had our rooms, but we haven't had a home. Raven made it a home by coming, so let's give her one."

It might have been the sweetest thing I'd ever heard. Tears rushed to my eyes, and I reached for him to join the hug I shared with Crew. Gunnar did just that. I was smushed between them and that was better. I needed the contact.

"What was home like for you, Raven?" Mace took a step toward us. "Can you remember? We could try to make the apartment similar."

I blinked. *Good question.* I didn't let myself think about it most of the time, but I searched back to the memories from when I was so, so young and small. "It was a house. To me, it seemed huge, but maybe it wasn't. I was just small. We had three bedrooms, and two were upstairs—my brother and I had those rooms, and basically the whole upstairs. My parents were downstairs." I remembered sneaking through the dark to find them at night after a bad dream. It seemed like such a long walk. "There was a kitchen." *Of course there was.* I had to think. "The walls were yellow in the kitchen. The floors were smooth but wood." I shook my head as the rush of emotion hit me the second that the memory did.

Stone used to laugh at breakfast. Every morning, he found something so funny. He'd just laugh and laugh. I could almost hear it...

The hug suddenly became too much, a trap I needed to escape. I pushed out of their embrace, seeking the air again. Tears poured down my cheeks, and I scrubbed them away with the back of my hand in annoyance. "Sorry, too much. What if you all die? What happens to me then?" I held out my hand. "Sorry, but don't tell me that you can't die, because they gutted Amias. I may not have seen it happen, but I pictured it a million times on my trip here. He died from it.

So, yes, you actually *can* die, and I know that you know it, because I would think you've seen more of your people die than you'd care to remember." I wiped at my eyes again, but I still couldn't see past the blurry sheen of tears. I sniffled and said, "I need to get a job, I think, so I can survive if something happens to you. So I can pay for things that I need, but the only thing I know how to do is this." I hoped pointing at the mark on my forehead was going to be suffi-cient, because I didn't want to say the word aloud. "And I'm sorry about this. I'm *so* sorry." I turned to walk away. "Give me a moment. I'll get it stopped."

Mace grabbed my arm. "I'll go with you, okay? I know just where we can go. We all have bad moments, and these are very real, valid questions you're asking. We'll figure them out. All of us, together."

Gunnar cleared his throat. "Anything I have, it's yours, Raven. All my credits. I'm sure you can have all of ours. That's what I see them do. The families around here that we've observed. I mean, Missy isn't working right now, because the babies are young and she has money—she just has credits. She has John's. That's how it works, right?"

I wiped at his eyes. His sweetness put a halt to my uncontrolled weeping. "It's really nice that they do that. I think my parents were the same way. My mom had just gone back to work running a fishery when Clarke arrived. She'd been home for years, and now that I think about it, I think that the man next door stayed home while his wife worked, because he used to take us all on playdates with his kids." What were their names? What happened to them? I'd prob-ably never know. "And yes, they share money, if that was how it worked for them. I don't know. But *they're* married. I'm not your wife and I'd never marry you to use your cred-its. If anyone ever suggested such a thing, or if you ever have someone you even think wants to marry you to use the income you've earned with all your hard work, get rid of them."

They all fell silent. I didn't know why, and I didn't have the wherewithal in that moment to figure it out. Instead, I looked at Mace. "If I'm too much, I can just go for a walk by myself."

"Never too much. You're always the right amount of much." He held out his hand. "Can I carry you like Ransom did? It's a perfect spot, but it's all uphill."

I batted at my face, wiping away the stray tears. "If you don't mind going at what I'm sure has to be my frustratingly slow pace, I could use the exertion of the walk."

"Raven. " His voice was low. "I'd never mind any pace you wanted. Sure, you can walk."

I appreciated that Mace kept his word. He never at any point trudged ahead of me or acted like the fact that I was obviously slower than him was a problem. At some point, I also stopped trying to go faster than was comfortable to prove something in my own head. We walked for about forty-five minutes when I heard a loud noise, a rumbling I couldn't recognize, and I stopped, catching my breath and looking around.

"Mace?" I wasn't crying anymore, but I hadn't spoken since my episode, so my voice felt and sounded rough when I used it. "What is that?"

He grinned. "Ah, she finally hears it. Come on. Just a little bit further, and you'll see it for yourself. It's safe. I'd never bring you anywhere that wasn't safe."

" Well, there went my idea of going on your jobs with you." I shook my head. "I'm kidding. What would I do up there, doing whatever you do in space?"

He tilted his head. "No, you absolutely can't come with

me on those jobs. Let's leave that for now. You'll like where we're going."

It was another ten-minute walk to the top, but the view made me instantly grateful we made the effort. I'm not sure if I read or heard stories of waterfalls, but I'd never seen one in real life before. A roar filled the air, the sound of the rushing water all consuming, as the beauty of the majestic thing took my breath away.

It was so beautiful. In the distance, the town flowed out of the forest and the lavender fields waved violet in another direction. The entire valley looked like some magical hideaway, lit by a strobing sky.

"Mace." I had nothing to say after speaking his name. It was just so...incredible.

A lake that led into a river stretched blue and unbroken beneath us, the water looking so cool and crisp after our hike.

"Can you swim?" he asked me as a response.

"I haven't in fifteen years, but I used to be able to a bit, in the way that children could. I don't know if I remember anymore."

He nodded. "Got it. Well, do you trust me?"

I blinked, focusing on him instead of the water, and for a second I was glad that the weather had normalized so the lightning was staying in the upper atmosphere and not down here with us. His hard profile seemed softened by his shaggy blond hair, getting a bit long around his ears. "Yes, I trust you." I meant the words. I did trust him.

"I'm going to jump in that water. Once I'm in, you jump to me. Nothing will happen to you, and you'll love it."

He pulled his shirt off followed by his pants and then his underwear. I caught my breath. Mace and I hadn't been intimate with each other, but he was gorgeous. I knew he would be, but all of his flesh revealed at once left me gaping at him. Mace seemed carved out of marble, sculpted to be perfect.

I grabbed at my shirt. If he was naked, I wanted to be, too. My mind stuttered when I remembered that meant throwing myself off the cliff and toward the waterfall. "I trust you, but this scares the shit out of me."

"It should," he said with a reckless grin.

I stripped just in time to watch him leap over the rocks' edge and into the water below. He was down in seconds, barely a sound made while he entered the water. For a moment, I couldn't see him, and my breath caught in fear. I couldn't save him, if he was hurt. But then he appeared, his head popping out of the water with a splash before he waved at me.

I lifted my hand to wave back. *This is nuts. I can't do this.* I'd sit down and enjoy the view. That would be fine. Still, I tugged off my underwear, and without giving it another rational thought, I closed my eyes and launched myself into nothingness.

Airborne before I even knew really what I'd done, there was a horrible few seconds of wind and weightlessness for me to reconsider everything before I struck the water. The water hit like a slap, startling me before it closed over my head, and everything went blurry. My eyes were open, a hazy uncertainty of cold water making me question my sanity. Mace's arms slid around me and before the thought to breathe hit me, we were back above water. I wrapped my arms around his neck and grinned at him, shaking my hair back from my face.

"That was...that was the best thing ever!" Exhilarated, I laughed and gazed up at the cliff, which now seemed way too far away. *I jumped from there.* I laughed again, amazed.

His smile was huge, when I turned back to look at him. "I know. I thought you'd scream but you were silent. Brave."

"Maybe just struck dumb."

He threw his head back and laughed. "Welcome to the Falls, Raven."

I remembered how to tread water but not as well as Mace. In the end, it was more fun to hold onto him and let him streak us through the water. Warm air washed over my flesh as the cool water almost sparkled across my body. And he was so happy just swimming with me that I had to kiss him, because to not do so would be one of the great tragedies of my life.

If I was being ridiculous, I didn't give a shit.

He kissed me back, holding onto me like I was the most precious person in the world.

Finally, I pulled back. "Thank you for this."

"Thank you for being willing to come without even knowing where we were going. That meant you trusted me. Then you did again—you jumped off the cliff because I told you to trust me. You told me you did. It's really what I wanted more than anything, and I didn't even really know until you told me that you did." He blinked. "You're magic, Raven."

I wasn't, but maybe he was. "Do you come here a lot?"

"I used to. Lately, no but I want to again. A lot. With you.

Just the two of us, okay? The others don't love it like I do. Ransom likes the mountains, but this isn't really his place. He likes to go west of the lavender fields. Crew walks to the coastline to think, and I'm not sure Gunnar is really a nature guy at heart. He'd rather take a hammer and fix something."

I kissed him again, lightly, right on the mouth. "This is your place."

"It was, but now it's our place. Okay?"

I was more than okay with that. "Mace, do you want to make love to me?"

I never really put it like that before, but it seemed apropos because Mace looked at me like I'd hung the stars. Like I was the kind of girl who could use the phrase *make love* and mean it.

Who could have waited to actually make love to someone like Mace?

"So much..." he said, his voice low. "But, Raven, I have to tell you I might be terrible at it. I don't even remember what I saw in that stupid machine. I might be...I might need you to be patient with me."

I knew what it took for a Super Soldier to admit to any weakness. Amias once told me they were born to be great at whatever they undertook, and if they weren't, they'd better not admit it if they didn't want to be decommissioned.

"Mace, I am not concerned in the slightest about how you'll be this first time. Besides, if for some reason it doesn't go well, we'll have plenty of time to practice until we get it right." And the idea of the practice pleased me.

He moved so fast, I shrieked, but he quickly sliced through the water toward the falls. "When we get to the stream, hold your breath and hang onto me," he said.

I tried not to feel too baffled at his abrupt change of conversation—perhaps he wasn't as interested in making love? I obeyed his directions, though, holding my breath and clinging to him as he dragged us beneath the waterfall.

We surfaced again, and the sound of the waterfall changed, echoing off the walls in a melodic way. "Where are we?"

"A cave I found." He grinned. "I don't know if anyone else has ever been here. I like to think it's only mine. The falls make it hard for anyone outside to hear us. No one knows we're here, which might be why I've never seen anyone else ever find this place. Although the constant ability to be spied upon is invasive, it's also a safety net. When I was struck by lightning, they heard it. If something happened in here, they wouldn't know."

Interesting. "So it's sort of dangerous and exciting?"

"Yes. But they're going to be mad at me. We all like to be able to hear you when we so choose. Distance can make that hard. They're not going to be happy I took you away today, but I don't give a shit. You've been through a ton. You got stuck here. You were nearly killed by a lightning strike, then drank bad water. You got kidnapped, delivered a baby, tried to kill Net, and then burned your hands. Then you killed Evans so he couldn't kill Ransom. And all of that after you just lost your brother and Amias, which meant you had to be able to travel the universe through space when you couldn't even read."

I quirked a brow at him. Well, if he listed it all out, I did sound more impressive. "Maybe I should be more tired than I am?" I joked.

He shook his head, pulling me onto the cave floor. "What it means is if you want to scream at the top of your lungs with only me to hear it—with no one around to know that you did—you can."

That was an incredibly sweet offer. Maybe it would have

been appealing...an hour ago. I was interested in making noise, but not because I screamed. I smiled at him, then twirled my fingertips on his chest. "Or we could make love, and no one could possibly overhear us."

He stared at me. "On the ground? I don't want it to be uncomfortable for you."

"It wouldn't be. Would the ground hurt you?" I didn't think it would. "Because if you wanted to lie down right there, I'll show you something I was thinking about."

I was being flirty and a little silly right then. After my anxiety crying, it was a small miracle that I could feel like this again. Or maybe I never had before? Everything was always so serious all the time. But not in those falls. It had been like bathing in joy. Doing it with Mace made it so much better.

He lay on his back right away. "Have your way with me, Miss Raven."

I laughed. "Well, I guess I'll do just that."

We were both totally naked, and I hadn't even given that a single thought. I laid my body flat on top of his right away, loving how warm his flesh felt after the coolness of the water. "This isn't too heavy? The floor isn't too awful?"

"The floor feels like a soft mattress. Anything is wonderful as long as I get to be with you."

I lifted my head to kiss all over his face. "I am going to make you feel so good. It's going to give me so much pleasure to do so."

Before he could answer me, I slipped down his body to take his cock in my hands. He was already slightly hard. It was gratifying to know that he could get hard for me just from the concept of talking about it. If he touched me right then, he'd find I was warm and ready for him, too, but I wanted to play for a while first.

I kissed him right on the top of his cock. His hips lifted, and he caught his breath. Beneath my mouth, he trembled, so I let my breath wash over the head. It was the perfect time to do just what I wanted. I took him down my throat and moaned when I did. Nothing ever tasted better than his cock in my mouth.

I lifted my head just enough to whisper to him. "At any point, if you want to fuck me in my mouth, and just lose it, you can."

I never would've imagined using those words on a Super Soldier, but I did, because Mace was right. I trusted him. Completely.

Once again, I sank my mouth over his hard cock, sucking hard and rolling my tongue. He moaned, a small sound that got louder as I increased my pressure, flicking my tongue against him. His hips bucked, and it took him down my throat even further. Yes, that was what I wanted. I'd told him to take me, to use my throat anyway he wanted. But suddenly it stopped, and he leaned back on his elbows.

"Not for the first time. I want to be inside of you. I love this. It's so hot. I can almost not fathom it's happening. You are a sexy goddess of light sent here to make me think that life isn't just pain. But I can't come in your mouth today. I have to feel you around me. I need to make you come, too."

For a person who said he might not be good because he didn't know what he was doing, Mace certainly caught up pretty quickly with what he wanted. I pulled my mouth away from him. I pouted, "Sometime will you let me? Just suck and suck on you until you come?"

He visibly swallowed, his cock jerking in my hand. "Yes, I promise."

I climbed back on top of him, positioning myself so I could slide onto his cock. I rubbed the head against my clit before slowly sheathing him with my body. He was thick, so I had to stretch to accommodate him. Mace, still on his elbows, let his head fall backward. "Fuck."

"Yes, that's the idea." I was being funny, at least in my own head, and he lifted his head to smile at me.

"I liked the other phrase better."

The *love* phrase. I nodded. "I think I do, too. I guess I just have a dirty mouth."

"This is heaven, Raven."

Mace said the sweetest things, but I didn't want to talk right then. I moved up and down his cock, grinding my clit against his belly on each downward motion. Surges of pleasure traveled through me, and my breath came faster. This was my pace, he wasn't taking control of these moments. If anything, he watched me with what I could only think of as reverence as I rode his body.

Finally, he lay flat down, raising his arms so I could grasp on to his hands, giving me something to hold onto while I bucked against him, hard. We were both silent except for the sounds of our breaths, which were in sync with one another. Finally, I had to let go of his hands because I needed to hold onto my breasts.

As I grabbed them, he shook his head. "No, I'm going to hold them."

Mace grabbed onto them and squeezed my nipples. Yes, that was what I needed. I cried out, my muscles clenching around him as I came all at once. Waves of hot satisfaction left me trembling in reaction. Pleasure rode me as Mace grabbed my hips and took over how we moved. He drove into me—once, then twice. He came on a long, low sound that resonated through the cave around us, echoing back in a symphony of bliss.

Warm air kissed my sweaty back, and the sound of the

falls fluttered into my consciousness. I lay flat against Mace's chest, listening to his heartbeat. It rushed when I first collapsed on him, but it slowed as his breath calmed.

I lifted my head, and he grinned at me. "Hi there. Wow."

"Wow is right. I can do longer next time." He stroked his finger down the slope of my nose. "Do you want to go again now?"

"I was the one who couldn't hold back. You just gave me just what I needed." I was rambling. "I'm getting a little bit cold." The air was warm but the cold water from earlier was finally starting to make me a little bit shivery.

"Oh. " He sat up fast, taking me with him. "Of course. Yes, you're cold. I'm the worst to not think about it."

I kissed his cheek. "No, you're incredible. I just got cold, or yes, I'd say let's do it again. Right this very second, in fact."

Things moved very fast after that. Whatever else I might have added was lost because Mace focused on getting me warm. "Arms around me. I'll make this as fast as I can. You're going to have to get wet again, but only very briefly, and shit we don't have a towel."

"I've been wet before. In fact, when we met..."

We were suddenly under the water. I thought we swam quickly before, but it was nothing to the burst of speed that blurred us hyperfast through the water. I gasped when we came up and he winced. "Sorry, I didn't warn you to hold your breath. I just keep fucking it up."

"Mace!" I kissed him roughly on the lips. "Stop. I'm not going to freeze to death. I'm just a little bit cold. I've been much colder than this. Take a deep breath. It's going to be fine."

His smile was small but got bigger in a second. "I just

want you to be wonderful every second of the day, because I am...since you arrived."

"I wish I could bottle what you say to me so that I could let it out and replay it all the time."

He hoisted me up. "All right. I'll get you dry and warm in a reasonable way. Then we'll go home and get ready for the night at the bar. In warm clothes, where you won't catch your death of cold."

"Okay. But only if you kiss me again one more time."

Mace leaned over. "I'd kiss you every day all day." He kissed me softly. "Count on it."

AFTER I CONVINCED Mace I could dress myself, he carried me home on his back. I didn't object, since it was nice to be close to him. I didn't watch the woods or the landscape change. Instead, I watched the sky. The colors of the lightning above us changed and swirled, constantly making a show for us. I didn't notice it all the time anymore, as though I'd just gotten used to it.

But it really was beautiful. A light flashed to the left, brighter than the others. It was sort of more yellow. "Did you see that?"

He shook his head. "See what?"

"The lightning was a funny yellow." It was gone, vanished in the darkness. "Not a streak lightning but more like one of those flashes."

He shook his head. "I didn't see it, I'm sorry. Was it pretty?"

"Not any more pretty than the rest of it, though it startled me for some reason." I put my head down on his shoulder. "Thank you for today, Mace."

"Don't ever thank me for anything."

I doubted that would be the case. I would probably thank Mace for the rest of my life for lots of things.

We arrived back at the bar, and although I wouldn't tell Mace, I did appreciate the hot water rinsing away the cold from earlier. By the time I got out, rain pounded a staccato beat on the roof. Thunder sounded and I winced. Net was dead, so I knew he didn't cause the storm. I knew they experienced their lightning and storm season, so I shouldn't expect it to be sunny. Would I hate the sound of the rain for the rest of my life?

I ran a brush through my hair and considered leaving the burnished length of it flowing down my back. Normally, I pinned it back in some fashion, but what if I let it air dry just once? I decided to find out, so I pulled on a black cotton dress one of the neighbors left for me. I wished for a change of shoes, and wondered if we could buy a pair somewhere after the rainy season. I knew some of the locals ran shops in the town, but I hadn't visited them yet—could there be a shoemaker among them?

Gunnar knocked at the door, jarring me out of my worries. "You okay?"

"Yep. I was just thinking I need some more shoes, but I'll be out in a second. Meet you downstairs."

I ran the brush through my hair one last time then opened the door to find Gunnar leaning on the frame. He grinned and said, "Or I could wait for you, because I just like to look at you."

I put my arms around him, sighing happily when his arms closed around me in return. "Hi."

"Hello." He lifted me up for a kiss. "It'll probably be a quiet night down there. The rain is really bad. It could just be us."

Now that's a thought. "What do we do when it's just us in the bar?"

"Well, we used to tinker around trying to fix things—making them worse, actually, so we have to pay Winter to come over and fix what we made worse." He grinned. "You haven't met Winter and his crew yet, but there are three of them. They come and go a lot, buzzing all over the planet to repair things. They're not here right now, but you'll for sure meet them when I break something...likely, badly."

I grinned. "Maybe you could dance with me? We could play a song from the jukebox, if we're alone. Maybe you could all dance with me."

"I'd love that." He grinned. "So would the rest of them."

Sadly, Gunnar was completely wrong. We were very, *very* busy. They came in large numbers that night, much like when Evans tried to kill Ransom. Why were they braving the weather? Ransom didn't know when I asked him, but he kissed my cheek. "Maybe they're here to see you again."

I couldn't be *that* interesting. It had to be something else. But I did notice plenty of girls around, which brought up a good question. I elbowed Ransom gently. "There are women around. Why did you wait for me? Like, why didn't you fall in love with Chanel or one of the other women here?"

He set down the drink he was making, and Crew grabbed it to deliver it to a table. "Because they weren't you, Butterfly."

"That's a non-answer." I dried another glass.

"Well, it might have to do with our circumstances. We were welcomed, but we tried not to overstep. The regular humans like us, but they don't particularly socialize with us. Chanel in particular is an excellent example. Her father is dead now—he took ill and didn't get better—but he really didn't like us at all. He was one of the few who voted to not

let us stay." Ransom shook his head. "He asked us specifically to stay away from them, so we did. They have a farm a
ways from here. After he died, Chanel and her brother
popped around a bit. They don't seem *as* hostile, but we're
not going anywhere near that. Besides...do human guys
have to explain why they like one girl and not another girl?"

No, they didn't, but what did I know? "I'm not sure. I
mean, I didn't exactly have a traditional background, either.
Sorry, I was just curious."

"It's okay." He kissed me square on the lips. "You're ours.
That's all there is to it. Period. It fit for us. I'm just glad it was
something you wanted, too."

Crew came back for another drink. "More than glad.
They just weren't ours, so don't worry about them. We're not
going to suddenly decide we want someone else. We only
want you."

That was really sweet. Thunder boomed outside, and I
winced. "This is normal?"

"Completely normal." Ransom shook his head. "It gets
increasingly bad and then it ends. It'll be intermittent. It's
not Net or anyone else messing with it. Just wet and noisy."

I was dead on my feet by the time we went to bed,
climbing in between Gunnar and Mace. The storm still
clamored on outside, raging with wind and thunder. I clung
to Mace while Gunnar hugged me from behind. "Will you
guys be sleeping tonight or is it one of those nights where
you won't, even though I need to?"

"We might doze," Gunnar said and laughed gently.
"Don't worry about that. It's very restful to be here with you
while you breathe. We love it, sleeping or not sleeping."

That was good because I wasn't sure I could have stayed
awake another minute if I tried. The bed dipping woke me.
Both Gunnar and Mace had gotten up, though it still looked

dark outside. I lifted my head and Mace bent to kiss my cheek. "Sorry we woke you, but it's better anyway. The rain caused flooding down at the coastline. People need help, so we have to go. But don't worry. Sleep for a bit. There will be a Super Soldier in and out of here all day to check on things until we get back. When we're finished, we'll come back."

I rubbed at my eyes. "I'm not worried about being alone. I don't think anyone here wants to hurt me or anything. Can I help somehow?"

"No. I don't want you anywhere near the floods. Get some more sleep, but if you need us, just start talking aloud. Whichever Super Soldier is patrolling here will hear it, and they can come get us. We'll be a few hours away."

Gunnar took my hand. "Or we'll stay, if you want us to."

"No, go. They need you." I rolled over. "I'm sure I can find things to do today. People to see. Be safe. How are you going to handle it while it's still raining?"

Cruz poked his head through the door. "Probably badly. See you later, beautiful."

Gunnar and Mace both left but Ransom sprinted back to kiss my shoulder. "Don't go outside. I don't want my Butterfly to drown in the rain."

Maybe I would spend the whole day in bed. Was that something I was allowed to do?

I closed my eyes, amused by the luxury of the idea.

I WASHED all the dishes and hummed to myself when Gator poked his head through the door. "I'm trading with Wave. We meet in the middle, then he'll be here. Anything you want me to tell your crazy four guys who are probably insane with worry because you're here alone?"

"Tell them I am fine, and I'm slightly reorganizing the kitchen to make it more aesthetically appealing, but I'll put it back if they don't like it."

He smirked. "I'm sure they'll think whatever you do is perfect. They love you. I know next to nothing about that, but that's what I see around, anyway. You just want the other person to be happy. Check on Raine later for me, will you?"

I looked over my shoulder. "I will."

If I knew him better, I might tease him about caring about what she needed, too. But I didn't, and I had no idea if their feelings for Raine ran that way, or if they were just nice because she needed somewhere to go.

I went back to organizing the shelves.

Maybe I never would've expected being smacked, but getting hit on the arm when I didn't even know someone was there shocked me. What the hell? I looked down where I'd been struck almost instinctively. A metal object stuck awkwardly out of my arm.

"Don't make me use it." A female voice drew my attention from the pain on my arm to the person who stuck it there. A blonde woman I'd never seen before held a device pointed at me. I recognized the markings on her head—she belonged to Clarke. "If I press a button on this device, it will cause you a huge amount of pain. I don't want to do that." She held up a device I did recognize. "No one can hear us here. This makes it impossible for them to hear us, not that they could right now anyway. There is a dead zone of time when they change places. I think I timed my visit perfectly. In fact. I'm sure I did. Raven, you're coming with me. Clarke wants you back, and I'm here to get you. Are you going to make this hard or easy?"

17

THE WHORE AND THE BOUNTY
HUNTER

I leaned against the counter and stared at her, twirling a lock of red hair around my fingertip casually. She was like me, except obviously...she wasn't. At some point, she likely started as one of Clarke's whores. Everyone knew the tattoo, even if they didn't know about Clarke—it meant we were available to have sex if you paid someone. Ransom knew it when we met, and he didn't even know Clarke.

But she intended to capture me and bring me *home*. That wasn't something we did. We spread our legs and said things like *oh yes, so good*. We didn't grab runaway whores and drag them home.

"Why are you doing this? *How* are you doing this?" The metal attached to my skin burned, so I waved it at her. I'd pull it off, but it might take all of the skin on my arm with it. They weren't meant to be detached by the wearer.

"I'm doing this because I have to, which is also how I have a ship, and Clarke has the technology to get through bad lightning storms. So, move. We're going. Now."

Leaving with her seemed like a bad idea overall. The

longer I stalled, the more likely a Super Soldier would notice they couldn't hear me. Then they'd come find out why. That was the plan. It had to be. I'd attack her, although I had no fighting skills, and she'd probably press that button to hurt me. Pain didn't frighten me, but what did she mean by *hurt*?

"What will it do? The thing on my arm?"

She scowled at me, some of her long blonde hair falling over her shoulder. "It'll incapacitate you. And it won't be pretty. You'll hurt for days. Ask yourself...do you want to go back to Clarke's ministrations in that much pain?"

No, she was right. Of course, she could be lying, and I wouldn't know. Did I want to risk it?

I began, "Listen, I'm...I get that you think you have to do this."

"I don't think it, Raven," she yelled at me. "I *know* it. Okay? I don't have any more choices than you do. So let's get the fuck moving."

I kept talking, even through what she said to me. "And it hasn't been very long, I know that, but I've made a life here. I didn't think it was possible, but I fell in love, and they love me back. Please, just go. Tell them I'm dead. What does Clarke even care? I'm nothing to him. I'm not an important whore."

She laughed. "Do you think he'd tell you how important you are? Raven, you matter a shit ton. He had someone lined up to buy you. Do you know how rare it is? One of your regulars wants to own you."

Which one? No, that didn't matter. I didn't want any of them. *Fuck. No.* They were all repulsive. "I can't just *go*. I won't do that. I love them. Do you understand?"

"Oh, Raven." She sighed, and for the first time, she looked human to me. Tired, even. "Men are just men. They don't really love us. They want us. They may even be nice to us for a while, if they want to fuck us. But make no mistake, they don't love us. Super Soldiers don't love at all. They're genetically coded to kill us. So, move." She grabbed me then stopped. "We'll even be kind and tell them you're leaving."

She pulled a paper out of her pocket and wrote on it, speaking aloud as she did. "This way they don't wonder. Dear, Guys, Sorry. None of it was real. I'm just a whore. We lie. XoXo, Raven."

I stared at the paper. They would know I didn't write them a note. I couldn't read or write. She'd actually done me a huge favor, so I let her drag me out. Just because my Super Soldiers couldn't hear me didn't mean others couldn't. I started to scream.

It didn't matter. No one came, and by the time we got to the shuttle that could make it through the lightning, I was soaked.

I never expected to stay there, and it looked like, in the end, I wouldn't.

WET AND SHIVERING UNDER A BLANKET, I stared at the blonde woman who piloted our shuttle. I wanted to hate her, but I didn't. Couldn't. She had my markings. Whatever happened to her, she wasn't any more in control of her life than I was . With a swift movement, she got up and left the control room. In a second, she returned with a bathrobe. "Get changed. You're freezing."

She didn't look particularly cold, but she also wore a coat. "I don't do wet very well. I freeze fast." I took the robe and turned my back to change. We didn't care about nudity at Clarke's, only now I did. *That's going to be a problem.* Who was I kidding? All of it was. I couldn't do my job anymore. Any of it.

"What's your name?" I asked her.

Maybe she'd tell me or maybe we'd be in silence for the rest of the trip. She kept the metal device on me, which was probably smart, since I might decide to crash us back onto the planet. Or I would have. It had been too long since we'd left orbit, headed back to Clarke's. I couldn't believe it. I'd actually decided that I could be happy, and it vanished.

"My name is Cambree." She looked over her shoulder. "I don't expect any sympathy from you, Raven. I'd hate me, if I were you. I hate myself a bit, but I really don't have a choice. I'm sorry."

I lay back on the couch behind me. "How does he make you do this? How did you even start doing it? I mean...I didn't know he had a fleet of us running around."

She snorted. "We don't have a fleet. They basically have me. I guess he sometimes sends out some enhanced to do things for him, but they always come back having seriously damaged the merchandise."

The merchandise. It was funny to think of myself that way again, yet as one of Clarke's belongings, it seemed apt. I pointed at the device she attached to me. "This is less permanently damaging?"

"Yes, and only one runaway has made me use it so far. Thanks for not being number two." She sighed. "As for why...I suppose you have the right to know. Funny, because you're the only one who has ever asked me. Clarke has my brother in cryo. Do you know what that means?"

I did, actually. "A long, cold sleep. They used to use it with the Super Soldiers, to transport them."

"That's right. Don't use that phrase, remember? Clarke

doesn't like it. Super Soldiers—they're enhanced. You should know better."

I closed my eyes. "I did. But, the guys I love? They don't like 'enhanced.' Sorry, you were telling me about your brother in cryo."

"Right." She sat down in her chair. Cambree was older than me. I didn't know by how much, but it was at least a few years, since she could read and write, and I obviously couldn't. She clearly forgot when she wrote the letter that was supposed to be from me.

"He was fifteen when they put him in to blackmail me. At the time, they wanted me to perform better as one of his whores. I'm really, really bad at it. They had complaints, but then Clarke decided my proficiency with the ships—I stole one and had to be recaptured before they put Danny in cryo—might prove a more useful way to torture me for the rest of my life."

She'd ripped me away from my lovers, so I shouldn't feel bad for her. Only I absolutely did . Before Stone died, I would've done anything for him. "What does it mean, that he's in cryo?"

"It means he's paused in time. He was fifteen, and he should be twenty now, but he's still only fifteen. Forever paused, unless I can get him back or Clarke has him killed. Those are the two options."

I couldn't imagine having my brother frozen, just to be used as a bargaining chip. My heart wrenched. "I'm sorry," I said softly, not really knowing what else to say.

Cambree shrugged. "It's not your fault. It's Clarke's. He's the one who makes us all do horrible things. And now I've done a horrible thing to you. I don't believe in love, but you said that you had it. That's over now, too, and that's on me."

I frowned. "But why do you keep doing it? We could go

back and get my guys. They'll help you. They'd do it anyway, just to be nice, but they won't even question it with me in play."

She sighed, looking down at her hands. "It's not that simple. Clarke can track us, even when we're in space. If I turn this ship around, he'll send more and more until he gets what he wants and that, Raven, like it or not, is you."

Her words hit me hard. I'd tasted freedom and love, but that was gone. In front of me stretched a life I wasn't sure I could tolerate ever again. Tears leaked from my eyes, and I batted them away just in time to see Cambree pretend she didn't notice them.

"Do you know who it is? Who's he selling me to?" There was bad and then there was much, much worse. A night with a person who wanted to hurt me for his pleasure, I could handle. A lifetime? I wasn't sure I'd make it.

Then again, my guys would know I got taken. If I escaped Clarke's compound, could they find me? Would they? It's not like I wore a tracker. Or maybe I did. But the guys couldn't use that to locate me, could they?

Maybe there would be a time when I could escape, and I could figure it out. I couldn't read, but I was smart. I'd find a way to get myself back to them, even if it took time. They waited years for Amias. Maybe they would wait for me, too. *Maybe. Maybe. Maybe.*

Too many maybes.

"I don't, but it can't be good, right?" *At least she's honest.* "Decent men don't buy women, so the fact he wants to buy you means he wants you under his control, where no one else can see you."

I feared she was absolutely right. I gave her a cockeyed smile and raised my brows. "No chance you could report me as dead?"

"I'll do anything for Danny, to save him, even if it means that I have to hurt someone like you. If it wasn't for Danny, I'd prefer to help. You have a month until he takes you. You have no reason to believe me, but if I can figure out a way to save you between now and then, I will."

A month. Anything could happen over that time, although I doubted very much that any of it would be good.

I HATED LOOKING AT CLARKE, but that wasn't anything new. He was tall, good looking in the way of all the Super Soldiers. They'd designed them to be beautiful, but when I looked in the eyes of my guys, I saw only goodness. In his, there was nothing. Maybe it had made him, ultimately, a better soldier than my guys ever were, but he hadn't been their leader. He couldn't control them, and they didn't think highly of him.

Right then, he was my nightmare. I ran away from his 'care' as he loved to put it, so I would be punished for my crime. *That's all there is to it.*

"You broke the rules, Raven." He said my name like we were close friends, when we'd only spoken exactly four times over my lifetime. Once, when he'd told me it was time for me to take my place as one of his girls. The second happened briefly in the hall, when I'd passed him after a client beat the shit out of me. The next two times were similar. Nothing more than a *hello* or worse *that client liked you.*

And now we're here.

"So did you." I should probably just drop my eyes and say sorry, but I wasn't in the mood. *Maybe I finally found a little backbone?*

He lifted a dark eyebrow. "How do you figure?"

"Turns out I'm worth something to you. A lot of money, actually. You promised us, if we became profitable to you, that you would let us use the med machines. I'm worth something to you, so much so that you sought me out on a planet in the middle of nowhere." He knew I left, but he didn't know who was there, or anything about that place. As far as he was concerned, I just ran off. "But you didn't let my brother use the med machine, so I think it's fair to say you also broke the rules."

He was quiet for a second, although I held no illusions that he listened to my words. Instead, he raised his hand and struck me so hard across the face that my ears rang. I hit the ground, barely catching myself with my hands.

"Maybe, where you were, you forgot yourself? Allow me to remind you. I am your better. Every enhanced in this room is your better. You are *nothing*. I'm selling you to a man named Peter Alpin. I presume you remember him? Peter doesn't give a shit if you come damaged, so you should remember your manners when you talk to me. Otherwise, I'll deliver you to him unconscious and nearly dead."

I could hardly think. The room blurred in and out of focus, but I'd heard him. And I knew Peter. *Yeah, he is the nightmare scenario, the worst possible person to want to buy me.* I wasn't going to live to escape, as I barely made it through the night we shared previously. Amias tried to go up against Clarke and he failed, so I didn't have a chance.

Hands grabbed me from behind, and I was held against Cambree's chest. "Don't do that to her. I didn't bring her here for you to beat her."

"Have all my whores lost their minds?" He looked at the man next to him, an enhanced man named Stocks. "Take her."

His goon grabbed Cambree and dragged her backward

by her hair, leaving me flat on the floor again. I lifted my head. "Apologies." There really wasn't anything else to say.

He sighed. "As I was saying, you ran off and caused me no shortage of problems. I can understand you wanting to run after your brother died, but I think the real problem is that I let Amias be nice to you for so long. This is what happens when I show my big heart. It always comes back and bites me in the ass." This time he looked to the right with his long sigh. "Take her to the doctor. Tell her no med machine. I want her to still be bruised when he comes for her. She can keep her alive, and if she runs off again or does anything I don't like, tell the doctor I'll take it out of her ass."

The enhanced I didn't know picked me up off the ground. At least he didn't drag me by my hair. But as I left, Clarke had a final blow to deliver. "I may decide you should work a few jobs between now and when you leave me. I might not, but be ready, in any case. It's so fun to watch you on the screens with your legs spread."

I hated him. Everything about him. The enhanced man set me down, but I saw none of the kindness of my men at home in his hard eyes. I blinked. Yes, it had become home, I realized. That was home, and this was hell.

When he set me down on a bed in the infirmary, he scowled. "Amias was always so full of himself, like he was too good to be here. I hated him."

"I'm sure he hated you, too." Something was wrong with my mouth. I just couldn't seem to keep it closed.

He lifted his hand like he planned to strike me. A familiar voice rang out, saying, "None of that. Not in here. I don't know much, but I'm sure Clarke didn't send her in here for you to damage his property more than she already has been."

The enhanced man lowered his hand. "He says no med

machine. She leaves in a month. Maybe she'll be used before that. Maybe not. If she gets away, he's taking it out on you."

She nodded. "Fine. Get out. Now."

"You can't throw me out." He snarled. Whoever he was, he had a lot of anger issues. Still, he turned and left. Apparently, although she couldn't technically throw him out, he left anyway. I giggled. Dang. I was really out of it from the strike to my cheek.

The woman looked down at me. "Hi, Raven. Do you remember me? We met a few times when you were younger."

"Yes." She wasn't technically a doctor, but she did her best, and I knew there was a story there. Stone probably knew all about her. He knew everyone's tale of woe. "Your name is Lydia, right? Lydia."

She took my hand in hers. "That's right. Here, let me help you sit up. I want to get a good look at you. Where have you been? Never mind. Don't tell me right this second."

Super Soldiers carried in Cambree, who was out cold. They dumped her unceremoniously onto a med table. Lydia touched my arm and left me for a moment to run over to Cambree. "What did you do?" She shouted at the man, but he left without a backward glance. I hated this place. It really wasn't a strong enough word. When had I gotten used to this kind of crap?

"Well," Lydia said, but I didn't think it was really to me. "He didn't say I couldn't put *you* in the med machine." She felt all over her body, pulling things out of her pockets. "This can't go in with you. Oh." She saw the silencer that let us talk without being heard, and she put it in her own pocket. "Come on, Cambree. I'm going to make you okay."

She pressed a button to lower the machine and then

gently rolled Cambree into it. With smooth moves, she programmed it and then hit a button which made the machine buzz and whir.

Without another word, she grabbed an ice pack from the freezer and came over to me, placing it on my cheek. The cold hurt more than it helped, so I tried to push it away, but she held onto it, keeping the pack in place.

"How badly do you hurt?" She sighed. "I'd put you in, too, if I could." As I watched, she lifted the device that made us silent to the enhanced in the area. "I know you have no reason to believe me, but Cambree is a good person. She really is."

I didn't actually doubt it. She just grabbed me when I'd been struck. She was in an impossible situation, but I let Lydia talk. My cheek hurt, so I didn't want to waste words.

"But she's brought you back here, and we only have seconds. Here is what I'm going to do. Number one, I am going to tell them that you have a bad flu and can't see clients for a while. It'll let me keep you in here, safe. It is the smallest thing, but I can do that much. I also want to tell you Stone and Amias are alive." When I jerked up, she held my arm and continued. "I've hidden them in cryo. Clarke has so many people in there, he doesn't even know who he has anymore. I don't have them labeled as Stone and Amias, they're under B12 and B13. I still have to heal them. They're just both in there as they were, almost dead, like when they got to me."

My pounding head increased but for other reasons. "What? Why did you do that? Are you...setting me up to make me complicit? What are you...?"

She shook her head. "No. Just the opposite. I'm sick of him winning. I could have saved Stone, and Amias would never have lost him and gone to kill anyone. I wanted to tell you, but then you were gone. I need you to know now. Whatever happens, I'll keep them hidden. I'll keep them safe, and if there is ever a time I can bring them back, I will. I promise you that."

I threw my arms around her and then groaned. *Ouch.* That really hurt. I did need the ice. "Thank you."

She put the device back in her pocket then placed her finger over her mouth to indicate I needed to be quiet. That was fine. I had plenty of things to think about, lots to contemplate. My brother and Amias were alive, sort of. They were still in bad shape, but they could be saved if we were lucky. Could we be? I lost everything when I lost the guys, but at least I still had something. I found the impossible, that which had permanently left.

I wiped at my tears. There were small, beautiful moments even in this mess. Whatever happened from then on, I had to believe that someday, they'd be okay.

A Super Soldier ran into the med bay. "Why can't we hear in here?"

Lydia blinked. "I have no idea. Do you want me to look at you? See if you're okay? Check your ears?"

He stared at her. "No. Two of us couldn't hear. Something..."

She shrugged. "Let me know if you want an examination, but for now, I have a patient. She might have the flu. Get out."

How did they keep her there? She was inked like the rest of us. Surely, if someone as brilliant as her couldn't get out, there would be no escape for me. I wanted to ask her but not with various Super Soldiers listening. We probably couldn't push the button again so fast.

Instead, I held the ice on my face and tried to think about my brother and Amias. The guys would be so happy to hear Amias was okay. Maybe he'd come home to them someday. Maybe he'd just walk into their bar and tell them hello. They could explain to him that I'd been taken and...

I closed my eyes. In that scenario, I wasn't home with them. Why couldn't my daydreams at least be happy? Lydia rushed around the med bay, and I watched her, remembering suddenly that Stone mentioned she was ten years older than me. Dark haired with brown eyes and high cheekbones, I thought her lovely, although she nervously gnawed her bottom lip a lot.

I owed her. If I lived through the next months, I'd try to find a way to thank her.

18

JUST TRYING TO SURVIVE

Eventually, Cambree came out of the med machine. She didn't have anywhere to be, either—Clarke could send her out on any number of miserable missions any time, but the three of us—Cambree, Lydia, and myself—were all together in the medical facility. We couldn't say much because we couldn't afford to have them discover the device that made them unable to hear us. Which meant we made pleasant small talk, and my anxiety ramped with each and every fake sentence.

When I couldn't stand it anymore, I hoped it would be worded safely enough, when I asked, "Did anyone get hurt when I left?"

Lydia looked up from the medical book she read at her desk. I should probably ask them to teach me to read. I bet they would. She shook her head. "Not really. Don't worry about it." Her smile was tight. I wondered what she couldn't say aloud. "Clarke is always fair and understanding, even when we make big, nearly unforgivable mistakes."

Cambree visibly rolled her eyes, and it was hard for me to hold back my laughter. *Okay, fair enough.* My "flu" was coming to an end. Someone could still select me from the book of available whores, then I'd be called upon to work for Clarke again.

Did Lydia have anything that could end my life? Was I willing to consider suicide? *No, not yet.* Just a fleeting thought, really. Something to wonder about. If Peter Alpin hadn't changed, I wouldn't be long for the universe anyway. I rubbed my face. I was scared, and I'd reached a point where I didn't mind the other women knowing.

Cambree got up and she hugged me. It was so surprising; I almost didn't hug her back, but then I did. She'd brought me back to the prison, but she was as much a cellmate as me. I had experienced *weeks* of happiness. Cambree never did. Lydia watched us with visible tears in her eyes.

The enhanced could probably hear we were upset. They wouldn't understand it, since tears didn't register as sensible, so they mostly left us alone with them. Amias could have explained it to them . I looked over at the cryo tanks stacked up against each other. I couldn't see inside of them, but he was in one of them. My brother, too. I'd keep it together for them and for the four guys who would want me to survive. I'd do it for me. I was worth something to this galaxy. I just didn't know what yet.

I'd figure it out. This wouldn't be my forever.

The internal pep talk helped. I would do whatever I needed for however long I had to, one way or another.

~

MY BELIEF in my abilities fled when the call happened. Lydia answered the ring on her tablet and turned to me. "Yes, she can go. Thank you."

She was pale as she regarded me. "There's a client here to see you. They want you to go."

I nodded, my pulse skyrocketing and my stomach hurting instantly. I really didn't want to go. Sex was private and should be consensual. I didn't want to do it on a view screen so Clarke could make more money off me.

Maybe Amias was right. Maybe I should have gone out in a blaze of glory like he did. Or like he'd tried to do, since he was frozen and might never be awake again.

I wiped at my few stray tears and steeled my back. *Okay. This was happening.*

I left Lydia's med rooms and headed to the dressing area. Four other women made preparations for similar meetings. We never looked at each other in these rooms, like we gave each other privacy while we still could.

But for once, I intended to break some protocol. "I think you're all amazing." There I'd said it. "Strong and beautiful."

All four of them turned to me with equal surprise on their faces. I didn't expect responses, and I didn't get any, beyond baffled expressions. I hadn't broken a rule, since Clarke wouldn't care.

I changed, looking at the tablet in the room as I did. It usually said the name and information of the guy we would service. I didn't know the one who claimed me—a Timothy Erad. I couldn't see more than his name. *Okay, Timothy, please don't be too awful.* Was I praying to the universe? Maybe. Would it make a difference? Never had before.

I put on my uniform—a sparse brown knit with holes intended to reveal my bare skin beneath the dress. I wasn't to wear underwear and didn't have any to put on anyway. Instead, I pulled my hair into the braids they required we wear and slid into the brown heels to match the outfit. We all looked the same for our clients. Regardless of our height or figure, the outfit made us all look wanting and available.

Tonight, it made my skin itch.

Two of the women in the dressing room had already left when I went to meet Timothy, but one had remained. "I think you're amazing, too," she whispered.

I smiled at her. Maybe we weren't too broken. *Maybe we can live through tonight and still have souls tomorrow?*

Steeling my spine, I walked down the hall, listening to my shoes click on the hard floor. Amias once told me babies could recognize their mother's footsteps coming down the hall. Did we ever stop and listen to our own footsteps? To think about where we'd been and where we might someday go? *Tonight, I have to do this.* Tomorrow, who knew where my feet would take me?

I was practically an optimist.

My shaking hands betrayed my confidence as I opened the door to meet Timothy. I sucked in a breath.

"Hello, Timothy." I didn't look at him yet. They liked it when our eyes were on the floor. "I'm here for your pleasure tonight."

"Uh, hello," the voice answered me. *Okay.* It might be his first time, but that didn't mean it wouldn't be a disaster for me.

I lifted my gaze and almost fell backward in shock. JoHanna's father? The man whose daughter I saved from poison looked mildly horrified as he gazed back at me from across the room.

His gaze went to the camera above my head, and if possible, he looked even paler. *Okay.* I shut the door. *What is happening here?* Did he want to fuck me? I never got that impression from him on his planet, where he seemed devoted to his wife and daughter. How did he even get off the planet, not to mention find his way to me?

A red light flashed, and he took a deep breath, holding up one of those devices again. They really were useful. "Twenty seconds until they notice they can't hear you. All their cameras just went down. Come sit here. Wait. That is what they said to tell you. Sit here. Wait with me. Be safe." He rushed through the words, his eyes rather frantic. "I was happy to help. You saved my daughter. I'm helping to save you and bring you home."

Realization dawned on me. *The guys are here.* "How? It's not time yet and..."

He let go of the device and shook his head, patting the sofa next to him as he sat down. I could sit. And wait. And be safe. That's what they'd told him to tell me.

JoHanna's father's name was Timothy, a minor and meaningless point for my mind to focus on when it couldn't quite stop jumping from thought to thought. An explosion sounded somewhere in the distance, and Timothy nodded. He lifted his hand and showed me his fingers in a countdown from five. Another explosion echoed in the distance.

They happened again and again after that. Shouts. Gunfire. I covered my ears. It was loud, terribly so, and I didn't want anyone except Clarke and his men to be hurt. Maybe I was a bad person for even wanting that.

Timothy rose. "I think it's okay to talk now. They said by now no one would be listening in here."

"How did they do this? The lightning." I ran a hand through my hair and started pacing the room. "I don't understand."

"Right." He got up, too. "The bad guy who poisoned my daughter—Net—he had a ship, and there were things on the ship. I'm sorry, I'm not being articulate. There were things. And they used them to make their shuttles work."

That made sense. *This is nuts.* "So the four of them, and you, came for me? That's impossible." Tears flooded my eyes again but this time they were happy. "I never would have dreamed it."

"The four of them? No, I mean, yes, they're all here. I mean...most of the planet is here. Some people who came, I haven't even met. They left two just in case, but they're all here. No one was okay with Clarke kidnapping you. You're ours. I mean, you belong to yourself, of course, but you are on *our* planet, which makes you our responsibility. They love you, and that gave the others all kinds of hope or something. No, it's not just the four of them."

My knees gave out and I would have fallen, but the door swung open. Gunnar was suddenly there, catching me in his arms.

"There you are." He kissed my forehead. "You're okay. Little overwhelmed? I've got you. Always." He kissed the end of my nose. "I'm sorry it took so long for us to get here. Are you okay?"

"Took so long?" I hadn't expected to see them ever again. I threw my arms around his neck and held on tight. "You're a miracle for my eyes to look at."

"Oh, Raven." He kissed my lips. "I cannot do without you. The four of us need you like we need air, okay? No one will ever take you again."

He kissed me all over my face until I was dizzy. When I finally pressed my lips to his it was the sweetest feeling in the whole universe. *Gunnar is here.*

I pulled back to find Timothy vanished. Where had he gone? "Gunnar, I have to tell you something. Maybe it's too late. Oh no."

He yanked me even tighter against his hard body. "What? Talk to me."

"Okay?" Mace was suddenly there, pressed against my side. "Why is she crying? Are you hurt? Did they hurt you? Who the fuck do I have to kill?"

"Oh," I threw my arms around him then. He smelled so good. *So familiar. So home.* "I was just going to tell him Stone and Amias are alive. The doctor—Lydia—she put them in cryo. They still have to be fixed, but they're there. In the med room."

"Really?" Gunnar laughed. "Fuck. Amazing. Okay. Let's go there. Nothing happened in the med bay. We never blow a hospital up." He took my hand and Mace took the other one. "Crew and Ransom and everyone has heard you. Let's go see the situation there."

When I reached their location, I found Lydia and Cambree huddled together in the corner. I let go of my guys' hands to rush to them. "It's okay. They're here to rescue me."

"And put a stop to all of this shit," Ransom added as he rushed into the room. "No more of Clarke and his crap, Butterfly. He's done terrorizing this planet." Ransom grabbed me and kissed me. "I don't know who he sent to take you, but if you see him, point him out, will you?"

My mind stuttered. What was I going to do about that? "Um, sure. If I see him." I made eye contact with Cambree. I'd just lied to Ransom, but if he noticed it, he didn't say a word. Instead, he picked me up in his arms and kissed me, hard.

We weren't alone, but he didn't seem to care as he lifted his head to talk to me. "I love you. Okay? It's a foreign word to us. Not one we expected to ever use, but I love you. We should have ended it years ago, and then we could have found you and brought you home where you would've been with us even longer, but we didn't know what was happening here. I'm sorry we didn't. I love you."

In the corner, Cambree cried, and they all turned to look at her. "They really love you. I mean...they really *do*. They did this whole thing for you."

"We do love her," Mace said and stroked a finger down my face. "She is our forever and our reason why."

"We love her so much," Gunnar proclaimed walking over to the cryo machines. "This is incredible. I haven't seen this kind of tech since Evander fell."

Explosions were still going off in the distance. A bizarre moment, I realized, with the dichotomy of my sweet reunion with three of them and the mess still happening out there.

Ransom looked at me. "Some of the others are helping the frightened women. They're not thrilled with us, because we're Super Soldiers, and I can certainly understand why. Hopefully, they'll soon figure out we're not here to take over where Clarke left off. We're here to remove him, the others, and give you back your planet."

"Really?" Lydia cleared her throat. "You're going to leave?"

"Yes." Mace nodded. "We have a home. We're going back there."

"Could I come?" Her voice shook. "Please. I don't want to stay here anymore. Not one more day here."

I whirled around into Mace. "She's a doctor, pretty much. I can explain later, and this other woman—Clarke held her brother in cryo to make her do what he wanted. Can you let her go? On a ship with her brother, so they can just go? On their way to wherever they want to be."

He nodded. "Of course. Just wait a minute, miss, until the bombs stop, and I'll see to it you can take off in peace."

"Really?" she outright sobbed. "But..."

"No buts," I practically shouted. "This is good news."

She sucked in a breath. "Okay."

I didn't know what they'd do if I admitted Cambree took me. She was a woman—they'd never hurt her or anyone else who didn't threaten them—but they weren't going to be happy about it. I just wanted her to be able to go. She'd find a way to make amends somehow, in the future with someone else. I didn't need it. I was going home.

"Stop right there." I winced. *Clarke*. It was Clarke. And he was there. A red light danced on my head. *Oh fuck. He has a gun pointed at my head*. "You little bitch, you..."

One second, he spoke, the next, he was flat on his stomach on the floor. Crew lay on top of him, holding him to the ground. "You were always *so* bad at this. A mediocre soldier at best. Do you remember me?"

Clarke actually whimpered, and I caught my breath. The man tormented us all, took over our planet, killed my father, let us die from things that we should have never had to face, and now he was what? *Crying* because Crew held him on the floor. I blinked. I couldn't really believe my own eyes.

"Not so tough when you don't have your group with you? Guess what? They're dead or they're no longer able to hurt anyone, so it's just you, me, and a few of my closest pals." He flipped Clarke over before he picked him up and shoved him into the wall, the structure shaking slightly. The room was so silent we could have heard a pin drop, yet Clarke didn't even move a muscle to fight back.

"You remember me?" Crew repeated his question.

My tormentor nodded. "Yes."

"I remember you. What a blowhard you were! What a ridiculous waste of space. You should have died on Earth and spared the universe putting up with the likes of you. We were given a chance when Evander fell. They wanted to put us down. We escaped, and we had the chance to be men, like the ones we saw who beat us. Like the humans who fought for their lives, their homes, and their families. Who said no to being hurt by us or anyone else who dared to come and try to take what was theirs. We had the chance to be like them, yet instead you went and enslaved a planet. You abused people with no chance of fighting back against you. You made yourself into some kind of demigod. Guess what? You're not. Gods can't die, but you can."

With a shaking voice, Clarke finally answered. "I wanted us to have what we *deserved*. We spent years under Evander's control. For once, I wanted us to be the ones with power."

"You don't deserve *anything*. The universe doesn't open and dish out things based on who deserves what. The people on this planet lived under Evander, too. They had their resources stripped, their people kidnapped. They finally had a break, and girl babies were being born. Then you showed up and destroyed them again. You hurt the love of my life. Took her from me. I don't care to hear your excuses or rationalizations. You're done."

With a twist of his hands, Crew snapped his neck like it was nothing. Clarke fell to the floor before Crew ripped his head off, throwing it aside. It was the same move he'd used with Net, only there was no fire to burn Clarke's remains.

We all stared until finally Crew turned to me. He opened his arms, and I rushed into them. He'd killed that man for me—for all of us, but mostly for me. It was all for me. I closed my eyes and let him hold me.

"I need to bring you home. No one will take you from it again without your permission." He kissed me, gently, like a caress. "But please don't leave. Please stay, because it isn't home without you. Either that or take me with you wherever you go."

I closed my eyes and pressed my head against his cheek. Clarke was gone. His palace was gone. His people were out of commission or dead. I wouldn't have to prostitute myself anymore, and neither would anyone else.

"He was selling me soon. A man...never mind. I want to go home. I want to go *so* much."

Crew scooped me into his arms. "Let's get things finished here and then we can go."

I woke up on their shuttle but we weren't in the air. I lifted my head and Ransom stroked my back. "Hey there. You don't have to be up. I'd rather if you slept for days and days."

I rolled toward him and put my head in his lap so I could breathe him into my lungs. He seemed so warm, so real, and I'd missed him. "Why are we still on the ground? The sooner I leave here, the better."

"We had some logistics to work out before we could take off. A surprising number of people wanted to come with us, for starters. Then we had to deal with the cryo situation. He had so many people locked up so he could blackmail other people. We had to figure out who is in there, who is sick, and who is just stuck in there. Your doctor friend is helping us sort through the cryos. Your friend with the brother left. I'm not sure what her deal was, but she hurried off. There are others... It's all just taking a little time, but we should be leaving..." His voice trailed off. "Soon. Right now, actually. They're coming. Stone and Amias are here—still in cryo, but with us. Lydia needs to treat them before we can attempt to wake them."

The shuttle was filled with my guys, so I forced myself to sit up. "What happened to Timothy?"

"He's with Gator. They're good friends, as they do some work together. He was so happy to help. Jumped at the chance. Everyone wants you with us. Chanel, who wants to be your friend, runs a boarding house. I think she's going to be full of women. Some others will have to step up, too, if we want to house everyone. It's going to be interesting." Crew sat next to me. "I need to look at you and just see that you're fine. You're pivotal. Essential."

They were too. "I thought...I thought that would be it. You were stuck. And then I'd be sold off, and you'd never find me in time, because the man who was buying me was intent on hurting me until he killed me. By the time you could come—and I sometimes thought maybe you wouldn't, because I'm just not used to anyone doing that for me—it would be too late."

Mace knelt in front of me. "We will *always* come for you, Raven. You're our family. Our love. The center of our hearts and our home. We would never not come for you, and we will never be too late."

"Thank you." I let my tears fall. I felt things and I didn't have to hide them. They wouldn't decide I was too much because sometimes I cried.

"Don't ever thank us," Gunnar whispered. "Let's just get out of here."

I was so glad to be going home.

THE STREET WAS the quietest I'd ever seen it. The bar's lights were off, and so were the ones up and down the street. They all came for me; everything was shut down. I had arrived on their planet soaking wet and terrified but determined. Now, despite the bumpy landing thanks to the lightning, I was home.

As we got off the shuttle, Crew bent over, and I climbed

on his back. They wanted to carry me around, to see that I slept and ate. For the time being, I would allow them to spoil me a little. I was tired—bone tired—but I was home, and I would heal there.

However long that takes.

"Is Raine okay?" I asked them, not caring who answered.

"She's very glad you're back. She offered to come by if we needed her, but it seemed best to have her stay behind with Kitty."

He was right. Their planet was magic. The people were, too. Maybe she and I could both find our way.

When they carried me upstairs to the bar, I missed the sounds of the music and the people talking downstairs. "Can we open tomorrow night?"

"If you want." Mace pulled on the end of my hair. "Whatever you want."

"Then I want to open. I want things to be as normal as possible as fast as possible, okay?"

They set me down in the bed and Gunnar took off my shoes. "Sure. Ransom can have a fight with someone and everything."

"Why am I the one who's having the fight?" He shoved Gunnar. "It could just as easily be you."

"No," Gunnar said as he sat down on the bed. "I'm a pacifist."

"Sure. Those were some real peaceful things you did when we lost her. You are a man of no violence."

Gunnar yawned then shot me a wink. "Maybe just for Raven."

19

SURPRISES, ALL AROUND

I knew Gunnar had already awakened and left the room as I got out of the shower. How did I know? The area outside of the bathroom felt empty. That might be nuts, and I might be wrong, but I would be surprised if that was the case. My men brought presence to a room, intense ones. Everyone else woke up except Gunnar when I slid into the shower, so I tried to be quiet. I knew it to be impossible, unless I had one of those little devices to hide voices...I immediately realized they'd hate that idea. I could practically hear them—they'd rather be awake and hear my heartbeat than asleep and not hear it. Some of them might even hear it while they slept, for all I knew.

Drying my hair took a long minute, so I stepped out with the towel around me. I needn't have bothered, since I was right—the room was empty. Besides, they all saw me naked. A lot. Still, wrapping the present for them seemed the least I could do, since they all so loved to unwrap it.

A motion out the window caught my eye, so I headed there to watch a bright blue bird swoop toward the mountains, climbing toward the sky. I smiled, as I hadn't spent much time looking out windows since my first day there. When I heard the knock at the door, I turned and said, "Come in."

Ransom leaned in the doorway, staring at me with a hot, possessive gaze. "Damn, that's beautiful. The sunrise. You. That towel."

I blushed, smiling a little because he *did* notice the wrapping paper. "Good morning. Did you sleep okay?"

They'd surrounded me on their big mattress, with Crew and Ransom the closest. Mace and Gunnar had slept on either side of Crew and Ransom, so I had no idea if they'd slept well. I knew I had , with all of them touching me.

"Did I sleep okay?" He grinned. "Yes. None of us slept the whole time you were gone, so I'd say we all needed to just pass out. There was no way any of us were going to rest without our Raven home. My sweet butterfly."

"Ah...look how poetic he sounds." Mace snuck past him, ducking into the room with Crew close on his heels. A second later, Gunnar joined them.

Ransom elbowed him. "You just wish you could say sweet things to her."

I looked down at my towel. I wasn't particularly dressed to see everyone yet. "What do we do now?"

"We go see your doctor friend. She is unfreezing her own brother, so he'll be up soon. Once she's finished with him, she'll let us know when we should expect others to be thawed out and fixed." Gunnar rocked back on his feet. "And we open up the bar, if that's still what you want."

Yes, I thought, smiling. I wanted to live with these guys on this planet that I loved. I'd heal there. I'd find myself there, I was sure of it.

~

LYDIA'S new place sat on the edge of town. When I arrived, one of the Super Soldiers painted the symbol for doctor next to the door. I didn't know him, but he smiled at us when we approached.

"Raven, this is Bomber. He's part of Wolf's crew."

I remembered Wolf, somehow connected to Druid.

"Glad you're back. It felt good to get rid of Clarke, like we finally did something worthwhile. Hasn't felt that way in a bit. Anyway, these guys were a nightmare without you. Don't leave them again."

I liked him. He was funny, and he made Gunnar groan, which made me smile. "Nice to meet you, Bomber."

"You, too."

We went inside, where Lydia checked the readings on a machine. She turned when we entered. "Raven, thank you for having guys who love you so much that they did this."

I opened and closed my mouth. "I think I'm as lucky as any person could ever be. And I'm also so glad you're here, too. How many came with us?"

"Ten." She smiled. "Others may follow. It's nice to be here. The air feels better. The sun... It feels like freedom, but I need to check with you fellows. I hear you're basically in charge."

All of them looked at Crew and he winced. "Listen, there were a few of us who are here who were in charge. Once we got here, somehow that became me. I'm not looking to do it, it just keeps happening, but I suppose, yes, I'm in charge."

"Then I have to tell you." She steeled her back. What was she about to say? "My father was Dr. Bourd."

The guys tensed around me. They might not have moved so others could tell, but I could. They didn't like that name. "He was the doctor who experimented on a lot of us,"

Mace explained in a low voice. Outside, it sounded like something fell over. I hoped it wasn't Bomber.

Lydia nodded. "He was a very bad man. I wasn't alive when he did what he did—by then he was just practicing medicine—but I've spent my life horrified by the tales. My brother was a baby when our father died. I don't know if he even knows what our father did. If you don't want me here, I understand, but I am determined to help people. I'm not a doctor, not technically. I need a certificate for that, and maybe I can get one now, but I know all the things he knew. I've studied and studied. I can help. Or I can go. Regardless of your decision, please let my brother wake up first."

Crew stepped toward her. "No one here will hold your father against you. You kept Raven's brother alive. Amias is alive. I don't know how many others you saved with your quick thinking and ingenuity. You're clearly a good person, but your father is a memory I'm happy to forget." He put out his hand. "That was hard and probably a little scary, since your experience with people like us was basically Clarke and those asshats. Welcome home, Lydia, for as long as you want to stay."

She teared up but then sucked it back with firmed lips. "Thank you. My brother needs a place to grow up. They stalled him at fifteen." That was something Clarke liked to do, I realized. Cambree's brother had been fifteen, too. "I think here is where we need to be right now." She cleared her throat. "Speaking of Amias and Stone, we need to wake them, but first they have to go from cryo to the med machines. Afterward, I just don't know how long it will be until I get them in there. I'll do it today. No matter what, I promise to have you here when they're waking up."

That was the best I could ask for.

On our way out, I took Gunnar's hand. "Do you think the

others here will agree with what Crew said? About Lydia's father?"

"They'd better, or we'll remind them why he's in charge."

I hoped that was good enough.

I WAS WASHING A GLASS, humming to myself, when Crew called me into the bar area. I set down the glass and headed out to see what they wanted. Abruptly, I stopped moving. All four of them were on their knees.

"Are you guys okay?" Were they hurt? "Do you need help? I can get Lydia..."

Crew put out his hand. "No. We're fine. This is just what we read that men do. They get on their knees when they propose."

My mind stuttered. "What?"

He cleared his throat. "We are here, on our knees, asking if you would be our wife."

I stared at them. "Really?"

"Yes." Ransom caught my attention. "We remembered what you said before you were taken, and about how your life would have been if Clarke didn't come to your planet. It never occurred to us that marriage was possible, but we love you. We need to be with you forever, and we hope that you feel that way, too. Would you please be our wife? Would you please be our forever?"

Mace groaned. "Always comes out with the better words. We all feel that way. Raven, will you?"

Gunnar nodded. "I don't think we've really told you what it was like when you were taken. We've hinted at it. And we don't want to burden you with it, but you should know it was like all of the light went out of the world. We saw that stupid note you obviously didn't write, and we could breathe again. You weren't dead, and you didn't leave on your own. Someone took you, and we're in the business of getting things back that go missing. We knew we could save you and bring you home. That is what you are, Raven. You make this place home by being in it."

I didn't try to stop the tears that flooded my eyes and dripped down my face. They were coming whether I tried to stop them or not. "Yes. Yes. I'll marry you."

They had made me a ring with four stones in it, which Crew slid on my finger, and then they were all kissing me. I could hardly breathe, but I loved the affection. There was nothing better than them in the whole universe.

"We could get married right now." Ransom jumped around. "I mean...we could. Unless you want a dress and a whole party. We want what you want."

Life was short, and I never knew what would come next. Did I want to wait for Amias and Stone? Sure. But I didn't know when they would be awake, and I wanted our marriage solidified as soon as possible. I wanted it to be official.

"Let's go get married." I stopped. "Who's going to do the ceremony?"

Crew grinned. "I thought maybe Gator could."

"Why Gator?" The choice seemed sort of random to me.

"Because he'll be really good at it, even though he has no idea he will."

It sounded like as good of an idea as any.

~

THREE WEEKS LATER....

"Is she...a prostitute?" a young man whispered to another one in our bar, and I glanced over to smile at Ransom. He still couldn't stand it when people noticed the mark on my forehead. With eleven other women sporting the same look as me, I was hardly alone in people having those assumptions about me. But Ransom hated it, and I was sure the others didn't care for it, either.

"No," the other guy answered. "Not on this planet."

With the lightning gone, more people came and went from the planet, doing various business or visiting friends and family. The influx of guests was great for the bar, but it meant strangers and their assumptions became part of our lives a lot. I walked over to kiss Ransom. "Go easy. I've got something to do."

"You okay?" He kissed me back.

I was better than okay. I was happy. "Yes."

With that, I left him and exited the bar. I'd probably have one of them tailing me by the time I got to Lydia's, so they'd know where I went. Sure enough, by the time I rounded the corner, I heard Crew's familiar whistle on the path behind me. I supposed I should consider their protectiveness invasive, except I'd just gotten kidnapped a few weeks ago. They were going to be a little overprotective for a while, and I didn't mind it. If they were still worrying this much about me in three years, we'd discuss it.

I stepped inside of Lydia's and looked for the privacy device. Lydia offered the use of the device to give her patients privacy in her office, and after some modifications by Wolf to increase the ease of use, she kept it out for anyone who might need it.

Wolf built things all the time lately, I thought, glancing at some new shelves on the doctor's wall. Her brother sat on a couch and smiled when I entered. He was a nice kid, but I knew she'd love to do something about the sadness in his eyes.

He sat reading a book that would probably be too hard for me even in a year, but I was determined. Someday, I'd get there.

"Hey," Lydia said, then patted the table in her med room and closed the door behind us. "What's up?"

I pointed at my forehead. "Get them off me."

Her smile fell, replaced by her professional expression. "Absolutely, if that's what you want. We put them on you, so I can take them off easy-peasy. Five minutes in the med machine, and they're gone." She opened the lid. "Hop in."

Five other machines buzzed in the room, two of which held people I loved. I'd be joining them for just a second, so I lay down in the machine. She hit a button to start the scan then shut off the machine. "Hold on. No med machine for you today."

"Why not?" I stared at her, confused.

"You're pregnant."

We stared at each other as my brain tried to process her words. Finally, I found my voice. "Not possible."

"Except it is."

She clearly didn't get it, so I explained. "Lydia, I was sterilized."

"I know. I watched them do it to you. You had the asshole who was there while I was still learning. Before he locked up Jack, and I had to do what they wanted, I used to say no."

I pointed at the area. "So how is that possible?"

"No one operated on you?" She shook her head. "Of course not. Did you get in a med machine that fixed it?"

I shook my head. "I got in one with burned hands, but that shouldn't have fixed my sterilization."

She walked over to one of the med machines, tapping it with her fingers to open a panel. "This is the one that guy Net owned. Your Mace gave it to me, so I had another med machine, but it's an odd machine. He had all kinds of settings." Lydia read something out of the panel then turned to me. "He was obviously very focused on fertility. Yes, any females who got in this machine would have their sterilization reversed, which is why you, Raven, are pregnant."

I sat down, my face hot and my mind spinning. Okay. This was happening. I never thought I could be a mother. It hadn't been on my radar. It was good news, just so wholly unexpected. "How far along am I?"

"Just two weeks. Even these guys can't hear it yet, only the machine could pick up on it."

I nodded. "Okay."

"Do you not want a baby?" She knelt down in front of me, her eyes kind.

"I do. I'm just..."

She waited a second before she suggested, "You're just dealing with an understandable amount of shock?"

"Yes. I guess. So, right, my tattoos will wait." They almost seemed a silly concern, in light of the new developments.

"No," she jumped off. "I can still take them off. It'll just take longer. I have a device. Stay right there." She looked over her shoulder, squinting at me. "It might burn a little."

Great. But I nodded and she headed to get the device.

Pregnant? What kind of mother would I possibly be?

ALL FOUR OF my guys waited in the living room for me. They stared at the door. Jack looked at all of them and then at me. "They let me show them my comic."

"That's really nice of them." It was. Seriously, so I teared up. I might be a crap mother, but they would kill at the dad thing.

Ransom pointed at me. "You said you were all right. You...got your tattoos off."

I rubbed the spots. She'd underplayed how sore I would be from the procedure, but it was worth it. "Yes."

"Jack," Lydia called him. "Come on, let's go eat dinner so you can get to bed."

"Okay." He jumped up. "See you guys later." They left together, going to the rooms they were staying in at one of the houses nearby. The locals were so happy to have a doctor they'd offered her a choice of homes to live in, but she'd told me what she really wanted, once it could be done, was to live upstairs from the med office. Wolf was working on that. He did like to build her things.

"So. " I sat down on the couch next to Crew. " That took a lot longer than we thought it would, because I'm pregnant."

There, I just said it. They all started talking, but the bottom line was they were thrilled. I blinked. They were happy about it. Confused, but elated. I grinned, some of my anxiety fleeing in the wake of their joy. If they could think it was a good thing, then maybe it would be. Maybe it *could* be.

They were, after all, the bringers of dreams. Even ones I hadn't known I had.

～

One week later...

"They'll both be able to hear you soon. Amias first, obviously." Lydia wore her white coat and spoke in her doctor voice as we stared at my brother and Amias. They both lay out cold, on tables in her med bay. "I waited to wake Amias later, so he'd wake up at the same time as Stone. I thought that might help them both adjust."

It was good thinking. I took Mace and Crew's hands as they stood next to me. I knew the moment had equal weight to them, as Amias was their brother like Stone was mine.

His eyes started to open, and he groaned. Crew dropped my hand to place a hand on Amias' shoulder. "Easy, brother. You've had a time."

"Crew?" His voice sounded rougher than usual. "How?"

"Long story. Just know that you're here. You're okay. And your husband is, too. It's all a bunch of really good news. You had to get better and now you are."

Amias sat up, despite the pressure keeping him down. He stared at Crew. "What about Raven? I sent a girl to you. She's very important to me. Did she get here? We have to find her, if she didn't..."

"I'm here." Any second, he'd hear our heartbeats, but he was too out of it right then. "I found your family and then eventually we all found you. They're my husbands now."

Amias' mouth fell open. "I hoped they'd take you in, but I didn't foresee marriage."

"Well." Ransom grinned. "You send us a gift in Raven, and we're not giving her up."

"I just have one question." Mace didn't sound joyful. "I get why you stayed after you met Stone, but why did you go there in the first place. Why would you ever have joined sides with that asshole Clarke?"

Amias swung his legs over the side of the machine and held his head like it hurt. "I got readings that there were a ton of med machines down there. I thought maybe I could steal one. Crew told me to find med machines. I figured, after the way I left, I couldn't come back empty handed. When I got down there, I saw what Clarke was doing and I wanted to get a full understanding of it so I pretended I wanted a job. He was happy to give me one. Then things changed because I met Stone. I couldn't leave him, or Raven, not ever."

Mace visibly relaxed. "Makes sense."

"Hold on." My brother's voice was soft, but it was there. "Did you say husbands? Plural?"

I grinned, filled with more happiness than I could've imagined. All of the love in the universe lived on this beautiful planet, where I was convinced, miracles could happen.

DON'T FRET DEAR READER. Book 2 is written and ready for you to order. *Advancement* is Cambree's story. You can grab it here: My Book

OTHER BOOKS BY REBECCA ROYCE...

Contemporary Romance

Redheads (completed series)

Redhead on the Run

Redheaded Redemption

Real Men Love Redheads

Reverse Harem Story (completed series)

Unconventional

Unexpected

Undeniable

Kiss Her Goodbye (completed series)

Hard Truths

Dark Truths

Deadly Truths

Stupid Boys (writing with C.R. Jane) **(completed series)**

Stupid Boys

Dumb Girl

Crazy Love

Science Fiction Romance:

Wings of Artemis (completed series)

Kidnapped By Her Husbands

Rescued by Their Wife

Crashing Into Destiny

Meeting Them

Reclaiming Their Love

Loving Them

Ship Called Malice

Saving Them

Dark Demise

Light Unfolding

Still Waters

Rising Tides

Lost Star

Pointed Arrow

Super Soldiers

Uncivilized

Advancement

Mirage (coming soon)

Illicit Minds

Illicit Senses

Illicit Connections

Illicit Alliance (coming soon)

Shifter World

Planet Bear

Planet Cat

Planet Wolf

Heart of the Nebula (writing with Heather Long)

Queenmaker

Deal Breaker

Throne Taker

Stranded Hearts (writing with Vivien Jackson)

The Girl Who Fell From The Sky

The Girl Who Crossed The Stars (coming soon)

Paranormal Romance:

Addalee Ackers

The Hunted

The Possessed (coming soon)

Trials of Blood (completed series)

Servant

Paramour

Flame

Last Hope (completed series)

Tradition Be Damned

Past Be Damned

Destiny Be Damned

Compassion Be Damned

Future Be Damned

Dragon Wars (completed series)

Forever

Eternal

Always

Evermore

Endless

Wards and Wands (completed series)

Hexed and Vexed

Curse Reversed

Meow, Baby (novella, co-written with Ripley Proserpina)

Tragic Magic

Why Yes, There are Witches (novella)

Safe Haven

Everywhere and Nowhere

Dimension X (coming soon)

More coming soon....

Soul Bound

Prisoner of the Dragons

More coming soon....

Shadow Promised

Strange Days

Weird Nights

Bizarre Years

More coming soon...

The Westervelt Wolves (completed series)

Her Wolf

Summer's Wolf

Wolf Reborn

Wolf's Valentine

Wolf's Magic

Alpha Wolf

Angel's Wolf

Darkest Wolf

Lone Wolf

Fallen Alpha

Alpha Rising

Alpha's Strength

Alpha's Sacrifice

Alpha's Truth

Alpha Enticing

Hidden Alpha (coming soon)

Cascade (completed series)

Haunted Redemption

Phoenix Everlasting

Fragility Unearthed

Persuasion Enraptured

The Swamp Princess (completed series)

Hidden

Pursued

Caught

The Coveted (writing with Ripley Proserpina)

Eyes in the Darkness

Voices in the Darkness

Return to the Darkness

Prison Princess (part of the Prison Princess world, writing with CoraLee June)

Young Adult/New Adult Urban Fantasy/Post-Apocalyptic:

The Warrior (completed series)

Initiation

Driven

Subversive

Redemption

Justice

Warrior World (spin off of The Warrior, completed series)

Deacon

Micah

Jason

Fantasy Romance:

Life of the Chosen

The Ritual

The Omen (coming soon)

The Storm (writing with Ripley Proserpina) **completed series.**

Lightning Strikes

Thunder Rolling

The Deluge

Stand Alone Titles

Under The Lights

No Quitting Allowed

Mr. Wrong

Bite Marks

Bitten Surrender

The Vampire and The Virgin

Crimson Lust

Call Me Crazy

The Men of Elite Metal

Gunmetal Lily

www.ingramcontent.com/pod-product-compliance
Lightning Source LLC
Chambersburg PA
CBHW011027260626
47153CB00020B/2964